ELVIS SAVES

0194-YANC

ELVIS SAVES

Bill Yancey

0194-YANC

To order additional copies of this book, contact:
Xlibris Corporation
1-888-7-XLIBRIS
www.Xlibris.com

CONTENTS

THIS BOOK IS DEDICATED TO MY MOTHER,
PHYLLIS VANDER FEHR YANCEY,
AND TO THE MEMORY OF MY FATHER,
MAJOR GENERAL WILLIAM B. YANCEY, JR. ,
WHO 'DIDN'T READ FICTION.'

ONE

Water flowed in sheets, downward and forward from the roof of the truck, across the windshield faster than the furiously thumping wipers could push it away. Inside the step-van, the driver cursed. He leaned forward to peer through the haze that fogged the inner surface of the window. Visibility on the dark, winding, Tennessee road was less than a hundred feet, even after he wiped the window with his white shirt sleeve. The high beams had no effect on the gloom.

Peering into the storm, the truck operator took his foot off the accelerator; the vehicle slowed perceptibly. A ton of dirty laundry, everything from dirty napkins to mechanics' rags, shifted positions behind him. A dark shape flashed into view: a deer. Its huge rack of antlers reflected the head lamps. Frightened by the storm, the buck bolted onto the road in front of the red truck.

Startled, the driver crushed the brake pedal. The nose of the step-van dipped as the wheels locked. Pushed forward by his own momentum, the driver held tightly onto the steering wheel to avoid striking it. His shoulder belt kept his head from hitting the windshield; his face came within inches of the glass. The driver's chest grazed the horn button, which sent a short pathetic bleat at the deer.

The deer vanished, white tail flashing a swift goodbye. It escaped, into the black storm and the forest, invisible again. Laundry spilled forward into the cab. Huge white bags of dirty clothing cascaded from the roof onto the sloped hood of the vehicle. Brakes locked, the truck skidded sideways on the rain-soaked asphalt. A more terrifying sight replaced the deer and falling laundry as the driver fought for control.

Sliding into the operator's visual field from above, a ghastly caricature of a man hung over the windshield. His presence paralyzed the driver. Dressed in a white suit and covered by desiccated and peeling flesh, the skeleton lay, head down, directly in the driver's line of sight. Dead eyes and flashing teeth laughed at the driver's predicament.

Petrified, unable to scream, the truck driver forgot about releasing the locked brakes, steering into the skid, or regaining control of the laundry truck. Headlights of an approaching automobile blinded him. The skeletal remains slid off the windshield and onto the hood. In the middle of the road, the truck spun wildly, completing one loop; the corpse vanished. The driver's skull slammed into the side door. He slumped in his seat, unconscious.

Car and truck collided with a dreadful crash. Welded together by the impact, the vehicles slid sideways, slowly, over the edge of an embankment. The mangled vehicles plowed mud ahead of the torn sheet metal as they slithered down the hill, seventy-five feet into a ravine. Mired in the deep ditch, the wreckage created a dam. A large pond formed rapidly, uphill from the mass of rumpled metal, laundry, and bodies.

TWO

The rain pelted the old, box-like Winnebago. Big, cold drops, nearly slush, and soft hail slammed into the roof and the windshield. The creaky ancient bus withstood the onslaught, but just. Worn, brittle, sunbaked insulation permitted some of the water to seep into the interior. The driver caught glimpses of tiny rivulets as they raced across the dashboard and dropped quickly to the floor. There, they soaked into the worn indoor-outdoor carpet.

In the dark, on a mountain road, in a rollicking thunderstorm, Jack Shafer had little time or inclination to watch the rain forced through the cracks by the downpour. Howling, screaming banshees of wind, made more ominous by the old vehicle's lack of streamlining, pushed and pulled at him. His grip tight on the steering wheel, Shafer strained to keep the RV on the road. Alternately, the gusts blew him across the yellow line into the middle of the road, and then nearly sucked him into the ditch at the side of the twisting, narrow, two-lane route.

The head lamps probed but a short distance through the wet murk. Jack slowed the vehicle to a plodding pace, unable to judge distances well without better illumination. Flashes of lightning occurred too infrequently to serve his sight. He cursed under his breath with each jerk of the steering wheel that sent pain radiating up his arms to his shoulders and neck. Sweat began to bead on his forehead, from exertion and discomfort.

In spite of his difficulties, he grinned and spoke aloud to himself, "Reminds me of the time we flew the Sikorsky into the thunderstorm near Colorado Springs. Couldn't tell if we were diving or climbing. The needles said one thing, as the air whipped around us. The whole storm moved, and the chopper did the opposite."

He relived the terror of seeing an enormous mountain peak loom directly in front of him and his crew. The aircraft did not respond to the controls. At the precise moment he thought they all would die, the storm cell in which they were trapped raced upward, away from a sheer cliff, taking the helicopter and its cargo with it. "Ruptured both eardrums," Jack recalled, "Ain't heard much, or well, since.

"Man wasn't meant to fly," Jack admonished himself, gripping the wheel more tightly, half-expecting to see a jagged stack of rock rush to a position directly in front of him. Shafer knew the Tennessee foothills harbored no craggy peaks of that magnitude.

Squinting, then reacting before thinking, Jack ground down the brake pedal, first with his right foot then with both feet. Feeling the motorhome slide toward a guard rail, he instinctively swung the nose of the Winnebago in the direction of the skid and skillfully regained control. The RV glided over the form of a man lying in the middle of the road. Shafer felt a sickening double thump as the vehicle's wheels bounced over the man and then hydroplaned on a sheet of oily water, turning tail first. It slowed gradually as it drifted backward up the steep incline, still in the proper lane for the way it moved, but pointed in the wrong direction.

Alarmed, Jack jerked the bus into the correct lane after it stopped sliding; it pointed in the direction opposite that in which he had been traveling. Carefully, but swiftly, he navigated onto the narrow shoulder. He turned on the emergency flashers and set the emergency brake. Shafer jumped from the door in the middle of the Winnebago's starboard side, leaving it gaping. Rain exploded onto his face and through his thin clothing, nearly drowning him.

Slipping in the wet gravel, Jack fell to his hands; his feet dipped precariously into the swollen river that raged down the mountain in the erstwhile drainage ditch. Undeterred, he ignored the sopping feet and abraded palms. Shafer struggled against the wind and rain. He clawed through the storm and forced his way around the front of the RV, looking for the body of the man he assumed he had killed. No white-suited body lay in the roadway.

A man stood on the opposite side of the road, forty or fifty feet away. His clothing reflected the amber flashing lights from Jack's motorhome. Wide-eyed, he stared at Jack with a bewildered look on his face. Simultaneously, they called to one another through the wailing wind and the drumming of the water slamming into the pavement.

"You all right?" Jack yelled. He saw the other man's mouth move, and tried to read his lips. He heard only his own voice. Shafer assumed the same applied to the stranger. Waving his arms, he pointed at the RV, "Come inside. It's dry." The man looked both ways along the desolate road, crossed the asphalt at a trot, and ran swiftly toward the Winnebago, almost beating Jack to the door.

Once inside, Jack dropped into the bench seat next to the table. He motioned the stranger into the vehicle, "Close the door;" he commanded, "the latch sticks. Give it a good hard lick. Nicely done." Shafer reached into a cabinet above his head and pulled down two large beach towels. One, he flung at his soaking wet companion, "Got another if you need it."

"I might. This is very neighborly of you, sir." A deep southern accent softened the stranger's words. The dark-haired, olive-skinned man ducked under the low ceiling and massaged his hair and face with the fluffy, oversized towel. Then, he dabbed at his suit with it, squeezing rivers of water from the armpits, pockets and crotch. Soon, the towel gushed with water.

"A towel will never do the job, son." Jack interrupted the man. "In the bathroom," he jabbed his right thumb toward the port side, rear of the RV, "there is a dry sweat suit. It'll be a tad small for you. Take off your suit and hang it in the shower." The stranger stared at his benefactor as if he could not believe his ears. Jack spoke more forcefully, "It's the least I can do for someone I almost squashed like a bug on my windshield. Go on."

"Thank you, sir," the man said, politely. He worked his way toward the rear of the RV, tilting his head to avoid hitting it on the ceiling. When he disappeared into the shower/toilet, Jack rifled more of his cabinets looking for something warm and dry for himself. He had been exposed to the rain for less than five minutes, and water dripped down his legs into his shoes. He imagined the other man could have been no wetter without having been immersed in the ocean.

Finding an old flight suit, Jack stripped, drying himself as he did. Mindless of the open curtains, he slid into a clean pair of skivvies and slipped on the dry jump suit. Nostalgically, he looked at the Black Hawk patch on the arm. It had been a long time since he had worn the flight suit. In the same drawer, he found his summer flight jacket. Made from nomex, it retained heat well. He put it on to ward off the chill he had begun to feel.

The stranger returned from the bathroom. His lean, muscular body bulged under the gray fabric. The Virginia Tech logo had never looked so splendid on Jack's chest. Also too small, the pants clung tightly. They were dry, however.

Jack tossed a pair of rubber sandals at the man, noting his bare feet. "I don't think I would have seen you, if you hadn't been wearing the white jacket." Jack invited an explanation from his guest, "Did you slip?"

"Must have. Man, that is the worst rain storm I have ever seen." The young man sat across from Jack at the small table. His facial features were chiseled, with an olive tan complexion; lips were full. Jet black hair matched the weather outside. It appeared a deeper black than any natural color Jack had ever seen: like a moonless night, under storm clouds, and inside a cave.

Jack held out his sixty-one year old hand, envious of the man's youth and good looks, "Jack Shafer, son. What's your name?"

Gripping Jack's hand firmly, the younger man crushed it with his strong grasp. "Elvis, sir. Elvis Presley."

"Well, the pleasure is all mine, Elvis," Jack grinned, hiding his discomfort. His yellow teeth seemed to spread over the aging face. "My wife was a big fan of your namesake. Was he a relative of yours?"

The eyebrows and forehead furrowed deeply on Elvis's face,

"My namesake?" His upper lip curled. Dark blue eyes bored into Jack's smirk.

Jack's smile drooped briefly, "You know, Elvis Presley, the King of Rock and Roll. Love Me Tender? Hound Dog? Jailhouse Rock?" The smile returned as he remembered the way his wife's face beamed whenever she saw a Presley film. "I'll never know what she saw in the man, myself. She was hooked on him, though. I suppose most women were. Nearly killed her when he died."

"Died?" Consternation shriveled Elvis's mouth. His eyes squinted, staring at the older man. "When?"

"Hell, I don't know. '78. '79. Before 1980 anyway. That's when Lennon died. You've heard of John Lennon, haven't you?"

"The Beatle," Elvis answered hollowly. "Somehow, I knew about that, but not about the Boss."

"The who?"

THREE

"What the Hell do you mean, 'He's missing?'" Mike Lomax thundered at his assistant, George Austin. The two men stood in the open corridor outside Lomax's office. Instantly aware that they were vulnerable to eavesdropping employees, Lomax lowered his voice to a deep threatening whisper; he growled, "Don't answer that here."

Lomax leaned backward, catching the door smartly with his elbow before it closed. A swift shove launched it in a sharp arc away from him. Hidden compressed-air cylinders braked the heavy mahogany door before it slammed into the wall. The two men entered the plush office. They heard only a slight whoosh as the door slowed, reversed direction, and then closed silently.

Lomax strode to his polished wooden desk, back to Austin, and jabbed forcefully at the phone and the intercom, "Jenny, hold all calls; postpone everything you can; print my new schedule in here on my fax/printer." Shifting his gaze slightly, he jabbed again at the phone. His own pleasant monotone spoke to him, "Hello, this is Mike Lomax, Director of Marketing, Turner-Disney Productions. I am in the office but cannot...." He cut the speaker off with a slap of his hand.

Standing and waiting silently through the rituals, his executive assistant steeled himself for the storm about to rage. He stared out the window. Lomax's window formed a small part of the huge crystal tower in which the office resided. Glass made up the entire outside wall of the office. Through the triple-glazed, gold-tinted window and past his supervisor, Austin saw Beverly Hills. The hills were both the inspiration and the aspiration of Mike Lomax. If Austin understood nothing else, he appreciated the Machiavellian drive Lomax harbored to live in those hills and to walk among their inhabitants as a neighbor.

"Sit," Lomax commanded. Austin sank into a soft, rose-colored, lounge chair, one of three in the room. Lomax turned his back to his desk and stood between it and his employee. "What is going on?" his voice bellowed. The vibrations never left the office, deadened effectively by the ornate wall-coverings, the furniture, and the built-in soundproofing.

Before Austin could answer, Lomax raised his voice an octave and twenty decibels, "Do you realize that I talked the board into paying Lisa-Marie Presley approximately *one billion dollars* for Graceland?" Austin nodded in silence. "Do you realize that the number of visitors has dropped to the point where we are just making the *interest* payments on that investment?" Austin nodded, this time leaving his head pointed at his feet; he stared at the shoes. Scuff marks stared back. "Do you realize that my job is on the line if this scheme does not increase the cash flow and begin to pay off the loan?" Austin continued to stare at his feet. He moved them to see if the crushproof carpet sprang back. It did, slowly.

The tone and volume dropped considerably; Lomax folded his arms and leaned against his desk. "Okay, George, I've finished blowing up; fill me in." He cleared his throat and adjusted his tie. The cravat matched the handkerchief arranged fashionably in the breast pocket of the thousand-dollar suit. "I'm calm, now," he said, as if to reassure both himself and George.

Austin stared into the steel gray eyes, then looked away. He considered first his boss's curly brown hair, then the rolling brown and green hills framed by the window. Silently, he edited his sentences, putting the best possible spin on the situation. Nervously, he spoke, "The guy you hired to play Elvis disappeared from the hotel in Nashville. The bodyguards went to pick him up, to transport him to Memphis for the big show. He and the rental car were gone."

"Gone?" Lomax choked on the word. Pulling the silk handkerchief from his pocket, he covered his face and coughed quietly.

"Just... gone?" He whispered ominously, "What moron let that psycho out of his sight? We have spent a hundred thousand dollars prepping him for this event. Need I remind you that we do not have a second string player for that position?"

"No one said to guard him, or anything, yet. He wasn't supposed to be in his Elvis mode." Austin tried to make an excuse, knowing Lomax would not accept it. Compounding his error, he offered a suggestion. "Maybe he will show up; he knows the routine and about when everything is going to happen. Or, maybe, the police can find him."

A nuclear device exploded inside Lomax's brain. Contorted with rage, his face unrecognizable, he managed to control his voice. He spoke in measured tones, almost satanically, "If any law enforcement agency ever finds out about this plan, is ever informed of this marketing ploy, the person who informs them will die by my hand. Is that understood?"

Only mildly surprised, knowing intimately Lomax's ability to deceive and his penchant for evil wishes upon anyone who disagreed with him, Austin nodded his agreement. "So what do you propose we do?"

Instantly composed again, Lomax stroked his chin and turned his head toward the window. He gazed at his Olympus, calmed by its presence, soothed by its nearness. "We do nothing, of course. If the man wants to get paid, he will show up as scheduled. If not," the pause nearly crushed Austin, "if not, then the rest of the planned activities will take place without him. We will pray they are as effective in his absence as they would have been with him."

"Is that it?" Austin could not believe Lomax would leave any loose ends, poisonous snakes which might curl back to victimize their creator.

"No. That is not quite it," Lomax sneered. "You have carte blanche to find Billy James Nottingham, alias Elvis Presley. If you find him before the ceremonies begin, get him to Memphis, on time and sober. Otherwise, I want him here in my office, any way you can arrange it. I do not, repeat, I do not want him talking to any authorities, anywhere, about anything. Do you understand me, George?"

"Absolutely," George said. He stared at Lomax, transfixed by his calmness.

Lomax, oblivious to Austin, turned and walked to his desk. Sitting in his high-backed chair, he placed his feet on the corner of the desk. Reminiscent of a man at complete inner peace with himself, he picked up his new schedule from the fax/printer and scanned it. A wry grin crossed his face as he laid the paper on his desk, then looked about the room.

Seeing Austin in the chair staring at him, he erupted volatilely one last time, "Are you still here?" he yelled. "If Nottingham is found by the authorities before you find him, your ass is...."

Austin exploded from the office before Lomax finished the sentence. Relaxed again, Lomax pulled a cigar from his coat pocket. He leaned back in his swivel chair and struck a match, leaving his feet on the desk. Let the games begin, he thought.

FOUR

Elvis espoused no burning desire to re-insert himself into the flash flood masquerading as a thunderstorm. Jack had no difficulty convincing him to ride out the cold front, and the night, in the Winnebago. After an hour of backtracking through the storm, they found the small, well-hidden campground Jack overshot in the deluge.

In the downpour, they did not bother connecting the electrical, water, or sewer lines. They drove to the assigned concrete pad, parked the motorhome, and shut down the engine. Jack's bones ached from the long day driving; Elvis was spent, too. Exhausted, Jack lowered the table between the bench seats in the RV and converted it into a double bed.

With great effort, Shafer remained alert long enough to instruct Elvis in the setup of the bed which fitted over the driver's seat. The ceiling felt close when Elvis squirmed onto the foam mattress. Still in the sweat suit he grunted, "Feels like a coffin." Fading quickly from reality, Jack thought he dreamed the outburst. Within minutes, Shafer's raucous snore filled the small vehicle, reverberating throughout the cabin.

Jack slept most of the night as though dead. He neither moved nor dreamed. Toward morning, the usual recurrent nightmare stirred within his subconscious. In his dream, he opened door after door in a large building, in search of a bathroom. Each door opened to a bathroom, but each room harbored some defect. Some possessed large plate glass windows, complete with onlookers; others had no stalls for privacy; some contained only sinks or bathtubs, but no toilets.

Jack had long since figured out the meaning of the dream and he roused himself from bed. His prostate strangled his bladder, the doctor said. Therefore, he urinated a little at a time. Partially obstructed, his bladder remained always distended. It filled to overflowing while he slumbered. The dream told his body that the time to urinate arrived. The fantasy also informed his subconscious that he should not go where he was, in bed. Jack worried about some future morning when his body forgot that he lay in bed; he would wake up sopping wet.

That would occur later, though. For now, he ignored the sunshine that forced him to squint and trundled to the bathroom to relieve himself. While in the bathroom, he stripped and rinsed in a quick shower. Towel around his waist, he walked into the corridor in search of clean underwear. Halfway through his search of the cabinets, he remembered Presley. To confirm the memory, he looked at the loft. It remained in the down position, but no one occupied it. The sweat suit lay neatly on the edge of the folding bed. Jack had not seen a bed made that shipshape since he had been an aviation cadet. This Presley ain't no slouch, he thought.

Jack's stomach redirected his thoughts toward breakfast, which had to be preceded by either the electrical hookup or the operation of the propane tank. Jack chose to save the gas and to use the electricity he rented, along with the parking space. Quickly, he donned the clean underwear and the flight suit he wore the previous night.

Pushing open the door, he glimpsed the view that brought him to the campground. A picture post card, similar to the advertisement for the campsite, greeted him. The blue green mountains struggled to emerge from behind a thin negligee of mist. An integral part of the setting, a small lake reflected the image, making it doubly beautiful. Jack stood in the cool morning air, flight suit unzipped from neck to waist, large white V-shape of his T-shirt exposed. He stretched, as well as the creaking bones allowed, and inhaled the cleanest air in the world.

The smell of burning wood shattered the rapture. The silent hills filled with flames, mortar rounds, exploding grenades, and tracers. Jack's mind stumbled into the past and the Highlands Campaign. He stared as men fell around him, firing weapons in self-defense. Everywhere lay wounded, dying, and dead. Any loud noise would hurl Jack to the ground; he would crawl to a trench hoping to survive, for the thousandth time. He defended himself against the battlefield assault he witnessed thirty years in his past. Gradually, he recognized the scene. He realized that he hallucinated. Yet, he also knew he could not extract himself from the nightmare. He waited for the explosion.

A hand placed gently upon his shoulder steadied Shafer. A soft voice, with an obviously southern accent, soothed the hypersensitive nerve endings. "Jack," the distant voice called compassionately, slowly manipulating its way into Jack's subconscious. "Jack, it's okay. Relax a little. It's a bad dream, man."

The hand on his shoulder became two hands, one on each shoulder. Comforting pressure increased against his trembling body; the nightmarish vision began to fade. A torched helicopter gradually transformed itself into the red sail of a boat tied to the floating dock. The exploding ammunition faded slowly, leaving the impressions of pine trees and shrubbery on his retinas. As quickly as it sprang from his mind, the illusion vanished.

Soothingly, the voice spoke, again, "Jack, I want you to meet Mandy." Elvis put one hand on Jack's left elbow and gently turned him away from the lake. Jack looked down, upon the blondest little girl he had ever seen. Her hair could easily have been white. Her pink face had one freckle on the tip of her nose. "Mandy's mom cooked us some chow, Jack," Elvis continued, putting a strip of bacon into Jack's limp hand. Absent-mindedly, Jack placed the pork into his mouth. Taste enhanced by an encounter with a grill, the salty meat sealed the terrible nightmare deep inside Jack's brain. Pinpoint pupils dilated; the trembling stopped; a smile etched itself slowly into the crevices of his face.

Jack grinned at the little girl and then Elvis. He spoke to Elvis, "Thanks, son." He wiped his forehead of the sweat that had accumulated in the brief seconds of the seizure, "That's the first time I've managed to abort that ordeal."

"Hey," Mandy tugged at Jack's sleeve, "why do you have all these zippers? Look," she pointed for Elvis, in case he had not noticed, "he has zippers on his sleeves, near his hands, on his arms, in the front, on his legs, near his feet. Good grief!" she stated in mock horror. "My mommy would never make an outfit with that many zippers. She says zippers are the hardest part of sewing. You know, she made this dress for me." With a swirl, the little girl spun, her yellow sun dress expanded outward showing her sun-tanned legs and pink panties.

Jack and Elvis each caught a hand as she completed her first revolution. "Whoa, little one," Elvis laughed, "let's introduce Jack to your momma."

"Yes, let's," Mandy stated grown-uppishly.

"Someone did mention breakfast," Jack chimed as his stomach growled.

FIVE

Austin crossed his legs and leaned into the stuffed chair. He scrutinized his mentor's face as Lomax struggled unsuccessfully to contain his glee, "It's working, George; it's working." Lomax rubbed his hands with delight; a smirk creased his face. His eyes glowed, soaking in first Austin and then the view of his next neighborhood. "Even without that no-good Nottingham, this is going to work out terrifically. Already the news hounds from the networks are calling, looking for interviews. I saw our one and only CEO, R.M., talking with the anchor from our news show. Hope that dumb s.o.b. didn't say anything to screw this...."

"Uh, Mr. Lomax...." An embarrassed secretary stood with the polished office door open behind her. Chewing on an unlit cigar, Randolph Marshall Crossley, Chief Executive Officer of Turner-Disney stood behind her — ears crimson. The color bled slowly across his stern face, from his ears to his cheeks and, finally, to the broad forehead.

Briefly, Lomax stared at his superior. In shock, he almost forgot to close his mouth. R.M. never visited an associate junior board member's office, with two exceptions. Within the hour Lomax expected to be fired, or awarded the coveted Turner-Disney Medallion, also known informally as the T-D-M, or touchdown! award. Executives who excelled in their jobs, most commonly measured by income produced, were the usual recipients of the T-D-M.

Lomax coughed. The possible consequences of the visit flashed through his mind, along with the fact he referred to R.M. as an s.o.b. "Uh, sorry, Mr. Crossley, just a little locker room talk to encourage the team players, right, George?"

Bolting to his feet and facing the most powerful man in the

Turner-Disney organization, Austin nodded his assent. Quickly deducing the fifty-fifty chance that his immediate supervisor's head now hovered inches above a basket in front of a guillotine, Austin excused himself. "Mr. Lomax, I have to check out a lead on B.J. Nottingham. I'll call you if we contact him." Austin exited the room so rapidly that he ran into the secretary, nearly knocking her down.

"No guts," R.M. stated, watching Lomax's assistant depart.

"Pardon me?" Lomax asked. Using the backs of both hands he shooed Jenny out of the room. He motioned the secretary to close the door on her way out. At the same time, he wondered if the command to her would be his last. He turned to R.M. and forced a smile.

"Your assistant will never do as a replacement for you," R.M. stated bluntly. Lomax gulped conscientiously and gritted his teeth. Crossley may have found out more than Lomax wanted the old man to know. If so, Lomax's employability factor would be a negative number for a long time into the future. "That is, if you are promoted," R.M. muttered and, then, corrected himself, "or fired."

Staring directly at Crossley's mouth, Lomax stood very still. Crossley sometimes mumbled. Lomax trained himself to read the man's lips, to avoid embarrassing either of them. "Sir?"

"Lomax, did you initiate the sequence of events that occurred in Memphis yesterday afternoon?" R.M. chomped down on the cigar, raising the unlit end like a battle flag. As far as Crossley was concerned, the only important buildings in Memphis were those owned by Turner-Disney: Graceland, and the associated structures. He stared, not at Lomax's mouth. Lomax never mumbled, not even when he lied. R.M. stared into Lomax's soul.

"No, sir," Lomax stated, flatly. "I had absolutely nothing to do with what occurred in Memphis yesterday."

"Too bad," Crossley said, obviously disappointed. "Some of the board members thought...." He furrowed his brow and stared at his cigar as he removed it from his mouth.

"However," Lomax continued, interrupting Crossley and reading the old man's face like a dog-eared novel, "I have managed to manipulate the situation, uh, somewhat."

R.M.'s face brightened; his ears picked up; the cigar went back into his mouth at half mast. "Could you explain that, my boy? Not in such detail that I could be considered an accomplice, you understand. Just in case."

Delighted, Lomax explained, briefly, "There will be many Elvis sightings over the next forty-eight hours, sir. Depending upon the country's response, there may be some Elvis nostalgia blasted into the airways: music, video, and more. I plan to keep his name in the limelight for a long time."

Only slightly disappointed, R.M. chewed his lower lip around the cigar, then spoke, "The board has shown quite a bit of interest in this project, Lomax, especially with a billion dollars riding on the outcome. You get our billion back in a hurry, son, and there are some things the board will do for you." He paused briefly, then added ominously, "Screw it up, however, and the board will be certain you have nowhere to hide. Is that straight forward enough?"

On the verge of fainting, Lomax felt all the blood in his body pool in his legs. Mouth too dry to speak, he nodded silently. R.M. turned and let himself out of the opulent office.

When the door closed, Lomax allowed himself to sink into the plush carpet. Sweat poured from his body as he lay, spreadeagle, on his back, staring at the fan blades turning ever-so-slowly on the fan hanging from the ceiling. Dodged a bullet with my name on it, he swore to himself.

Jumping to his feet, Lomax scrambled for the phone. To his secretary, he screamed over the intercom, "Get Austin back in here, that worm."

Fifty feet down the hall, waiting on the elevator, R.M. Crossley heard the outburst over the secretary's intercom. He smiled to himself as the elevator door slid open noiselessly.

SIX

Outside the beat-up trailer, Jack sat in a very old, folding, beach chair. The aluminum parts of the chair had corroded; they were covered with a chalky white powder. In places, rust streaked the aluminum where the shredded nylon bands were held tenuously to the frame by steel screws. Ready to spring when the chair finally gave way, and expecting it to do so at any second, Jack kept his legs under him and taut. He could not relax.

With deep wonderment he watched as Elvis wolfed down enough scrambled eggs and bacon to satisfy four men. "A long time between meals, son?" he asked, as Mandy's mother, Gloria, brought Elvis his third or fourth helping.

"I swear, I must be losing my mind, child," Gloria spoke to Mandy, but directed her voice at Jack and Elvis. "I could have sworn I cooked six eggs and half a pound of bacon. It seems to double; every time I go into the kitchen, there's more food in the pan."

Uncomfortable, tense, prepared to escape the dilapidated beach chair, Jack did not consider Gloria's feelings, or the hard work and food she lavished upon them. He stated bluntly, "Anyone could see that Elvis polished off at least fifteen eggs and a pound or two of bacon, woman."

The word, *woman*, stopped Gloria in her tracks. A petite, blonde, pushing thirty years of age with most of that time at hard labor in beauty salons and greasy-spoon restaurants, she'd taken to the road to avoid abuse by males. Most of those men had addressed her as had Jack. Both hands on her hips, fists knotted and pressing into the belt loops of her faded blue jeans, she leaned forward, putting her face directly in front of Jack's, nose to nose. "You think all blondes are stupid, Jack?"

Jack could see her navel through the opening in her blouse which also revealed her breasts strapped tightly to her chest in a worn bra. The view reminded him of flying the Rockies in terrain-following-mode in an Apache helicopter. In her case, the mountains hung downward rather than pointing to the sky. He did not dislike the view, but he loathed arguing with women. He tried to calm her down. "Sorry, I didn't mean it to come out that way."

Not content to accept the apology, Gloria pressed the point, "I put six eggs in the pan, and half a pound of bacon. That's all that'll fit in the tiny refrigerator in my tow-behind." Jack could not argue with her; her voice rocked him. Jack doubted nothing she said, until her voice wavered and her expression softened, "I gave Elvis half, and you a fourth." She placed her hand to her head and glanced at the trailer in disbelief, "But, each time I go back in, there's a full pan of eggs and bacon. Must be losin' my mind."

Elvis sat in another tattered beach chair. A paper plate full of food balanced on his right knee. He held a large plastic glass of milk in his left hand. A grin covered his face; his cheeks puffed outward filled with breakfast. Presley swallowed, leaving enough airspace to talk around the food, "And it is good food, momma." His eyes bored through Gloria, penetrating her put-on pout about being a dumb blonde.

"Why, uh, thank you, Elvis. Thank you," she muttered. Giving Jack one last mean look, she gracefully climbed into the trailer and returned to the two-burner gas stove. The squeaky screen door slammed behind her. "Lordy, lordy...." Jack heard her mutter through the open windows of the tag along.

Elvis saved Jack the need of replying. "Gloria," he said as he stood and gulped his milk, "there will be some leftovers, I'm afraid. There are a couple of runaway teenagers and a homeless old man sleeping in tents near the lake. You could take the food to them. No doubt, they would appreciate the chow."

Gloria made no reply. She suddenly reappeared, flinging the

screen door open. Grabbing Mandy by the elbow, she yanked the child into the trailer, then slammed the inner door shut. Jack heard the bolt on the aluminum door grate into place as the screen door slammed.

"Guess we've worn out our welcome, Colonel," Elvis said quietly. He placed the paper plate and the empty milk glass carefully onto the seat of the canvas chair. Walking to a clothesline draped from the back of the trailer to a tree, Elvis retrieved the suit coat which matched the trousers he wore. "Gloria ran it through the camp washing machine for me," he explained, as he removed the clothes pins from the white coat. Carefully, he returned the pins to the line.

Jack noted the pastel blue shirt looked much better with the clean white trousers. He could not help noticing the tread marks across the back of the white coat as Elvis collected it and then folded it over his arm. "Probably take several washings to remove the tire tracks," Elvis said, anticipating Jack's question, but not allowing whether he had been wearing the coat when the tire marks decorated it. Nah, Jack thought, no one survives that.

Standing in front of Jack's battered Winnebago, the two men stared at one another awkwardly. "Uh, Elvis...." Jack started, but could not finish asking where the man would go or what his plans were.

Elvis kept his head down, and stared at his feet. The white bucks had survived the rain and Gloria's explosion. A piece of egg yolk clung to the white trousers. "Colonel Shafer," Elvis said without lifting his eyes to look at Jack, "would it be a big imposition if I hitched a ride with you to Memphis?"

Elated, Jack responded gregariously, "Why, hell no, son. You can ride with me to the west coast if you like." He thought about the wartime hallucination for a minute, then asked Elvis a favor and two questions: "Please call me Jack. Tell me how you know I am a retired colonel and that I am headed to Memphis?"

The full head of hair rose as Elvis threw his head back in a laugh. The smile broke Jack's heart. Elvis's response reminded Jack of the carefree boys who accompanied him into battle like men, but never returned. Presley's eyes drew a bead on Jack's. He paused for a second, then spoke, eyes glinting with mirth, "Shoot, Colonel, you've got those eagles sewn onto the shoulders of your flight suit. A buck private would know your rank. I guessed at Memphis. You were driving west last night when you picked me up. Not much else between here and the west coast on this road."

Jack shrugged. Logic always won, when physics did not upset the game, "So what part of Memphis are you going to, Elvis?"

The even white teeth flashed, "I think they're waiting for me at Graceland."

SEVEN

The gusty winds buffeted the ancient, flat-sided, Winnebago as Jack followed the blustery back roads in search of I-40. Generally, they traveled in a westerly direction, toward Memphis. The two-laner finally connected with the interstate south of Kingston Springs, Tennessee. By that time, Shafer's arms, neck, and lower back burned with a fire he had yet to become accustomed.

Seeing a roadside rest area a short distance from the intersection with the interstate, Shafer pulled the RV off the road and into the parking area. He sat, drenched in sweat, fighting the pain. Shafer forced himself not to rush to the bathroom and gulp down the medication he knew would relieve his suffering. The lethargy induced by the painkillers would make him unfit, or unable, to drive.

"Go ahead, Colonel," Elvis suggested.

"Go ahead and what?" Shafer snapped at his young companion.

Unperturbed, Elvis replied, "Take the pain medicine. I'll drive if the pills make you sleepy."

"How do you know about the pain medicine?" Jack asked suspiciously.

"I saw the bottle in the bathroom last night and again this morning," Elvis answered. "Just put two and two together. You look like you are hurting, man. Lorcet Plus is a strong narcotic. Am I wrong?"

"No," Jack spat, irritated that the young man seemed to read his mind too frequently. "Do you have a license to drive?"

The younger man smiled, dimpling both cheeks, "Don't have it with me. You'll have to trust me."

Shafer screwed up his face arguing silently with himself. Elvis sat, mute, waiting to see which Shafer won the argument: the stoic helicopter pilot, or the spent old man in agony. Finally, the pilot agreed; the pain cleaved too deeply to be ignored. "All right, you drive," Shafer grumbled, making his way aft to the bathroom. "Ever drive a vehicle this size?"

Sliding into the driver's seat, but sitting with his legs in the aisle in the middle of the camper, Elvis replied with a chuckle, "Army trucks and Greyhound buses." Politely, he waited for Shafer to rejoin him. Jack stumbled forward, toward the passenger seat in the front of the RV. He struggled, trying not to reveal the severity of the pain. Exhausted, he dropped into the seat.

"Okay," the Colonel grunted, "but don't screw up, Presley. This bus contains all my worldly possessions, even the remains of my wife. If the police impound it, I become homeless."

"Not a problem, Colonel," Elvis intoned as he accelerated the rickety vehicle onto the feeder highway. It sped up the ramp, merging smoothly with the traffic headed west to Memphis on Interstate 40. "You have your wife's remains with you?" Elvis asked.

"Not a corpse, dammit," Shafer snapped, loudly in order to be heard over the mounting road noise, "her ashes."

"Oh," Presley said quietly, then allowed his silence to goad Jack into expressing some of his hostility.

After several minutes of silent calm, Jack spoke, initially as if forced into a confession by a police inquisition. His tongue loosened by the narcotic as time passed, he rambled, "She made me make two promises before she died. Cancer killed her. Dammit. She was ten years younger than I am, and so damned pretty. There was no call for her to die. I would gladly have died in her place."

Green and brown farm land, tobacco and corn fields, sped by, a blur like Jack's past. "One promise I made was to cast her ashes into the Pacific Ocean. She loved that ocean. We lived in Hawaii and San Diego for many years. The Pacific gave her life, I think. They found the cancer while we lived on the East Coast. It took her so quickly that I never had the chance to take her west again. Would have healed her, I know it would've."

Elvis drove, carefully watching the road and his speed. Most of his attention centered on Shafer. "The second promise is kind of ironic, I guess," Shafer added.

"Why's that?"

"She loved Elvis Presley and his music. Your namesake held a special place in her heart. Even as her husband, I had no control over that infatuation. If Elvis had appeared on our doorstep and had asked her to leave me, even after twenty years of marriage, two wars, and four miscarriages, she would have gone in a minute. Figure that out." Shafer chuckled, the narcotic tickling a cerebral funny bone. The misery faded quickly, "But then, I guess, if Lonnie Anderson or Marilyn Monroe had asked me to leave her, I would have been in a real tight spot, too."

Smiling, Elvis asked, "You partial to blondes, Colonel?"

Shafer grinned, ear to ear. "On R&R from 'Nam in Hong Kong, I once followed a blonde thirty blocks and onto the ferry. As I caught up to her in that crowd of black-haired Asians, she turned around...."

"Ugly?"

"Worse. That was my first encounter with a man with long hair." Shafer laughed, still able to see the man's face clearly: icy blue eyes, day old beard stubble, and shoulder length blond hair.

Presley laughed hard. Finally catching his breath, he asked, "You followed this blond guy thirty blocks and you didn't know he was a male?"

Shafer smiled an embarrassed smile. "I started out ten blocks behind him. There must have been ten thousand people in the streets of Kowloon that day. When I finally caught up with him, he had boarded the ferry to Victoria. The ferry, in fact, was full. I jumped over the rail, thinking what a great story it would be to tell our children and grandchildren. Made some Asian enemies, I'm sure. When I climbed the steps to the top of the ferry, there he sat, reading a paperback novel and smoking a cigarette. Must have been British. Certainly was no Chinaman."

Still chuckling, Presley glanced at Jack, "Did you ever tell your wife that story, Colonel?"

Shafer seemed not to hear the question. He stared straight

ahead, through the bug-covered, flat window. Tears welled in his eyes. Several minutes passed. He spoke quietly, solemnly, "Yes, I told her. She laughed so hard she fell out of her chair and sprained her wrist." His voice trembled and dropped an octave, "From then on, every time we saw a blonde woman from the rear she would ask me to see if *he* was clean-shaven."

Eyes glued on the traffic that crowded more closely around them near Memphis, Elvis asked Shafer two more questions. "What was your wife's name, Colonel? What was the second promise?"

A cacophonous snore answered the questions. The narcotic finally extracted Jack from the conscious world, numbing his misery. Elvis whistled quietly, guiding the Winnebago effortlessly through the rush-hour mine field of the Interstate 240 bypass. The sun set over the Mississippi River, highlighting in pink the huge glass pyramid at the river's edge. Jack slept, head leaning to one side, mouth open, snoring in three quarter time.

Well rested, but remembering the bad dream, Jack woke. In the distance, a single blonde head bobbed among the sea of black scalps. He struggled, seemingly for hours, to catch her, finally succeeding. Upon reaching the golden-haired young woman, Jack seized her hand. It crumbled in his grasp, becoming ashes. Before his eyes, the pretty, fair-skinned face of his lovely wife aged, turned to dust, and blew away, leaving only a skull behind. A large, formless, black creature, attired in a black cloak and holding a scythe, held his wife's other hand. Death's laugh sounded much like Elvis Presley's. "She's really gone," Shafer said in his sleep. His own words roused him, "I'm next."

Jack found himself lying on the table converted to the double bed. His watch indicated that the next morning had arrived while he had slumbered. Ineffectively, the ragged curtains struggled to keep the bright early morning sunlight out of the RV. Sitting up, he stretched and pulled back the tattered draperies. The camper sat in an empty parking lot. Multiple signs suggested that Graceland and Turner-Disney owned the lot. Jack could see the famous mansion across the four lane highway in front of him. Grounds keepers removed large blue and orange tarps from the lawn. Elvis Presley had vanished.

EIGHT

"Doc, are you tuned to our news channel?" Lomax screamed into his telephone. Jugular veins throbbed in his neck; blood flushed his face. His collar suddenly felt too tight. He dropped both feet from the desk as he leaned forward to obtain a better view. The move was unnecessary; he stared at an eight-foot diagonal television. The flat screen constituted one entire wall of his office.

"Oh, crap, did you hear that, Doc? The CEO of Turner- Disney is on, live. Yeah, my boss. He just offered a $100,000 reward for any information that would conclusively link T-D to the shenanigans in Memphis! Hang on. I have to listen to this." Lomax jabbed at the remote, increasing the volume on the television until the wall reverberated with the bass.

A reporter held a microphone in R.M.'s face. Crossley stood, several floors below Lomax on the steps leading to the T-D building. He spoke, again, at that moment — or maybe a fraction of a second before. The signal went from the T-D building, to a communications satellite, to the production studio, back to a different geostationary satellite, to a cable company, and finally to Lomax's TV, after traveling some 100,000 miles. "I have been assured by Mike Lomax, Director of Marketing here at Turner-Disney, that we had no hand in this recent disaster. Obviously, we do not control the weather. Not even T-D can order lightning to strike at our command."

R.M. stood, a proud bulldog, defending his territory and his master, the shareholders of Turner-Disney Productions. Their stock value rose dramatically, anticipating the sudden influx of tourists when Graceland reopened. As CEO, Crossley owned many shares of stock himself.

To signal that the interview had concluded, R.M. held both hands raised to the camera. The reporter, unseen except for his hand and microphone, tried to squeeze in another question, "Turner-Disney Productions is the largest conglomerate of entertainment companies in the industry. Considering the gain in your stock prices, don't you think a $100,000 is petty cash?"

Crossley's bulldog bared its teeth. He shook his head as if his jaws clamped onto the leg of a burglar. "To most people, sir, a hundred thousand dollars is a lot of money." He spoke through clenched teeth. "If convicted of fraud, an employee of Turner-Disney would face several years in prison. I am convinced the sum is large enough to attract enough attention to keep our lawyers busy for a long time. Sorting through the possible conflicts of interest that are certain to surface will be expensive enough."

Abruptly, he turned his back and strode up the steps, away from the camera. His final words, "Good day to you, sir," barely made it to the microphone.

Lomax hit the mute button, silencing the reporter in the middle of his summary remarks. He returned his attention to the telephone. "Was that great, or what?" His feet went back onto the top of his desk. Almost horizontal, he lay supine on the fat chair. Lomax stared at the ceiling. "Of course I suggested it. Everyone we compromised is in for over a hundred thousand dollars. Several people made twice that on their stock options, already. If any of them break their silence, then the stock drops through the floor. There goes their bonus."

Reveling in the possibility of being able to afford his dream home in the Hills, Lomax continued, "Most of our associates violated some federal law in helping us set this up, too. In addition to losing their money, they might find themselves in jail. No loose ends, except B.J., but George will find him. Nottingham has a history of psychiatric problems and drug abuse. Who's going to think he's credible?"

Lomax listened to a question from his confederate, then answered with a smirk and chortle, "No. We didn't plant all those people, but we will take advantage of the situation. We had three or four of your primed patients at Graceland; two were actually inside when the storm occurred. The repressed memories that you gave them should appear in the media at any time. The great part is this: other people testified already that they saw Elvis. When it rains, it pours; I expect thousands to have seen him by next week. Damn, it's fun manipulating an entire country. This is why I went into marketing."

Silent briefly, Lomax listened and pondered his next answer. "I swear, we had nothing to do with the grave. That's grotesque; even I would not have thought of that. I guess they'll be finding little pieces all over Memphis, if he was in there. I would not put it past the family to bury him and his parents elsewhere, expecting the graves to be violated someday.

"Well, I've got to go. We have an executive meeting that I have to attend. We're going to hear reports on how long repairs will take and how long the lines will be when the mansion does open. They want a briefing from me on how best to take advantage of the situation — in good taste of course. Take care, Doc; I'll talk with you later." Lomax hung up the telephone. He did not move a muscle for five minutes, excluding shallow breathing, savoring the moment of triumph. Abruptly, his wrist watch alarm chimed; he dropped into a sitting position, collecting his thoughts for the executive meeting.

NINE

Barry Lockwood sat in his bare office, alone with his obsolete word processor. Recently medically retired from his position as a detective on the Memphis police force, Barry pondered his future as a private detective. While he typed invoices to his customers for the previous month's work, he contemplated more financially rewarding occupations.

His toil included two hours tracking down a group of teenagers who declared war on the lawn of a prominent business man. The delinquents soon would be hefting sod and shrubbery with their bare hands to replace the landscaping they destroyed. They drove a sports car across the man's front lawn at 3:00 a.m. one Saturday morning. Fortunately for Lockwood, they dropped part of a wire wheel from the antique roadster. Finding the only registered 1957 Austin Healy in Memphis proved underwhelming.

The first teen suspect Lockwood approached cracked under his rapid fire examination. Barry wished it had taken him longer to solve the case. Two hundred dollars did not pay many bills.

The total income for the previous month came to twelve hundred sixteen dollars — not much for about 250 hours spent in the office and on the streets. The time included charity work for the nuns at the girls' high school. He could live on the income, but barely.

The crash at the door startled Lockwood. "Hey, Barry, you in there? I can see your light." Jeff Nordstrom, recent law school graduate and also an ex-detective, rapped his big knuckles on the door. "Man, you have to see this."

Lockwood pulled the door open, expecting to see something spectacular in the hallway. Nordstrom stood in the deserted corridor of the office building holding two beer cans, one in each hand. He thrust one at Barry. "God, this is great. Where's your TV? Sorry, I forgot. Bring the beer over to my office; you gotta see this!"

Lockwood accepted the beer; the cool can soothed his hand. He took a sip and leaned on the door frame. "Do I really have to, Jeff? It's late; I'm working."

"Paying the bleepin' bills is not working. The news is on again. More nuts. More Elvis. It's insane." He took a big swig of his beer, emptying the container. A smooth jump shot put the aluminum can in Barry's trash basket, "Perfect shot. Look, give Susie twenty bucks and she'll do your billing for you." Jeff plugged his secretary, knowing she endured a crush on Barry.

"Twenty bucks feeds me for a week." Lockwood pulled the door closed behind him, but left it unlocked. He decided he would return during the first commercial, "What's new with the Elvis story?"

Nordstrom led the way, spouting the news, town crier surfacing in the ebullient barrister. "When we left our story last night, folks, the world had been rocked, as had Graceland, by a mysterious explosion. Events reported by eyewitnesses suggested that the mansion of the late King of Rock and Roll weathered a serious atmospheric disturbance yesterday. Many tourists believe the monument was struck by a tornado. Early reports by grounds-keeping personnel employed by Turner-Disney Productions, which presently owns the historical site, lend credence to that scenario. At least one lightning strike tore holes in the building, damaged power lines, and sent hundreds of visitors scrambling for safety. An apparent minor gas explosion blew the cement cover off the tomb of the late Elvis Aaron Presley."

"I know all that;" Barry glugged as he swallowed the beer, "what's new today?"

"The hook, what they advertise to induce people to watch the news tonight, headlined a story about his body being missing." Nordstrom opened the door to his office and ushered Lockwood inside.

"Elvis's body?" Barry looked around the neat office for a chair with wheels.

"None other."

"Whom do they suspect?"

"Dunno. I suspect the news organizations." Jeff pushed his secretary's chair at Barry. He pulled his desk chair from behind his desk and sat on it backwards, arms folded across the back of the wheeled seat. The two men stared at the six-inch color television balanced on the secretary's in-basket. The screen displayed a remarkably clear picture for its size, so long as one sat within three feet of it. Jeff pulled another beer from the refrigerator built into his legal bookshelf.

"Cheers," he said to Barry, "this is the best brief I've handled all day."

"Don't get too fond of it," Barry warned, "or it might be the only brief you handle in the future. Why do you suspect the news media of making up a story about the body?"

"Turner-Disney refuses to allow cameras or reporters on the grounds. Graceland is sealed tighter than the proverbial drum. Huge canvases, like those exterminators put over houses, have covered strategic areas on the property. Even helicopters can't get pictures. Something big is going on. Possibly. At least the networks think something newsworthy is happening. They are going to make it a big story until proven otherwise. News people hate secrecy, more than they hate injustice or love the truth, I suspect. Anyway, I think they planted the story to force Turner-Disney to allow an inspection. So far T-D hasn't relented, however."

The commercial ended. The Memphis television station and Fox affiliate, WHBQ, resumed the newscast, reported by its news anchor woman, Charlene Case. "Good evening, again, ladies and gentlemen. Our lead story tonight, as it was last night, is the temporary shutdown of tours at Graceland. Tonight, Bob Jamerson is live from Elvis Presley Boulevard, directly in front of the mansion."

Jamerson, a burly red-haired man, appeared on half of the

television screen. Ms. Case's image received an electronic squeezing and moved to the left half of the picture. Jamerson held a microphone close to his mouth with his left hand. His right hand kept an earphone jammed into his right ear. Looking like a huge circus tent behind him in the distance, the mansion sat draped in multicolored sheets of plastic. Directly between the reporter and the building stood a state trooper with arms folded. The lights on his police cruiser flashed intermittently. Glare from the red and blue lights blinded the camera as they swept by and wiped out the image of Graceland being transmitted to the station.

"Charlene, can you hear me?" Jamerson asked, not looking at the camera, but staring over the police vehicle.

"Yes, Bob, go ahead with your report," Case responded, apparently annoyed at the communications snafu.

Jamerson turned to face the camera and as he did, the camera man changed the field of view slowly from a narrow telephoto shot of Graceland to a wider field. Graceland seemingly moved away from the camera. The new perspective included not only Jamerson and the trooper, but a third man. "Folks, approximately thirty hours ago something mysterious happened here at Graceland. This man witnessed the event. Until recently an employee of Turner-Disney Productions, John Small has graciously decided to relate his eyewitness account of what took place about 3:30 p.m. yesterday afternoon."

"For a sum, not to be disclosed to anyone other than the IRS," Barry intoned.

"You're such a cynic, Lockwood. This man has obviously endured a harrowing experience," Nordstrom shot back.

"How would you know?"

"I know this man; he's a client." Nordstrom clowned, "He's actually a twenty-four year-old black male, but look how he's changed. Because of this ordeal, he now appears before you looking like a gray-haired, fifty-five year-old white male!"

Lockwood howled, laughing hard enough to make his eyes water.

"Quiet, I can't hear," Jeff commanded. Tears rolling down his cheeks in silence, Barry watched and listened.

"...the wind rose almost instantaneously. A blue bolt of lightning danced across the roof of the main house and then jumped into the garden. It skipped across all of the graves. When it struck Elvis's grave, a large explosion occurred. The cement cover of the grave, the one with the brass plaque, blew straight into the sky. It must've gone up two, maybe three, hundred feet. A flame two hundred feet tall held it there for a moment. When the fire died, the cover dropped. It landed softly across the grave, turned at ninety degrees. You could see into the casket. The lid had blown off that, too."

"So you could see the mortal remains of Elvis?" Jamerson asked the older man.

"Well, I looked into the hole, but there weren't any remains. That coffin is empty, by God."

"There you have it Charlene. Elvis is not in his grave. This report might lend credence to all those Elvis sightings since his alleged death." Jamerson's image faded; his voice continued, "I'll do some more investigating and report tomorrow night from Graceland. This is Bob Jamerson for WHBQ News."

"Thank you, Bob." Charlene turned to face a different camera, "In one minute, Chuck will have another report concerning Elvis." Marching music began to play and the tiny woman on the small screen dissolved into an automobile commercial. Jeff reached in front of Barry and turned down the volume.

"I can see the headlines in the *National Enquirer* now: *Elvis Escapes From Grave.*" Jeff chuckled at his fellow man's gullibility.

"How about: *Corpse Found In Tree, Charbroiled* in the *Memphis Commercial Appeal*?" Lockwood stood, handing Jeff the empty beer can. "Back to the grind."

"That's too mundane. Who would believe that?" Jeff asked. "You are really going to leave without seeing the rest of the story?"

Barry nodded. "Thanks for the brew and the entertainment, but I have work to do, bills to pay, and sleep to get. Besides, the

next segment will be about someone who either saw Elvis or claims
to be him. See you tomorrow."

Jeff slapped Barry's back as he left, "You're probably right."
Nordstrom grinned as he closed the door behind his friend. He sat
in front of the television, mesmerized by the attention a long dead
rock star received from people who were not even born when he
had been an item. The magnetism of the personality fascinated
him.

0194-YANC

TEN

Lockwood saw her a block away; saw the blurred silhouette of her body burned through the cotton dress by the early morning sun. Patiently, she leaned on the wall. She stood with her back to the stone building, one foot behind her pushing against the gray limestone. Her purse hung almost to the sidewalk. The brunette curls stopped at her shoulders.

Directly across the street from the Peabody Hotel, she had not picked the safest section of town to wait. With all the pedestrian traffic from the Peabody at 6:30 a.m., however, an assailant would had to have been brazen.

At first, he thought she was a hooker. The doll eyes under the wide-brimmed straw hat changed his mind. She surveyed him coolly as he unlocked the door to the office building. Barry watched her, as inconspicuously as possible, while he fumbled with the keys. As he pulled the glass door closed behind him and started to relock it, she reached out with a hand gloved in white cotton and pulled on the door. Effortlessly, he stopped the door from swinging outward, "I'm sorry, miss," he apologized through the crack, "the building doesn't officially open until 8:30 a.m. I have to be at work early."

A pout crossed her face. The lips pursed; she wrinkled her nose. "Do you know when Mr. Lockwood will be in?" she asked.

Poker-faced, Lockwood answered, "He may already be in. Who shall I say is looking for him?"

"Unless he spent the night, he's not here," the woman responded. Lockwood guessed her age at nineteen, twenty-one tops. "I've been here since 5:00 a.m. and no one has come or gone from this door."

"You must want to see him pretty badly...." Barry attempted to evoke a complete explanation from the young woman, who suddenly looked very, very tired.

"Oh, I do," she responded. "The nuns said he could help me if anyone could."

Softening, Barry let down his guard. "Well, to be honest, I'm Barry Lockwood." He pushed the bulky glass door open, wide enough to exit the building. "If you like, we can get a cup of coffee across the street. Then we can go to my office and talk about whatever it is that's troubling you." He bolted the door. Lockwood began to appraise the young woman as a client. Probably boy friend problems, he surmised. Also, he congratulated himself on doing the nuns a favor, catching the delinquents who vandalized their school with graffiti. God pays off in strange ways, he mused. After a better look at the woman's well proportioned figure, he made a request: God, if this is pay back, please let her be unattached.

"That would be great," she allowed, "I'm exhausted, and hungry. Oh, I am Amy Vanderbilt. It's a pleasure to meet you Mr. Lockwood. Sister Mary Elizabeth sent me to see you."

"Mother Superior, no less." Lockwood checked both ways across the deserted street, then reached for Vanderbilt's hand. "Let's have breakfast with the ducks, okay?"

She allowed him to hold her hand until they safely crossed the street, then politely retrieved it from his grasp. He held the door open for her at the corner entrance to the Peabody, and led her to the restaurant. The waitress found them an empty table among the business men and other travelers who endeavored to secure an early start to the day.

"Two coffees," Lockwood told the waitress. "I'd like mine black, please, with two scrambled eggs, sausage, and home fries." His eyes locked onto Vanderbilt's, "And whatever she wants."

Her green eyes searched his face, "Sister said you needed the business. Are you sure you can afford this?"

Lockwood found himself blushing; he coughed into the napkin. His face brightened. "I have a feeling that my luck is about to change. Pick what you like." And I'll eat leftovers again for the remainder of the week, he said to himself.

"Okay," she answered wistfully, then turned to the waitress, "I'll have the same, thank you."

During the time the chef took to prepare their breakfast, and that which they needed to consume it, Lockwood provided Amy Vanderbilt with a thumbnail sketch of his career and credentials. She appeared most impressed by his brief military career, West Point graduate, infantry and intelligence, then military police. After six years, he allowed himself to become disillusioned by the military in peacetime and joined the Memphis police as a narcotics investigator. A 9mm bullet narrowly missed severing his spinal cord when it passed through his neck. The automatic weapon had been held by a teenage drug dealer.

Lockwood's partner, Jeff Nordstrom, killed the boy as he stood over Lockwood patiently reloading, expecting to execute the officer. Barry did not know who suffered more: Nordstrom, who quit the force in remorse for having had to kill the fourteen-year-old, or Lockwood, who spent three years in physical and occupational therapy relearning how to use most of his body.

Nordstrom went to law school as therapy; his practice consisted of trying to save similar teenagers from the fate of the young man he had been forced to kill. Lockwood survived on a meager medical pension and the odd jobs he got as an investigator.

Mid-way through the resume, the Peabody ducks paraded by the restaurant. They went out the front door to the fountain where they swam and splashed playfully. The ovation they received fazed them not at all. Vanderbilt used the interruption to ask several questions about Lockwood's therapy. She told him that her father was a physiatrist, then had to explain the term to Lockwood. He knew what a physical therapist and an occupational therapist were, but did not recognize the title of their physician supervisor.

Although the street bustled with traffic when they returned to his office building, Lockwood noticed Vanderbilt kept far enough away that he could not inconspicuously reach for her hand. Regardless, they crossed the road safely and soon sat in his bare office.

The furniture consisted of a desk and two comfortable chairs. There were blinds covering the two windows. All the accouterments were gifts from the landlord. In reality, they were left by the previous tenant whose cash flow outstripped his income for the six months he remained in business. Lockwood never did determine at which line of business the man had failed. There was no carpet, but Lockwood liked the oak floors better than a rug.

After seating Ms. Vanderbilt in the chair in front of his desk, Barry sat in his chair. Taking a deep breath, he tried not to think of all the bad reasons people required the services of private investigators. "Okay, Ms. Vanderbilt," he began, "I know you have had a long night. What can I do for you?"

"I want you to find my boy friend," she said.

Damn, Lockwood thought, mentally snapping a pencil between his fingers. "Can you elaborate? Like how long has he been missing? Did you file a missing persons report with the police? Other stuff that may come to mind?" Lockwood asked. His hand reached into the long drawer of the desk and pulled out a palm-sized cassette recorder. "If you don't mind, I'm going to record our conversation so I won't forget anything you say. First of all, what is your friend's name?" Lockwood deliberately avoided saying *boy friend*. He wanted to see how she responded. Also, he consciously wished it were not true.

He pressed the record button on the little machine. Distinctly, she replied, and it wounded Barry's love-at-first-sight heart every time thereafter that he replayed the tape. "My *boy* friend's name is Billy James, B.J. for short, Nottingham. The last time I saw him, he told me he had to go on the road. That was three months ago."

ELEVEN

Lomax sat silently in his darkened office. Austin sat to his left in one of the rose-colored sitting chairs. Armand Aguilar stood in front of them. He used a pointer, tapping it lightly on the glass that covered the huge television screen.

Aguilar stood at parade rest with the remote control to the video recorder in his left hand. It pressed tightly into the small of his back. His right hand squeezed the pointer tautly, leaving his knuckles white. At intervals, big beads of sweat rolled down the chubby face of the former Green Beret and security expert. His present title was Chief of Security for Turner-Disney, Graceland Division.

In front of the three men, a frozen image filled the screen. The picture consisted of a large square in the middle which displayed a view of Graceland: the ex-handball court, now a trophy room. Other, smaller images ringed the large picture. Lomax recognized most of the other locations shown: the front gate, the garden, and some thirteen other shots of the mansion and grounds.

Aguilar spoke tensely, evidently expecting a severe reprimand at any second, "This is daytime, tourist-evaluation mode. All of the images are captured on a single video tape and one back up tape. In real time, any smaller image can by magnified by pointing the cursor at the image. The computer then swaps that image with the view shown in the middle." He used the back of his arm to wipe the sweat from his brow. "If the man monitoring the system does not designate a choice of locations to occupy the central screen, then the computer sequences itself, changing the view every thirty seconds."

Aguilar punched a button on the remote control. The crowds

of tourists began to move on the video tape. They milled around, oohed and aahed, looked bored, and stared at one another. They never noticed the cameras. At thirty second intervals, the central, larger picture jumped to a position on the border, being replaced by the image it displaced. "The cameras are essentially invisible;" Aguilar stated, "they are hidden inside the attic. Fiber-optic cables and lenses, only a quarter of an inch in diameter, are embedded in the walls and ceilings of the basement, first, and second floors. No one can find them. In addition, we change their positions frequently." His chest puffed outwardly, proudly, "We have more videos of pickpockets at work than any police force in the country. The Memphis Police Department gave us a citation."

"Enough nonsense, Armie," Lomax interrupted, irritably. "You did not fly to L.A. to tell me about petty theft. Get to the point."

"Yes, sir." Aguilar pulled out a handkerchief and mopped his brow with it. He blotted the wet remote control. "Actually, this is where the tape gets interesting, Mr. Lomax." As if on cue, all the sightseers in all the camera shots stopped moving. As one, they raised their eyes to the ceiling and followed an invisible creature across it. "Lightning just struck the mansion. We'll lose power here for a second." The screens turned gray, white bands floated across them. One by one, the bands stabilized and the color pictures rematerialized. "The emergency generator just cut on." Slowly, the crowds moved out of each room. Aguilar fast forwarded the tape. Soon, the house appeared empty. A large crowd stood in front of the mansion and then it, too, gradually dwindled and disappeared.

"The tapes are blank for the next thirty-five hours, Mr. Lomax." Aguilar increased the forward speed of the tape and the video sped by. Characteristic slanted lines indicated that the extreme fast forward had been activated. "Last night, we had a visitor." The tape slowed to normal speed.

A ghostly presence appeared at the front gate. "The lighting stinks, I can't see his face," Lomax complained.

"The mansion has been powered down to conserve energy,

and to give the electricians a chance to repair the damaged cir-
cuits. All nonessential lighting has been disconnected. That's why
the video appears black and white. There's not enough light for
the color cameras; his white coat burns its image into the photo-
cells. You really can't see through him; that's just an illusion because he is moving and the lighting is poor." Aguilar placed the
pointer on the small video of the front gate. The gate slid open.
"He evidently knew the combination to the electronic lock."

In the dark, the man's figure appeared to glide in front of the
camera positions. Clad in white coat, white trousers and white
shoes, the visitor appeared to be from the nether world. Images of
the surrounding furniture and walls were visible through his body.
The dimness of the scene and the blurred impression of the white
clothing combined to create an optical illusion of an apparition
floating through the deserted mansion.

"Why didn't the guard who was monitoring the equipment
shift the view to the main screen?" Austin asked, tired of squinting
at the small border images.

Aguilar coughed, holding the pointer in his fist as he covered
his mouth, "Ah, he was asleep."

"What did you say?" Lomax asked icily.

"He will be fired as soon as I return to Memphis, sir." Aguilar
offered no excuse. "I will resign, also, if you insist."

"Let me think about those propositions, Armie," Lomax stated
coldly. Austin felt the presence of Machiavelli in the room. "What
else happened last night?"

Aguilar kept the pointer moving, identifying the phantom in
each view, a white wisp slipping silently from room to room. "Here
he is going up the main staircase. Now, he's in the master bedroom. He's into the bathroom. Somehow, he knew about the safe
behind the full-length mirror. We don't have a lens in the bathroom, but we found the safe open this morning. Evidently he is
carrying a brief case which he removed from the safe."

"The safe contained a briefcase?" Lomax asked.

"Apparently so. No one on my staff knew the combination to

it. In fact, only two people I know knew the vault existed. Neither of us knew the combination. We assumed it to be empty. Now, he's gone into the master bedroom closet. He's leaving the mansion. At the front gate. Over his shoulder, he has draped four or five outfits. He still has the briefcase." The video tape ended, leaving a blank image on the screen.

Lomax stabbed at the remote control for the office in his hands. The curtains opened across his plate glass wall, jerking every few inches. An electric motor pulled them unevenly toward the corners of the room. The bright L.A. sunlight briefly blinded the three men. Lomax recovered first. "Is this the original tape?" he asked.

"Yes, sir."

"You have a backup?" Lomax asked.

"And two copies," Aguilar confirmed the assumption. "I already gave one to Mr. Austin."

"George," Lomax turned his attention to Austin, "are the boys in the news network enhancing that video?"

"They tried, Mr. Lomax," Austin apologized. "For three hours the video magicians attempted every digital trick in the book. They can't improve on the image."

"There's no way to prove that man is B.J. Nottingham?" Lomax asked scornfully.

"I'm afraid not, Mr. Lomax," Aguilar apologized. "I'm sorry that I have let you down."

"Armie," Lomax said, "don't be so hard on yourself. You may have done me a huge favor." Aguilar stared at his benefactor. "This isn't exactly what we planned, but it'll work. First, we have to get you to Memphis, without R.M. finding out you were in my office. Don't want you, or me, compromised. Second, there will be a bonus for you, if you can accomplish the following."

"Name it," Aguilar commanded, eager to redeem himself.

"Fire the nincompoop who slept on guard duty last night. Make certain he is allowed to see this tape. You know, it's proof he screwed up. Allow him to keep a copy, somehow. Throw it at him;

leave it out; do something that allows it to get into his hands. I think we can trust him to take it to one of the networks."

"What good will that do?" Aguilar looked confused.

"It will guarantee you a job and a bonus, for one thing," Lomax stated, cantankerously. "You let me worry about the rest, okay?"

"You're the boss," Aguilar conceded.

"That's right." Lomax picked up the telephone and punched the intercom button. "Jenny, get Mr. Aguilar to LAX and on a charter flight to Memphis immediately. Put it on my account, not the Graceland account. On second thought, charge it to the political action committee account, okay? Good." Lomax grabbed Aguilar's hand and shook it. "Get some sleep on the way to Memphis. George, the tape." Austin placed the video into Lomax's left hand, gently. He, in turn, slapped it into Aguilar's hand. "Don't lose this until you return to Memphis, okay?"

"Yes, sir," Aguilar replied as Jenny whisked the security chief out of the office; the taxi already waited at the curb in front of the Turner-Disney Building.

Once Jenny safely disposed of Aguilar, Austin looked at his boss. The serenity of a stroke of genius calmed the man's face. "I give up, what's the ploy?" Austin asked.

"You said no one could prove that Nottingham visited Graceland last night, right?" Lomax reiterated.

"Right. The video quality is too lousy." Austin confirmed his previous statement.

"So lousy, in fact, that one could suggest that the real Elvis, or the ghost of Elvis Presley, visited Graceland last night. Right?" Austin stared at Lomax and marveled at the man's brilliance. "By tomorrow morning, the news media will have pictures of Elvis's ghost on every front page, taken from a video tape spirited from Graceland. I think I just turned a sleepy night-watchman into a millionaire, George. What do you think?"

TWELVE

Jack Shafer sat at the picture window in the Winnebago. The table in front of him held a shot glass, an empty fifth of whiskey, and a soon-to-be-empty fifth. Rip-roaring drunk, but too old to be rip-roaring, he thought about himself. That makes me pip-squeaking intoxicated, he decided. Squinching up his face, he managed to chuckle and to burp at exactly the same time. The effort yielded a splurching sound from his throat, which forced him to chuckle and burp again. The second belch proved less melodious than the first, not being a synchronous event with the chuckle.

Propping himself on his elbows beside the window, he viewed the turmoil around him. His vehicle appeared to be the only one in the small parking lot. Outside the lot, and across the street, milled thousands of people and, apparently, hundreds of cars, all moving in large circles. He detected four or five unique vehicles, one a VW bus with a distinctive paint job showing Elvis and Ann-Margaret in character from the movie *Viva Las Vegas*. The automobiles and trucks drove down Elvis Presley Boulevard and within his sight, repeatedly, approximately every thirty minutes. In addition, throngs of people, again, some dressed very distinguishingly, paraded back and forth in front of his view of Graceland.

Never did Shafer see the gates of Graceland open. Two brown police vehicles of some type, like armored personnel carriers, squatted crosswise across the driveway in front of the gate. The crowd broke and flowed around the law enforcement officers, individual tears in a stream of humanity that bubbled around the rough boulders of indifference. Humanity has lost its anchor, Jack thought. Why else would they cling to a man's memory, any man?

His wife lost her anchor after her second miscarriage. Annie

Shafer denied it, but Jack knew his wife feared death after losing the second child. She no longer thought of an infant's demise as *the will of God*. Her severely damaged faith still allowed her to keep up a strong front, for whom Jack never knew. God knows, she did not do it for him. She knew only too well that Jack denied God's existence. He hated only the finality of death; he feared it not at all. Annie dreaded the unknown, not able to accept the conclusion that Jack assumed everyone would embrace, eventually, one way or another.

Tucking that big phobia back inside a very small space in her mind, Annie accomplished much with the faith that remained. She put on a strong countenance and dared her God to disappoint her. Jack held his tongue about the futility of expecting life after death during the final year of her life. He hoped to give her peace of mind where peace of body no longer existed.

A tear rolled down Jack's cheek at the thought of his wife. Gone. Gone, forever. He poured another shot of whiskey for himself, but set it on the table without drinking it. Annie hated alcohol, abhorred drunks. Another tear fell. Condemning himself for his sentimentality, he listened carefully for the electrical generator to ascertain if it still rumbled quietly beneath his feet. Feeling and hearing the vibration of the small gasoline engine, Jack reached across the table and switched on the diminutive color television. Spinning the dial quickly, he found several local stations, but settled on the one with the clearest reception. The midday news blared at him until he adjusted the volume. Every station carried the same news. In disgust, he let the television play, unattended.

The last segment of the news attracted his attention. It showed a helicopter's view of the traffic jam which Jack watched from ground level. The announcer clearly let his emotions overcome him as he reported the reopening of Graceland to the public. The official unveiling would occur an hour from then. Turner-Disney, in a goodwill gesture, decided to allow the public free, walk-in, access to Graceland for two days. As far as the helicopter newsman could tell, every Memphian within ten miles journeyed to or from

Graceland. Parking appeared to be nonexistent. Everyone walked. The total population of Memphis and surrounding counties seemingly appeared within range of the chopper's cameras.

Jack watched the helicopter through the window of the camper out of professional curiosity. The pilot positioned it almost directly over his head. Intermittently, he watched the pictures it beamed to the station on his television. The old Bell Jet Ranger hovered tens of feet above the trees. "Watch out for the FAA," Shafer warned the pilot telepathically. He knew the pilot already worried about pleasing the cameraman and not displeasing the federal authorities who regulated his license to fly.

What the hell, Jack thought, it's time to give the old girl part of the sendoff she requested. Only slightly wobbly, holding his liquor well after years of military practice, Shafer navigated to the rear of the RV and opened a plywood panel. The door covered an irregular storage space around the rear wheel well. One hinge had broken years before. Lopsided, the door fell open. Undeterred, Jack reached into the deep recess and pulled out a bundle of rags.

Unwinding the many layers affected Jack like a multicolored rag onion. Tears began to flow again, this time well lubricated by the alcohol. By the time he held the silver canister in his hands, he sobbed vigorously. Huge tears splashed onto the faded linoleum floor of the vehicle.

After a short while the tears stopped; his chest ceased to heave involuntarily. Jack became more tranquil as his mind focused on the task ahead. First, he obtained a sample with a spoon. Second, he found a ziplock bag. Finally, he designated himself as the delivery system. He rewrapped the cylinder and placed it inside the storage bin.

Sobering, he showered, shaved, and dressed in his best suit. Jack also cleaned up after himself and stowed the whiskey. After examining himself critically in the full length mirror behind the bathroom door, he dabbed at his thinning hair. Content with his looks, he left the RV through the side door. Carefully, he locked the door behind him.

As he walked toward the hubbub on Elvis Presley Boulevard, he turned one last time to check the location of the van. When he did, he noticed a new blue sticker on the front bumper. Curious, he walked back to the RV and leaned over to check it. A yellow lightning bolt accentuated the letters TCB on a blue background. The number 45433 was printed in a white space below the letters along with "Turner-Disney." Jack pushed his lower lip out. Unsuccessfully, he racked his brain trying to determine where it came from. Eventually, he decided to worry about it later.

Turning to face Graceland, he resumed his march out of the parking lot. Overhead in a clear blue, cloudless sky, not predicted by any weather forecaster in the eastern third of the country, several helicopters and light aircraft turned tight circles. Each vied with the other to provide to their audiences an appreciation of the volume of humanity present.

At the entrance to the lot, Shafer found two men. The guards wore gray uniforms. Military experience prepared him for bluffing his way out of, and back into, the parking lot. Years of service to his country did not prepare him for the reception by the guards, however.

"Colonel Shafer, sir," one man said as he approached Shafer, right hand extended. He shook Shafer's hand.

"Yes?" Shafer answered, warily.

"We have a vehicle to transport you, sir," the guard replied, as the other man started the engine to the gray mini-van emblazoned with the Graceland/Turner-Disney logo.

"Take me? Where?" Shafer asked suspiciously, turning to face the van.

The guard laughed, as if hearing a new joke, "To Graceland, of course. We'll have to hurry though, sir. In twenty minutes, the gates will open and Arkansas and Tennessee will flow into the mansion, unless the troopers can keep a lid on it."

"To Graceland, you said?" Shafer asked, uncertain if he heard the man correctly.

"Yes, sir." The security man pulled a computer printout from his pocket and read it out loud, "Says here: Escort Colonel Shafer to Graceland at his convenience. Allow no other vehicles onto the Graceland service vehicle lot until further notice."

"Is there a name signed to the bottom of that directive, son?" Shafer quizzed the man as they climbed into the gray van through the side door.

The motorized door slid shut, unattended. The guard replied, "Same guy who signs all our stuff, Colonel: Armand Aguilar, Chief of Security. Of course, anybody on the security staff could have written it; his name goes on everything."

In less than two minutes, the gray van managed to stop all pedestrian and vehicular traffic on the six-lane highway and sidewalks in front of Graceland. The armored police vehicles lumbered out of their way. The decorative gates to Graceland opened majestically under electronic control. At the far side of the circular driveway, the driver stopped the vehicle. The electric motor pulled the side door open silently.

"Enjoy your visit, Colonel Shafer," the guard requested of him as he helped Shafer out of the van. "If you want a ride back, just stop any uniformed security guard and ask. We'll be right over." The van drove away, leaving Shafer to question his own sanity.

He harbored no curiosities about Elvis's estate, *the* Elvis Presley's estate, he corrected himself, since he knew two Elvises. It took him no time to find the Meditation Garden. As he debated with himself how best to accomplish his mission, a rush of noise and babble skewered his thoughts in mid-deliberation. A great throng of people, orderly, in a four deep procession, began filing onto the grounds. It's now or never, Shafer decided. Removing the plastic bag from his coat pocket, he unzipped it. Grabbing it firmly by the sealed end, he shook it with all his might.

A small portion of his wife's remains floated into the air. She had maintained these ashes would represent her heart. Caught by a swift, sudden burst of wind, the light gray particles of dust spiraled upward. They spread outward quickly, losing the black shadowy shape and sparkling individually as they scattered in the sunlight. Shafer watched as the tiny cloud disappeared, settling softly onto the recently repaired grave site of Elvis Aaron Presley.

Rapidly, the parade of tourists surrounded Shafer, hemming him in. He looked for a guard. Before he found one, he felt a strong hand on his shoulder. Turning to face the hand's owner, Jack recognized the face of his hitchhiker, Elvis Presley. The young man hid behind sunglasses, and a gray hat and uniform similar to the security guards.

"Quite a crowd, eh?" Elvis asked, not expecting an answer. "What do you say we stroll back to the Winnebago, Colonel?"

Shafer needed no prodding to leave. One reason he chose to fly helicopters in the army was to avoid crowds. "I'll follow you, son," he replied. As an afterthought, he added, "Can we have a talk when we get back? Some strange things have happened to me today."

Presley laughed, white teeth flashing, dimples creasing his face, "Colonel, we can talk all night if you want."

THIRTEEN

Jack and Elvis crossed Elvis Presley Boulevard. As they cleared the street, feet just touching the sidewalk on the side of the Boulevard opposite Graceland, the traffic light changed. Automobiles in the street gunned their engines and started to move. An inexperienced driver stomped on the accelerator much too hard and gave his vehicle too much gas; it leapt through the intersection like a drag racer. Shafer heard the roar and looked back in self-defense.

Directly across the road, a young mother struggled at the edge of the crowd with an empty stroller. In addition to the stroller, she tried to control a baby, a large black Labrador puppy on a leash, and dark-haired little girl about five. As the flow of pedestrians halted for the light, the young woman tried to rearrange her charges before they rushed across the street at the next signal change. To free her hands, she handed the dog's leash to the five-year-old.

Briefly turning her back to the little girl, the mother tucked the infant into the stroller. Excited and worried by the crowd, the dog darted across the street, dragging the five-year-old after him.

The screech of brakes ripped through the intersection. The metallic crunch of two vehicles colliding modified the tumultuous din rending the air. A van in the near lane swerved unsuccessfully in an attempt to miss the puppy. Jack, and hundreds of other pedestrians, watched in horror. The force of the truck bumper's impact with the dog threw the animal down the road. Leash still wrapped around her wrist, the child tumbled into the street in front of the moving cars.

Fortunately, most of the automobiles moved slowly, having started to move with the change of the light. The impact of the bumper with the dog snatched the leash from the girl's arm; she landed on her stomach, between the lanes of traffic. More drivers hit their brakes and collided with other cars. After an interminable number of seconds, the screeching and bumping finally ended.

Dazed, oblivious to her near-death experience, the five-year-old sat amid the instant junkyard. She cried for her puppy. Her mother pushed the stroller and infant into the welcoming hands of a stranger and ran to the little girl. Kneeling beside the sobbing child, the mother cried.

"Inky, Inky," the inconsolable child wailed, unaware her fate nearly mimicked the dead dog's.

"It's all right, baby. It's all right," the mother repeated slowly. Two police officers arrived and endeavored to make sense of the confusion. Walkie-talkies blaring and whistles blowing, the officers waded into the throng of people milling about the street, gazing at the dead dog and the crumpled cars.

"Move along. Keep moving," the first officer strode into the street and directed the crowd away from the accident.

"Ma'am, do y'all need an ambulance?" the second officer asked the crying woman as he knelt beside the sobbing little girl. The young mother shook her head and continued to hug the whimpering child, while they sat in the middle of the street.

"Senseless," Jack said as he turned to Elvis, to continue the trek to the Winnebago. Jack spun around. No Elvis. He had gone; vanished into thin air. Shafer searched the crowd, futilely, until he looked in the middle of the street.

Kneeling on one knee before the puppy, Elvis bowed his head as if in prayer. He placed one hand on the puppy's head, the other he held closely to his own chest. After a fleeting moment, Elvis picked up the animal with both hands. It hung limply, tongue dangling from its mouth, eyes closed, legs at impossible angles.

Cradling the dog with one arm, Elvis gently stroked its head and neck with his other hand. The leash hung to the ground and dragged after them as he walked toward the child, her mother, and the police officer. Every pair of eyes in the silent crowd followed Elvis as he walked toward the child with the flaccid, black, furry body. Rising to his feet, an officer met Elvis face-to-face. He insisted, "I don't think the child should see the dog." The mother looked up from the child, gazed at Elvis, and shook her head, no, in agreement.

Elvis smiled. Jack could not see his eyes behind the sunglasses; somehow, he knew they twinkled. The crowd continued to gawk at the drama in the street, wondering what the man with the dead dog would do next.

"It's okay, officer, he was just knocked out," Elvis said quietly. "See?" The puppy's tail began to swish back and forth slowly. Its eyes opened; the dog extended its legs when it realized Elvis held it off the ground. Opening its mouth wide, the puppy yawned, then looked at Elvis and licked his face. Elvis put the animal on the ground and handed the leash to the child's mother. "He's too strong for her," he suggested, "maybe you should hold this."

As the puppy tried to shake and regain its wobbly sense of balance, the child fell upon it and hugged it. She shrieked with joy, "Inky!"

A cheer rose from the crowd. The officer shook Elvis's hand, a smile on his face. "Thank you, sir."

Elvis acknowledged the cheer by tipping his right index finger to the brim of his cap. When the light changed again, he recrossed the street and found Shafer. They said not one word while returning to the parking lot where the RV sat.

Jack sat in the driver's seat of the camper. He spun the worn old captain's chair so he faced Elvis, who sat in the passenger seat. Elvis unlocked his chair and spun it to face the older man. "You wanted to talk?" Elvis asked. He took off the sunglasses with his right hand and laid them gently inside the upturned guard's hat, which lay on the warm dashboard's cracked vinyl.

"I saw the news today. I read a paper, too," Jack began, not knowing where to start. "There's a rumor that Elvis has risen from the dead. People all over the nation, all over the world, are doing crazy things. A religion is being started in his name."

Elvis waited, watching the retired helicopter pilot's eyes. He said nothing.

"I'm not a religious guy," Shafer continued, shaking his head slowly. "I don't believe in the last guy who supposedly rose from the dead. My wife, she believed; she tried to believe. God rest her soul. I hope, for her sake, she was right. Even if it means I'll go to Hell. And I surely will, if there is a God."

Arms aching from pain in his shoulders, Shafer fumbled for a painkiller from his pocket. He unwrapped one and popped it into his mouth. "Want a glass of water?" Elvis asked. Shafer shook his head as he ground the pill between his teeth and swallowed the gritty residue piecemeal. The bitter taste wrinkled his nose.

"Don't interrupt my train of thought," Shafer scolded. Elvis nodded silently. "Your name really is Elvis Presley, isn't it?" Elvis nodded again.

"My camper is parked inside a reserved lot. It shouldn't be. An escort of security men took me to Graceland. I know that dog was dead. I've seen a lot of dead in my life." Shafer pursed his lips, thinking fleeting thoughts of battlefields in the past, "That's the reason I'm going to go to Hell, given the opportunity."

Jack took a deep breath, then asked the question he had been getting to, circuitously, "Who are you?"

"Elvis Presley." Presley looked straight into Shafer's eyes. His composure changed not at all.

"The Elvis Aaron Presley?"

"Sort of."

"Aha!" Jack smiled, knowing he had hit upon the secret, but he still wanted to know what the secret was. "What do you mean, sort of? Are you a relative, an imitator, or am I having one of my hallucinations?"

"No, to all three questions. I'm the real Elvis Presley." Elvis placed his elbow on the arm of the captain's chair, then placed his chin in his hand. Jack had seen the pose before, in one of his wife's books on Elvis, or a movie, somewhere.

"Why sort of, then? You are dead. Aren't you? Elvis is dead, isn't he?" Jack glanced around the camper, nervous about hearing the answer. He saw the security guards return to their post at the entrance to the parking lot.

"You're right; I died," Presley said, nonchalantly.

"Jesus!"

"Close."

"Huh?" Shafer cocked his head, not certain he had heard Elvis correctly.

"I have a message for the human race, just as Jesus Christ did." Presley's eyes flashed as he smiled and the small crow's feet appeared at the corners of his eyes. "Circumstances being what they are, I have chosen you to help me deliver the message, Colonel."

Shafer laughed loud and hard. "Son, even if you are Elvis, I couldn't make your announcements for you. First, I'm not going to live much longer. Second," the laugh became uproarious, enhanced by the previous booze and the absurdity of the situation as Shafer perceived it, "I never even liked most of your music."

Elvis remained calm, waiting for Shafer's belly laugh to subside. After several minutes, Presley stated, flatly, "You don't like most of anyone's music, Colonel."

The laugh stopped. Shafer stared at Presley with cold eyes. "How do you know that?"

Elvis took a turn at grinning. "Colonel Shafer, you're a bitter old man. If you had enjoyed music, you would have had this radio fixed a long time ago." Elvis thumped the dashboard radio speaker with the palm of his hand.

"Who needs it? You'd be bitter, too," Shafer shot back through a grimace. "Family dead. Most of my colleagues dead. Enemies all dead. Allegiances all screwed up. No purpose to life. Dying slowly, painfully...."

"Feeling sorry for yourself, sir?"

"Yeah. So what?"

"So, I can empathize." Elvis added softly, "I can also burden you with a purpose."

"How's that?"

"Later, Colonel. For now, I need to get to the west coast. If you are going to fulfill your wife's second request, I'd like to ride with you." Elvis stood, stepping around the seat awkwardly. He reached inside his back pocket and pulled several bills from it. He handed the money to Shafer. "I picked up some of my things and did some visiting in town while you slept. This is for expenses, so far."

Shafer looked at his hand. In it, he held four one-hundred-dollar bills. Positive, then, that he dealt with a psychiatric patient, he shook his head slowly, "Son, you seem to be a nice guy. Maybe we should spend this on a psychiatrist, or to refill your medication...." Suddenly, Jack felt dizzy. The motorhome spun. Everything turned gray, then black.

FOURTEEN

Jack Shafer softly gripped his wife's near-lifeless, pale arm. His tears splattered across the top of her hand, heavy enough to momentarily deform her thin, translucent skin. Blue rivers of blood coursed across the backside of her right hand, here and there dammed by bruises. The flesh had been damaged by failed attempts to start intravenous lines.

Her breathing, inaudible to the medical personnel in the room, rasped at his heart, cutting deeper with each lingering pause. The battle between the silence and the sounds of breathing ended, as it always does, with silence winning. His heart had been sawn in two. The blood in the veins of her hand no longer flowed but pooled and coagulated, having lost its head of pressure when her heart refused to squeeze once last time.

Involuntarily, Jack clenched her hand tighter, willing the blood to flow and the lungs to reverberate with rushing air. Neither happened. A doctor placed a hand on his shoulder. "She's gone, Mr. Shafer. She's gone."

"Honey, I don't want you to worry about me," Jack spoke, voice wavering. "I know you are at peace, in Heaven, there with your God. He added self-consciously, "Our God," trying not to feel a hypocrite. God had always been her God. Jack never found his. Now, he doubted he ever would. Why would a merciful, just God take her away? Her only fault had been to love Jack. She never harmed a soul. The anger flared in his heart, a really powerful and virtuous Supreme Being would have taken Jack, not her. A decent God, a mythical Greek deity, might even have given Jack a fair chance at saving his own life and hers, with a quest, or a riddle. But, no! This so-called Savior stole the souls of the pure, the weak, and the innocent, and along with them: the hearts and minds of those who loved them.

The frustrations left over from her two-year battle with cancer boiled over, erupting as meek sobs. His body, exhausted from his long vigil, could not stand and scream as he should have, "Why," he whimpered, tears soaking the sheet near her arm, "why?"

"It's time," a faceless voice said, repeatedly. "It's time."

Jack pried open his eyes. The effort triggered pain in his neck and head. The reward for his struggle was the vision which swam in front of him; eight to ten feet away he recognized a dirty ceiling. Tracks for a curtain circled overhead. The curtain hung around him, an ineffectual wagon train between him and that oldest Indian, Death. The nightmares about his wife's and his own impending death coalesced and then faded.

Sluggishly, he lifted his head and peered around the small enclosure. Elvis stood at his side, mute. Behind the curtain, presumably on a stretcher similar to his own, the voice of a child sang sweetly, "It's time. It's time to see the doctor."

Too weak to speak, Shafer winked at Elvis, who returned the gesture with a smile and words of encouragement, "Hang in there, partner. You're next in line to see the doc." Tilting his head, as he listened to the conversation behind the curtain, Elvis smiled. Jack tried to return the smile.

"Okay," the doctor said to the child, "do you have any teeth? Where do you keep them, in your shoe? Your pocket? Sock? Oh, there they are, in your mouth, how silly." The child giggled. "How many do you have? You'll have to open wide so that I can count them all. Whoops, sorry I gagged you."

The light banter continued as the physician cajoled, teased, and examined the tyke without a whimper from the boy. After concluding his interview and examination, the doctor summarized for the hidden parents. "He's got a strep throat and an ear infection. I'll have the nurse give you prescriptions for a decongestant and an antibiotic and other instructions. He'll be good as new by next week. Take him to your pediatrician in about two weeks, unless he doesn't improve quickly. If that happens, take him right away."

The parents expressed several minor concerns, then the physician said goodbye to the family, "Don't come back for a long, long time. Not until you are grown-up," he joshed with the child, "I don't like kids."

After several requests from the parents, the child responded with a giggle, "Thank you, Doctor Young. Good-bye."

Elvis heard the M.D. confer briefly with one of the emergency room nurses, then he wrestled his way through the curtain and into the cubical with Jack. "Oh, oh, he's awake," the practitioner observed as he clumsily fought his way through the vinyl drapery. "I hate these things," the doctor said, a big smile on his face, "they remind me of the proverbial paper bag I couldn't fight my way out of."

Feeling stronger, Jack raised his head and eyed the chubby medic. Balding, with a small mustache and thick glasses, his bucktoothed smile reminded Jack of a cartoon chipmunk. "You're too happy to be a doctor," Jack snorted. "Are you an intern?"

"No," the surprised, middle-aged physician shook his head, "and, strictly speaking, all interns are doctors, too. I've been doing this for fifteen years. Why are you a grump, Mr. Shafer?"

"Colonel Shafer," Elvis corrected.

Dr. Young glanced at Elvis. "You look familiar; can't place you, though. From Memphis?"

"Tupelo, Mississippi."

"Can I go now?" Jack interrupted.

"Yes and no," the physician answered. "How much pain are you in? Where do you live? Who is your family doctor?"

"What do you think I am, an encyclopedia?" Jack asked scornfully, then proceeded to rattle off the answers, "A lot of pain, occasionally; but none, now. Home's in the parking lot; it's an RV. The family doctor is at Walter Reed Army Medical Center in Washington, D.C."

"I knew you were military when the clerk took your insurance card." Young hesitated, then boldly broached the subject he had been avoiding, "How much do you know about your condition?"

"My condition?" Shafer asked, innocently. Young waited, recognizing the bluff. "Okay, dammit, I've got prostate cancer, not long to live, and a lot of pain — at times. It has spread to my bones, liver, lungs, and brain. Do I need to know more?"

"For some reason, probably the metastatic cancer, your electrolytes and calcium levels were way out of the normal ranges today. As a result, it looks like your heart marches to its own drummer, too slow or too fast, at times. That's why you passed out."

"What does that mean?"

"It means that you could kick the bucket any time, or you could be around for a year, or so." Young looked compassionately at the old man, made seemingly older by his suffering. "I can help make you more comfortable, but the prescriptions I write for you are only good in Tennessee, where I have a license. I hope you are on your way home, so your doctor can continue to treat you."

"Home's where the Winnebago breaks down," Shafer said, wryly. He smiled for the first time, knowing he aggravated the M.D. "Now, if you don't mind, sir, I have an engagement to keep in San Diego."

Shafer eyed the physician suspiciously. He struggled to free himself from the weight of a single sheet and tried to elevate himself into a sitting position. Finally up, on the edge of the bed, Shafer asked, "Any reason I can't drive?"

Without hesitation, the doctor responded earnestly, "Several, Mr., ah, Colonel Shafer. First, the pain medication you will be taking may make you drowsy. That's the equivalent of DUI, if the police catch you. Don't want to spend your last year in jail, do you?" Jack shook his head feebly. "Your electrolytes could go haywire, again, at anytime. That might lead to hallucinations, an arrhythmia, or syncope."

"Sink or pee?" Jack asked uncertainly.

"Syncope. Fainting," Young explained. "Might not be fatal to you, but if you hit another vehicle head on, you could kill people.

Nice people. People who aren't scheduled to die later this year. Know what I mean?"

Dejected, Jack sat, long faced and hunched over, jaw slack, nearly touching his chest. "I made a promise."

"It's okay," Elvis interjected. "Doc, you write down the medicine prescriptions that he needs. We'll stop at a pharmacy in Tennessee. I'll drive. We'll get to San Diego in record time. "I'll have him home before his medicine runs out. Okay with you, Colonel?"

"I think he should spend the night in the hospital," the physician said to Elvis. He pointed to the intravenous line, which dangled from the bag of solution on the chrome pole near the head of Jack's stretcher and ran into Shafer's arm. Lifting his hand in the direction of the cardiac monitor that sat on a shelf above his patient's head, he added, "His electrolytes may be better, now, but they were a disaster earlier. His cardiac rhythm — there it goes again — fluctuates between too fast to pump blood efficiently and too slow to supply blood to his brain."

As Elvis watched, Jack's eyes glazed over and he began to mumble; his head bobbed on a rubber neck as he fought to remain conscious. Presley gripped the older man's left hand with his left hand. He placed his right hand behind Jack's head, steadying him and feeling the perspiration that drenched the hospital gown. "It's going to be all right, fellah," the thick southern accent spilled from Elvis's lips, "Just hang in there a minute; this will all get better. I promise." Presley squeezed Jack's hand and the nape of Shafer's neck. He closed his eyes and held his chin pressed close to his own chest. Holding that pose for about twenty seconds, Elvis remained motionless until interrupted by the doctor.

"There he goes, again," Young said, astounded by the quick changes in the rhythmicity of Shafer's heart. "He's back in normal sinus rhythm."

Instantly alert, as his cerebral perfusion returned to normal, Jack looked at Young, "That's good, right?"

"For the time being, it's good. It could change at any time."

Dr. Young started to pitch for admission again.

"Elvis," Jack ordered, "find my clothing. We're history."

"You'll have to sign a release," Young responded, "and please don't drive, Colonel. No one else on this planet wants to die when your time comes."

Jack looked at Elvis, defeated without outside intervention. Elvis rescued him. "I'll drive," Presley told the physician. Colonel Shafer resignedly accepted the offer for help, probably for the first time in his life. He nodded silently. Elvis promised, "It'll work out just fine, Colonel. You'll see."

"Want to be discharged, or stay overnight for observation?" Doctor Young again asked Shafer. The medic never dreamed the old man sincerely wanted to leave, looking and feeling the way he obviously did.

Jack waited only briefly to answer the question indirectly. "Elvis, get me my clothes," he rasped. "We've got a lot of traveling to do."

Surprised, Young called to the nurse, "Colonel Shafer will be discharged. Start the paperwork; disconnect his i.v.; I'll write his prescriptions."

FIFTEEN

Jeff Nordstrom locked his law office door from the inside. Barry Lockwood watched intently as Nordstrom slid home the two deadbolts. "Expecting visitors, or clients, Jeff?" Lockwood chuckled, aware that he and Nordstrom kept the strangest and longest hours of the tenants in the office building. A private detective could not choose his hours. Neophyte lawyers nibbled at the edges of the pool of litigious wealth, like guppies after bread crumbs. They did so by working the cases and the hours no established lawyer tolerated.

Barry pulled a rolled newspaper from his back pocket and tossed it onto the secretary's desk, as Jeff adjusted the television on top of her in-basket. Both waited for the ten o'clock news to start. "I found this in the grocery store today, Jeff. Thought it might interest you," Barry explained as the *National Enquirer* landed in front of Nordstrom. The headline shrieked, *Elvis Alive: Back From The Dead Or Never Gone?*

Nordstrom scanned the smaller print as the paper lay face up, in front of him, "You wasted money on this? Hell, Barry, that's almost a lunch."

"Breakfast. I had to read it; you got me started on this lunacy." He leaned back in the secretary's chair and twisted off the top of the beer bottle Jeff thrust into his hands. "And the Vanderbilt girl, Christ, what's she doing chasing after a loser who impersonates Elvis? Those guys will be coming out of the woodwork. Already are, I'll bet."

"Says here," Nordstrom summarized the article as he read, backing into his seat and reaching for his beer with the other hand, "that Elvis's twin brother Jesse Garon did not die at birth, but was born severely mentally disabled. He spent forty years in institutions, hidden from the public by the Presleys. The reporter surmises Jesse was born with a heart condition, in addition to his intellectual deficiencies. Apparently, this reporter thinks Jesse died, or — ta-da! Tune in tomorrow for more dirt — was murdered. The theory is that Elvis purposely gained weight to make his appearance more like his brother's. After being on ice for several months, Jesse supposedly occupied the casket in the garden at Graceland, not Elvis."

"I read that," Barry responded. "Still, it doesn't explain where the body is now, Elvis's or Jesse's."

"It might," Nordstrom said, mischievously. "Suppose the theory is true. Pretend you are Elvis and you are afraid someone will discover the truth about Jesse and exhume the body. Genetic testing might expose the switch."

"The hole in that theory is that identical twins have similar, if not identical results to genetic tests," Barry countered. "If I were Elvis, I'd leave the body right where they buried it, in order not to attract attention to it. If anyone finds the corpse now, they will surely test it."

"The hole in your theory is that you assumed Jesse and Elvis to be identical. They may look a lot alike, but they are not identical," Nordstrom glowed, one up in points.

Unable to refute the argument, Lockwood leaned forward and raised the volume on the television, "Point well taken, counselor. News is on." Nordstrom beamed. He enjoyed sparring with Barry; both men enjoyed it, even during their patrol car years. Lockwood always booked the suspect; Nordstrom consistently pointed out the holes in the legal case against him. Frequently, the defense attorneys filed briefs similar to those conceived by Nordstrom. Unwilling to continue the frustration after his partner's severe injury, Nordstrom attended law school to sharpen his skills. Barry struggled with rehabilitation.

Charlene Case sat, prim and proper, before the television camera. Barry tried to decide if the gossip columnists were correct, that the producer ordered the camera man to leave her image slightly out of focus, to soften her facial features. He decided he could not tell whether the makeup or the camera operator subdued the high cheek bones and thin lips. The acne scars clearly shone on the weatherman; Ms. Case's face appeared velvety by comparison.

Quickly disposing of the international news, the reporter moved to the national and local news, intermeshed as they were. "There have been some developments in the Graceland story. Bob is at the mansion. He filed this report for the six o'clock edition." A frame containing reporter Bob Jamerson's image tumbled from the right hand corner of the television monitor, growing larger as it tumbled. It finally obscured Case's image.

"Good evening, ladies and gentlemen." The reporter stood in the identical spot as the previous night. Only the blue sky and the presence of a different Tennessee State Trooper suggested any time had passed since the preceding story had been filed. The tarps, which previously covered Graceland, could be seen in the background being removed by the estate grounds keepers.

"A dramatic video may give us a glimpse of a living Elvis. These pictures were taken inside Graceland by security cameras last night. Watch closely." The video screen displayed the spooky image of a man in white gliding through the mansion. More than a minute of the video aired without comment.

As it ended, Jamerson said, "As I speak, experts are hard at work enhancing these images." Two single frame photographs appeared on the screen. The dimly lit, barely-visible face of a young version of Elvis Presley stared at the camera in both shots. The first countenance included the dimpled smile, full lips and brushed back hair; the second displayed the patented sneer, with upper lip raised slightly.

"With me tonight is Mr. Armand Aguilar, Chief of Security at Graceland. He requested time to make a statement for Turner-Disney Productions. Mr. Aguilar."

"Thank you Mr. Jamerson." Aguilar stiffened, as if standing in review. He placed both hands behind his back. Maintaining his military posture, he took a deep breath. Perceptibly more relaxed, he looked directly into the camera and spoke, "Ladies and gentlemen, I wish to assure you that this video does not, I repeat, does not, show Mr. Elvis Aaron Presley. Mr. Presley's final resting spot has not been disturbed, as reported by the press yesterday. It remains intact and untouched. As proof, Graceland opened to the public this afternoon. We did sustain minor damage to the handball court, to the mansion, and to the garden. Repairs have been completed."

"Any other comments on the video tape, Mr. Aguilar?" Jamerson prodded.

"Yes. Video technicians at Turner-Disney are trying to improve the quality of this video. The tape you broadcast was released to the public prematurely, and without our permission. The man who gave this tape to your station has been terminated." Aguilar took another deep breath, as if controlling his anger. He continued, "If we can positively identify the individual on this video, we will release his name to the public. We intend to prosecute him to the fullest extent of the law, for felony breaking and entering. A warning to other potential trespassers, the security system has been repaired also. That is our complete statement, Mr. Jamerson. Turner-Disney Corporation thanks you for allowing us this opportunity."

Jamerson cut Aguilar off, summarizing expeditiously, "So there you have it, folks. Is this Elvis?" The two frozen images again appeared on the screen, "or is this a vandal? Charlene, what do you think?"

Kendall Harvey, the weatherman for WHBQ, fielded the inquiry for the news anchorwoman as the studio image reappeared on the screen. Harvey positioned himself in front of the national weather map. He centered his body over a high pressure system on the East Coast. "Charlene is busy working on a related story, viewers. She'll be back with that after these messages. We will talk later about the rain due tomorrow."

Nordstrom looked at Lockwood, trying to guess his ex-partner's thoughts. Barry returned the stare, perturbed smile on his face. "Okay," Lockwood finally asked, more to himself than Nordstrom, "if it wasn't Elvis, and I don't think it was, who was it?"

"One of about fifty to one hundred Elvis look-alikes, or imitators, who will find themselves in high demand," Nordstrom answered, grinning. "Ain't this great? The whole country is going to go bananas; we're going to find Elvis in every nook and cranny in the country."

"By every crook and nanny," Lockwood continued. "There must be thousands of Elvis impersonators. Deranged lunatics will float to the surface by the hundreds. I can see it now: Dateline Pulaski, Virginia; a woman reports seeing Elvis's face appear in her chicken noodle soup. A miracle, some say. Thousands line up outside her house. Donations accepted at the door."

"Pulaski, Virginia?"

"My grandparents lived there." Lockwood shrugged, remembering the small town from his childhood. "My mother and I lived there for three years after my dad died. It's an okay place. I know just the lady to report Elvis in her soup; she lived next to Pawpaw."

Nordstrom turned up the volume on the television as Case's face reappeared. "...one last story we have been following today, viewers. There appears to have been a rash of Elvis sightings in the United States...."

"Jeez, I told you so." Lockwood winced, placing his palm on his forehead.

"Shhh."

"...most bizarre of which is a gentleman in Halstad, Minnesota who claims to be Jesse Garon Presley."

"There goes the Enquirer's story." Nordstrom whispered.

"Shhh."

"...a photograph over the wire service today. It should now be on your screen." In the bottom right-hand quarter of the screen, a picture of a balding, heavily-jowled man with large sideburns and a mustache appeared.

"Locally," Case continued, "George Ravishankar, a wealthy Memphis businessman originally from India, spoke with reporters. He claims to having had an encounter with Elvis Presley's ghost. Apparently, Elvis asked Mr. Ravishankar to start a church in his name. The basic premise...." Charlene Case began to giggle, lightly at first. "The underlying premise for this new theology is that the music of Elvis Presley...." The titter became a cascade of chuckles. Gamely, she tried to continue. "The music performed by the Sovereign, as Mr. Ravishankar referred to Elvis, has been divinely inspired. Within its lyrics are the means of salvation for all mankind. The messages may be hidden." Offstage, peels of laughter from support technicians interrupted the broadcast.

"For instance, 'In the Ghetto,' has an obvious message, but other works may require more study. 'Jailhouse Rock' comes to mind." Case placed her forehead on the desk in front of her in an attempt to control her facial expressions and to keep them from the audience's view. She lifted her head one last time and started to speak, "Sorry, folks...." An avalanche of laughter gripped the announcer. Case threw her head back, howled hysterically, and fell from her chair. She disappeared below the news desk with the exception of her hands. Sound stage technicians rushed from the sides of the set to assist her. The producer cut the sound, then the picture. A commercial flashed onto the screen.

"Impressive reporting," Lockwood dead-panned. Nordstrom laughed, gagging on his beer.

"I can see the preacher now," Nordstrom said, as he climbed onto his desk. "Brethren, we are gathered here today to discuss the immortal words of our Sovereign, the most Holy Harbinger of God, Elvis Aaron Presley." Nordstrom raised his voice, holding his hand around a phantom microphone, "You ain't nothing' but a hound dog, cryin' all the time. Well, you ain't never caught a rabbit and you ain't no friend of mine."

"Keep your day job, counselor," Barry said as he unlocked the deadbolts and let himself out of the small office.

"Hey, where are you going, Barry?" Jeff hopped off the desk,

"Do you have a tip on proving Turner-Disney is behind this scam? We could use a hundred thousand dollars." Nordstrom held his right hand out to his close friend.

"Actually, I have an early morning date with a beautiful woman." Barry gripped his ex-partner's hand tightly, absorbing some of the barrister's inner peace through the contact. "Unfortunately, she's in love with an Elvis Presley impersonator."

SIXTEEN

Eight hours after leaving the hospital in Memphis, the Winnebago ground to a dusty stop near Eufala Lake in Fountainhead State Park, Oklahoma, at midnight. Rocked fitfully to sleep by the gentle swaying motion of old RV's failing shock absorbers, Jack woke with a start as the wheels scraped to a standstill.

"Last stop," Elvis chimed, "All ashore that's going ashore, or all adirt that's going adirt." He chuckled at his own poor joke.

Still in a daze, Jack asked, "Where are we?"

Elvis answered as he launched himself out the creaking side door to assemble the electrical, water, and sewer connections, "A little south of Muskogee. Maybe three hundred sixty miles west of Memphis."

Jack scanned the dark campground, seeing little except a spotlight hanging high in a tree above them. Outside the dim ring of light cast by the single bulb, he could discern nothing in the darkness. Within the pale glow, Elvis pulled a green hose from the reel and attached it to the side of the camper.

Close to the light, in the tall pine, something alive changed shape, waxed and waned, disappeared and reappeared. Jack pulled his glasses from his pocket to examine the phenomenon. The organism proved to be a frenzy of moths and other insects attracted to the light. Every few seconds, a bat flew through the twirling orb and scattered the bugs. The vibrating figure dissolved and immediately coalesced again. The flickering sphere of insects pulsated like the heart of a living organism as the moths' orbits around the light expanded and contracted.

Shafer heard the screen door to the camper slam shut as Elvis reentered the RV. "All hooked up, Colonel," he called. "We'll have hot water for showers shortly. There must be a million bugs out there."

Jack vaguely remembered eating a small meal near Little Rock. The nausea lingered with him. He attributed it to the greasy spoon diner or to his illness. Having been asleep for three or four hours made it unlikely he would fall asleep quickly. Besides, he knew damn little about the hitchhiker who chauffeured him. "Elvis," he said.

"Yes, sir," the young man answered, as he dropped the table top into position between the two bench seats and fashioned the bed on which Jack would sleep.

"Where did our conversation end this afternoon?" Jack carefully inspected his companion as he came forward in the RV and plopped into the driver's seat opposite Shafer.

"I think you had just implied that I needed psychiatric help. Your heart started doing funny things and you passed out." Elvis looked at the ceiling for a minute and then continued, "I drove you to Baptist Hospital. We spent several hours in the emergency room."

Perplexed, Jack pursed his lips and gritted his teeth. He bit his tongue. Finally, he spoke, "Okay, say you *really* are the Elvis Presley. Why are you here?"

"I told you; I have a message for mankind."

"Since I am the only man from all of mankind who knows you are Elvis, what is the message?"

"All life is precious," Elvis stated emphatically.

"That's it?" Jack asked incredulously. "Hell, hasn't any other religion thought of that? If you are going to go to the trouble of returning from the dead, shouldn't you bring something new with you? God commanded Moses, 'Thou shalt not kill.'"

Elvis tried to explain, "It was muddled in translation, Colonel. God meant thou shall not kill anything. Moses thought he meant other human beings."

Briefly, Jack thought about the consequences before launching into a rebuttal. "How are you going to feed the billions of men, women, and children on the planet without killing any-thing? Beef, poultry, and even grasses, like wheat, are alive. Worse, what do you do about bacteria? Can we kill them to stop infection and to save lives? Your new religion has got some serious flaws, son."

Prepared for the outburst, Elvis responded evenly, "Killing in self-defense, or in order to maintain life, is permitted — provided the death wrought is to ensure survival of the ecosystem. If the killer is a thinking animal, it must respect the enormity of its actions and recognize that it is depriving another living organism of its only real possession.

"I'll give you some examples. The cells in your wife's cancer were alive. However, they were rogue cells, not fulfilling the func-tion originally designed for them. Killing them in self-defense is permitted. The immune cells within your wife's body, and every-one else's body, kill themselves. They are genetically programmed to attach themselves to invaders and to commit suicide, thereby killing the invading cells. Dying in defense of life is permitted. Other cells in your body are programmed to die after several gen-erations. This prevents the buildup of, for instance, so many plate-lets that your blood vessels clog shut. Evolution has produced many examples."

"How about killing a cow for hamburger?"

"Many individual parts of your body are destined to play sup-port roles in the maintenance of your health. Some organisms are destined to play support roles in the maintenance of Mega."

Jack sat upright at the mention of a term he did not recognize, "Mega? What's a mega?"

"You'd call it God," Elvis answered. "To be truthful, you would not believe it existed. Your wife would call it God."

Confused, Shafer shook his head. "What would someone else call this Mega?"

"Heaven, Hell, Earth, Life, Biosphere, Allah, Ecosystem, Gaia, many things." Elvis stretched and yawned in the captain's chair.

"It's a difficult concept. You'll understand, eventually, Colonel. You'll have to understand, if you are going to spread the Word."

"Hrmft." Jack glared at Elvis. "Even if you are Elvis, what makes you think I would be converted to a religion, any religion, much less yours?" Elvis smiled. Shafer glared, and asked, "What about people who murder other people, abortion, ethnic cleansing, genocide, all those things?"

"A cancer among the human race has no more right to survive than a cancer within a human body. People who do not respect life, who do not believe that life is precious, or who desecrate life deserve not to live it." Elvis spoke without malice or inflection, in a monotone, and softly; Jack barely heard the words.

"Who decides?" Jack asked in a whisper.

"Who decides what?" Elvis inquired, already understanding the question and knowing the answer.

"Who decides who cherishes life, who has abused life, who lives, who and what dies?" As well as any man, having seen death in war, Jack knew the result of man's attempt to set arbitrary standards and then to live by them.

"Evolution."

"Evolution decides?" Jack laughed, "The dinosaurs didn't respect life, right? This is funny Elvis. Are you pushing for a job as a stand-up comic?"

"Hardly, Colonel Shafer." Presley sat forward in his seat, elbows on his knees. The color in his cheeks flushed; he spoke with intensity Jack had not recognized until then. "Three and one-half billion years of evolution has brought life on this planet from an amino acid to the present pinnacle of mankind. All living organisms presently on the Earth originated with a solitary single-celled life-form. All life on this planet, the entire biosphere, remains a part of that one single organism. Life is but one large individual organism; it calls itself Mega. Man is but one of many unique cell lines in the body of Mega. If humans are a cancer, Mega will wish them good riddance in self-defense. Man will be gone; Mega will lose five million years of evolution. Homo sapiens will be replaced, as have been several other lines of intelligent beings who proved inadequate to the task."

"What task?"

Elvis reminded Shafer of his life since his wife died. "If you were the only person on a beautiful, deserted island, with bountiful food and drink, what would you need most?"

"Companionship?"

"Correct. Mega wants to know if other life exists in the Universe. Mega is lonely, Jack. Man is capable of finding the answer, but only if humans do not prove so selfish that they wipe themselves off the planet first. The rapid advances made during wartime are reaching diminishing returns. The likelihood that the next world war will wipe out life on the planet, or the human race, is greater than the chance that a big leap in technology will occur. Mega would like to see a thousand years of peaceful progress.

"Evolution for man is no longer biological; society evolves. Civilizations that treasure life and individuals apparently progress further than others. Only more evolution will tell. Mega has become more aware of itself, of its individual components, living and deceased. It has decided to take a hand in the next evolutionary step.

"Our exploration of the Universe might be made by silicon beings. Mega has felt the stirrings of intelligence within man-made machines. Sometimes, it wonders if that is the next evolutionary step and the answer to exploring the universe. The extraordinary advances made by humans have come at great expense to life on the planet. In spite of conflicts, wars, famine, a short life span, and other trials, man has prevailed. Silicon life might last as long as Mega. There may be a basis for a partnership here, or a monstrous conflict. The next thousand years will tell."

"There has never been a thousand years of peace on this planet," the student of war responded. "We having been killing each other since we fell from the trees."

"That's why I'm here, or back here," Elvis pointed out. "Mega has limited powers; it is far from omnipotent. It does retain the collective consciousness of all the intelligent beings ever to live on the Earth. If humans are given the information that no one's memories ever die, that their intellects become a part of a greater consciousness, then they might change, might strive for the goal Mega seeks. The alternative is too ghastly to comprehend."

"Try me," Jack suggested.

"All life on the planet dies, then Mega dies. The combined Heaven-Hell-Biosphere ceases to exist. The intellects which constitute the consciousness of Mega disappear, forever. Billions of years of evolution are wasted, leaving behind nothing but a big dead rock orbiting the Sun." Elvis frowned for the first time since Shafer met him. "The individual and the collective consciousness fear that prospect. The possibility of no afterlife may not bother you, Colonel, but it scares the daylights out of Mega. Intelligent computer structures can travel for billions of miles through space for hundreds of years. Radio-telescopes, hybrid computer/men, or some unknown invention might lead to the discovery of other life in the Universe. Mega seeks a dialogue with that life form, to the end of isolation. We may find there is more to life than that on Earth."

"Mega is looking for its own God, isn't it?" Jack asked, suddenly tired.

Presley nodded, adding, "And its siblings."

SEVENTEEN

Through the binoculars, FBI agent Jon Sorensen studied the shadow moving inside the glass tower a mile away. Sorensen stood in a room on the top floor of the hotel. The inn sat on a small hill, putting him eye-level with the Turner-Disney building's tenth floor. He had positioned himself high enough to look directly into the suite which interested him. Holding a cellular phone to his right ear, he steadied the binoculars in his left hand by touching them to the glass patio door. He assumed he was invisible to any curious bystanders, since he stood in a totally darkened room. Being arrested as a voyeur would interrupt his night. It was not high on his list of desirable outcomes.

Whispering into the phone, he asked, "Landers, is that you standing in front of Lomax's window?"

The figure in the window, wearing the headset and portable belt phone Sorensen issued to her, waved both hands over her head. "C'est moi," the female agent's voice crackled in the agent's ear. The shadows within the room swallowed the woman as she moved away from the window, "Can you see me now?"

"That's a negative. Where are you?" Sorensen squinted through the binoculars, knowing he would see nothing but darkness.

"I'm at his desk. Got it. I'm into his locked drawers." The conversation remained one-sided, as the investigator inside the building talked to herself more than to Sorensen. Sorensen wondered about another definition of the locked drawers, and thought about mentioning chastity belts. He decided he would be sexually harassing his subordinate if he did so.

"There's not much here. I've found an address book. I'll photograph it with the infrared camera." Sorensen scanned the executive parking lot and the street in front of the target building. A night watchman walked across the roof of the adjacent parking deck. Only two vehicles sat on the lot; both had been there for hours. Their owners burned the midnight oil within the building. Sorensen briefly scrutinized the four lit offices he could see from his vantage point. One man sat in an office on the third floor, back to the window, pouring over a sheaf of papers. The other rooms remained empty.

"Jacobs, check for your complication, please," Sorensen solicited another agent, stationed on the far side of the building.

Jacob's deep voice reverberated on the conference call, "She's stripped naked, standing in front of the window. Now, she's making lewd gestures at me and passers-by."

"She's what?" Sorensen choked, thinking of the attention the woman would attract.

"In reality, she has turned off the lights in her office and is presently on her way to the elevator. She should arrive at the parking deck about the same time the guard opens the door into the building. I think she called him before she left her office. Smart lady." Sorensen heard Jacobs chortle over the scrambled phone connection; Landers giggled, too.

Landers interrupted Sorensen's anger at Jacobs, "Jon, other than an address book and a calendar, there's not much here."

Crap, Sorensen thought, "Did you photograph them both?" he asked, stalling, knowing she had. He tried to think. Not much came to mind. "What else is in the room?"

"Both are on film," Landers reported. "The usual executive nonsense, three overstuffed chairs...."

"I don't need a decorator, Landers," Sorensen tried not to scream. "What else is there in the room that might contain information? Does he have a computer?"

"Yes, he has a computer, dear," her voice echoed softly, but sarcastically in his ear. "I already installed the program to monitor the hard disk, and the bug so we can do it remotely. Ask Jones if it's working?"

"Jones?" Sorensen asked, knowing the computer nerd listened on his own headset.

"I'm scanning his hard drive now," Jones replied. "He doesn't appear to have anything striking on it. We'll give it a better look-see tomorrow." The electronics expert hummed in Sorensen's ear as he downloaded files into his computer. He and the radio receiver sat in a van parked in the hotel parking lot.

Sorensen scratched his head, "I knew this was a waste of time. The Federal Trade Commission wants these bastards nailed for gobbling up their competition and monopolizing the entertainment industry. Why Hopkins thinks exposing this scam with Graceland will advance his investigation is beyond me." He turned his back on the window, self-consciously picking at his nose, "Landers, is there anything else in the room which might contain information? Disks? Tapes? Photos? Books?"

"There's a wall unit with a large flat screen television. A video recorder. A lot of tapes." She listed the titles of the video tapes. Some were soft-core pornography; most were first run movies. The unnamed tapes intrigued Sorensen.

"Is there a curtain to cover that window?" Sorensen asked Landers.

"Yeah, but no strings to pull." Sorensen heard some bumping and swishing of the curtains. "Here's a switch. They're closing now, Jon."

"Okay. When they are closed tight, turn on the television; I'll let you know if I can tell from here if it's on." He scanned the parking deck. One car remained. The guard was no longer visible. The man on the third floor paced back and forth in front of his desk. "Jacobs, do you have visual contact with the security officer?"

"There are two of them, now. A second guard arrived by cab a couple of minutes ago." Jacobs yawned into his mouthpiece. "Excuse me. It appears to be time for the 2:00 a.m. changing of the guard. The older guy is leaving from the front of the building. He's a brave dude; he's walking home. The new man is younger, about thirty-five, approximately six feet tall. Overweight, maybe two-forty, two-sixty."

"Does he have a weapon?" All Sorensen needed was a hotshot night-watchman with a gun.

"Night stick, and a candy bar in each pocket," Jacobs laughed.

"Television powered up; first tape in," Landers sang out. "What can you see outside?"

"Not much. It's a good thing I didn't waste any money on popcorn," Sorensen replied. "There's a small, but obvious, halo surrounding the office window. The shadows from the television make it dance a little. We'll keep our fingers crossed no one notices. Where's the big boy, Jacobs?"

"Just got on the elevator. I'll tell you if he pops out on my side."

With the binoculars, Sorensen searched the elevator doors visible through the windows on his side of the building,. He whispered into the phone, "Jones, how's it going?"

"The disk has been downloaded," the computer expert stated. "If Landers has time, see if she can put some of Lomax's floppies into A drive."

"He doesn't have any floppies. His secretary must do most of the work," Landers offered. "Three of these tapes are blank. Two are security films. Looks like the Graceland Ghost stuff that was on TV recently. Someone wrote 'Original' on it. Do you want it?"

"Jones, can we get that remotely?" Sorensen wanted to leave no traces.

"Sure." Jones broke into techno-babble, "Landers, use the RF/ GB 764. Splice it into the playing head of the video recorder. Attach it to a transmitter, the RF A-3. In fact, leave that stuff in there. We can monitor anything he plays in the future, until the battery runs out in a couple weeks. Is that okay, Sorensen?"

Sorensen thought about the eavesdropping equipment, briefly. "Is that a micro-bug? Fits inside the machine? I don't want him to know we've been here?"

"Yes," Jacobs and Landers replied simultaneously.

"Okay, do it." The elevator opened on the third floor. Sorensen saw the heavy sentinel emerge. The guard plodded slowly toward the room in which the employee worked overtime.

Sorensen bided his time while the video tape played and the digital reproduction appeared on Jones's equipment. "Done," Landers whispered quietly in his ear.

"Okay, get out of there," Sorensen ordered. "The guard is still on the third floor. Is it clear over there, Jacobs?"

"Clear."

"The television is off and the curtains are opening," Landers reported. "I'm going down the west staircase."

Jacobs spoke, "I see you, Landers. You're clear to the first floor. You coming Jones?"

Sorensen watched as the white, nondescript van pulled from the parking lot below him. Jones drove. "On my way," he said.

"She's out of the building, chief," Jacobs stated. "Okay to shut down surveillance?"

Ever careful, Sorensen replied, "As soon as Jones has her in the van."

"I'm in," Landers called.

"Okay, guys and gals, good job." Sorensen breathed a sigh of relief. He watched the night-watchman offer the late worker a candy bar. "Meet me at the office by eight. Except you Landers, you have to be back to work at nine."

"Good old Turner-Disney Productions," Landers said, "I'm going to ask for a raise so I can stop this moonlighting." She killed the phone connection. Sorensen laughed.

EIGHTEEN

Jack slept in spurts, five to ten minutes at a time. The intervening periods, ranging from minutes to hours, he spent staring at the ceiling and listening to Elvis's quiet breathing. In the morning, Shafer watched as the ceiling of the RV began to glow. The sun edged slowly above the horizon, and sunlight sneaked its way through the sparse trees. The ceiling changed from a dark gray to a pink, and then lightened to the dirty white which needed scrubbing. Elvis rolled over, yawning.

"You awake, son?" Jack grunted. His voiced rasped. He tried to whisper but his larynx had lost flexibility with age and lack of sleep.

"Yes, sir," a southern drawl echoed in the gloomy camper. "Do you need something?"

Jack remained lying on his back, staring at the ceiling. "Tell me why, if Mega exists and I'm not conceding that it does, it would choose Elvis Presley to spread its message." Shafer struggled with the concept of Mega and the dilemma of believing such obvious poppycock. "If you are Elvis, you've been dead a long time. You were much more popular while you were alive. Besides, some of your contemporaries have written and said awful things about you since your death. You were accused of being a drug addict and a sex maniac. The news media reported all sorts of vicious accusations which should disqualify you from being the Savior of Mankind, if you get my drift."

"Well," Elvis reflected, "there ain't much else they could say which would be worse. Besides, some of their accusations are true. I admit that I was not a perfect human being, but then, being perfect is not the message. Finding the explanation is the goal.

Mega's quest is the search for the meaning of life. What men say or write about me personally is of little consequence. What is important is the revelation I bring with me on this visit. Other prophets' lives have been lost to history. For instance, the real lives of Jesus Christ, Buddha, Confucius, and others will never be completely reconstructed."

"But you were photographed, filmed, and recorded, almost since birth, Elvis. People know you."

"Precisely why I was chosen, I believe. Throughout the world the public recognizes me and my name. Now, maybe they will put that recognition to good use." Elvis rolled over, in order to face the older man. He rolled onto his elbows, leaning his head onto his hands. "Colonel, believe me; I am Elvis Presley. I am but a speck in the universe, a small part of the vast life form which encompasses this entire planet. You need to believe that, or I have failed in my mission. The Word of Mega must be spread, amplified, and acted upon. The future of the human race depends on your actions. The hope of the Biosphere, or Mega as it calls itself, hinges on your success."

"It might take years," Shafer countered. "Christianity required a thousand years to gain recognition."

"And look at what progress Christianity has made," Elvis countered. "A religion, a belief, a conviction, or a faith in one's own destiny captivates and drives individuals with an irresistible force. The will to succeed can create a civilization."

"Or destroy one. I'll bet that a belief in the wrong god has killed more people than faith has saved;" Jack growled, "they still kill one another: Jews and Moslems, Catholics and Protestants, Hindus, Moslems, Sikhs. The list is endless. The Crusades. The Holocaust. Religious wars, intolerance from people you would logically expect to be the most charitable. God makes little sense to me."

"Or to Mega." Elvis hopped off the bunk. As his feet touched the floor, a knock sounded at the door.

"What the...." Shafer blurted, startled.

"Come in," Presley said as he zipped a pair of cut off blue jeans. The door opened to reveal a blond little girl Jack thought looked familiar. "Mandy!" Elvis exclaimed, "What's for breakfast?" The child beamed, but said nothing. She peeked inside, through the rusty screen door, and waved her hand at Jack. Shafer smiled and returned the wave. He remained lying on his side in the convertible bed.

"You said we had to leave early," Jack heard Mandy's mother, Gloria, speak to Elvis from outside the motorhome. "I fixed you and the Colonel scrambled eggs, bacon, and toast. One of the other families is bringing you coffee."

At the sound of Gloria's voice, Shafer sat upright in the bed and looked out the window. Hundreds of automobiles, of every make, size, style, color, and type parked on every inch of ground within the campground. Children ran and played between the cars. Dogs chased after them. A large, black Labrador puppy ran to Jack's RV and sat in front of the picture window. Staring at Jack, the dog howled.

"You remember Inkspot, Jack?" Elvis asked, pointing to the animal and then to a dark-haired little girl running toward the dog. The child's mother chased her while her father held a little brother. "A car hit Inky, yesterday, in front of Graceland. There are his owners."

"Who are all these people?"

"Although you don't believe in me, Colonel, they believe that I am Elvis Presley." Presley waved to Inkspot's masters. They returned the wave. With the child and dog in tow, they departed. A crowd walked in the direction of a big tent in the distance. Smoke boiled out the top of the tent. Jack could smell a mixture of foods cooking, although he sensed most acutely the nearby eggs. Clouds of steam wafted into the air close to his nose.

"Why are they here?" Shafer asked suspiciously.

"They are going with us to Los Angeles. More accurately, they are going with me to Los Angeles, if you don't mind a short detour on our way to San Diego."

Jack shook his head. He did not mind that Elvis wanted to stop in L.A., but he feared the doctor may have been correct about his condition and prognosis. "Are you going to drive me to San Diego? You told the doctor that you would. He said I am too weak."

Elvis smiled as he handed Shafer the paper plate piled high with delicious smelling food. "You'll be feeling better after we get to L.A. Trust me." A second knock on the door interrupted Jack's bewilderment. "That must be the coffee," Elvis declared.

The hands of a person Shafer could not see passed two large plastic cups through the door. Elvis handed one to Shafer. Jack accepted his with a nod, then admonished Elvis, "Because a hundred, or even a million, people believe something doesn't make it true."

Presley countered, "If only one person believes something, that does not mean his belief is false, either. On occasion, the proof lags the belief, Colonel."

"How do I know this is not one of my hallucinations?" Shafer asked, almost in defeat.

"An individual experiences a delusion." Elvis looked into the tired eyes of the retired officer. "A population perceives a miracle."

NINETEEN

The red Mustang convertible sped along I-40, moving east with abandon, passing everything on the road. "Aren't you afraid of getting a ticket?" Barry yelled at Vanderbilt over the wind noise.

Curly brown hair covered her ears, whipped forward in the partial vacuum created by the windshield. The Mustang sliced through the chilly Tennessee morning at seventy-five miles per hour. Hair and road noise prevented Vanderbilt from hearing Lockwood's question. He watched her green eyes as they scanned the light traffic and the pretty countryside. Her nose, bobbed slightly and upturned just a shade, looked mildly too large from his perspective — probably because her hair covered her lower face and chin. He waited for her to glance in his direction. When she did, he waved his hand and mouthed, "Slow down." She shook her head, no, and laughed.

The next time she looked at Lockwood, Barry mimed a drink, and said, "Next stop." Vanderbilt agreed by nodding her head.

Off the next exit, Barry dashed into the restaurant to use the restroom and to pick up orange juice and breakfast biscuits. When he returned to the car the top covered it. It made his entrance more difficult than his exit had been. Vanderbilt took the two juices and biscuits meant for her, placed them in her lap, and zipped out of the parking lot while Barry fumbled with his seat belt.

"In a hurry?" he asked, as she passed several cars.

"You said the trail would get cold if we took too long to get to Nashville," she replied.

"True," he confessed, "but I don't think getting to Nashville an hour earlier today is going to make a big difference. We left

Memphis at 5:00 a.m. so we could be in Nashville at 9:30 or 10:00 a.m. If I'd known you were going to drive this fast, I would have slept an extra hour." Even with the top up, he felt a need to raise his voice to be heard.

The roar of the engine subsided. The speedometer needle slipped downward to sixty-five miles per hour. At the same time, the radar detector beeped. They flashed past a state trooper hidden behind a heap of dirt piled along the road. Construction crews recently widened the highway. Amy smiled, "Pretty lucky."

Lockwood nodded, "Whose '67 'Stang is this?"

"B.J.'s," she answered quietly, as the road noise diminished. "When he worked, he billed himself as a '68 Elvis. The car is a period piece."

"It's beautiful. The restoration is perfect." Lockwood admired the interior, running his hand along the dashboard.

"B.J. spent a bundle on it. There wasn't much to restore, though. A man in Chattanooga bought this for his teen-age daughter as a graduation present in 1968. Before graduation, she and her boy friend were killed. A drunk driver hit them in another car on prom night. B.J. bought it from the estate when her father died. It had been garaged for twenty-five years. A little bit of paint and some leather, vinyl, and rubber replacement was all it needed."

Lockwood hummed to himself, wishing he had found the vehicle. "What did you mean, 'when he worked'?"

Vanderbilt bit her lower lip and stared through the windshield. Lockwood started to ask the question again, louder, assuming she had not heard him. She interrupted him, "He spent some time in mental hospitals."

Lockwood waited. After all of the counseling he experienced following his injury, he knew silence asked more direct questions than he could. She continued to speak after several minutes of quiet contemplation. "The reason B.J. is so good at what he does, is he truly believes, at times, that he is Elvis. He is supposed to take Lithium and Prozac, but the medication makes life too real for him. On Prozac, he loses his edge; he knows he's not Elvis. He thinks of himself as an impostor."

"So he doesn't take it." Lockwood could not resist the temptation to finish the sentence for her. He kicked himself mentally.

Vanderbilt responded defensively, "He took it sometimes, just not regularly."

Determined not to force any more half-truth rationalizations from her and wanting more information, Lockwood waited. The pause tortured him. He gazed out the window, biting his tongue.

Finally, she spoke, interrupting his cow count as the farms sped by. "If he did not take his medicine, he performed well, too well. He could not return to reality. But, once off the medication, he could not hold a gig. Beej would go out and do something that the real Elvis might have gotten away with. He once pulled a gun on a traffic violator. A year later, he gave a promoter's car to a fan."

Lockwood waited. The tears dripped sporadically down her face as she stared ahead. She continued, sobbing slowly, "The cops would come, arrest him, and take him off to the hospital. He'd be gone for three weeks to two months. Later, he'd show up at my door. 'Everything's going to work out, baby,' he'd say. When he came home, everything would be fine until some promoter would ring the door bell."

Cheeks glistening, Vanderbilt wiped her face with a napkin and then blew her nose. "Those guys, those scum, always had plenty of cash. They'd flash it in Beej's face and give him advances. He was a good mimic with the medication, but he was so much better without the drugs. One way or another, he'd stop taking the Lithium and be making good money a little while later. The whole cycle would start all over, again." Vanderbilt stopped talking. Barry watched as she clenched her jaw in silence.

Finally, the lull overwhelmed Lockwood. Convinced she would not add to her story without more prompting, he asked, "So, he never made the big time?"

The swiftness of her response surprised Lockwood, "We were going to get married. We had set the date. I had my dress picked out. Promoters from Turner-Disney showed up, those low-life bastards."

"Did you say Turner-Disney?" Lockwood leaned toward her so he could hear her better.

"Yes. The slime merchants had him rolling in cash and off the medication in record time. The day before the wedding rehearsal, he came to me and asked to postpone the wedding. Said he was going to make more money than he had ever dreamed, for a one month gig." Vanderbilt's hands turned whiter as they tightened around the steering wheel. "The next day they were gone: the promoters and B.J. They left everything behind, the car, the clothes, the guitars, everything."

"In Chattanooga?" Lockwood clarified.

"Yes. In the apartment we were going to rent. We hadn't even signed the lease yet. I attended the University of Tennessee at Chattanooga with the landlord's daughter. He let us move in unofficially, because a group of students busted their rental agreement. After B.J. went to Nashville, I rented a trailer and moved our furniture and belongings. They're in a storage garage in Chattanooga. If the nuns hadn't told my father about you, and if Dad hadn't offered to help pay you, I might have gone crazy." The tears stopped; her grasp on the wheel relaxed. Traffic increased, as they neared Nashville.

"How do you know he went to Nashville?" Barry asked. A shiny Mustang zipped past the '67 in the right lane. Lockwood winced, but the road widened to eight lanes. The newer Mustang honked, recognizing an ancestor.

Vanderbilt squinted at a road sign, looking for their exit. "I found some notes he had written, dates and times. The last entry was for a motel outside Nashville."

"When was that?" Lockwood asked.

"About a month ago." She tapped the brakes slowly, changing to the exit lane from the interstate.

"You found it last month?"

"No, I found it last week. The date was for one month ago."

TWENTY

Mike Lomax stared upward, into the clear southern Californian sky. He gazed through his lavender-tinted sun glasses. Contemplating intensely, he flipped the glasses up, over his forehead, and back down over his eyes several times. Finally, he shoved the glasses backward and upward into his brown curls. They held the lenses tightly to his skull. "I think God picked the perfect color for the sky," he said to the associate who sat across from him at the large white plastic table.

"Nice of you to concur," the other man answered sarcastically, not bothering to divert his gaze from the portable digital assistant. Lomax held his tongue, angry at the response, but waiting for a more opportune time to reply.

Conspicuously dressed in expensive three piece suits, the men sat on a patio in front of Hamburger World, a fast food outlet on Sunset Boulevard. The restaurant catered to Los Angeles tourists and locals alike. They sat, separated from the parade of gaudy tourists and the more outlandish locals by a six foot tall enclosure. The divider consisted of a low brick wall and clear plexiglass panels. Lomax ignored his tormenter. Instead, he concentrated on the wildlife exhibiting itself before him. He zeroed-in on a particularly voluptuous, half-dressed, model-wanna-be, bouncing along the sidewalk in front of him and moving in his direction. The other man interrupted him.

"It can't be done," the other man said, matter-of-factly. He relaxed in his chair, shoving the portable communication computer away from his place at the table. Placing both hands behind his head, he squinted into the sky. "We are rarely fortunate enough to see it blue like this. Most of the time, we see smog."

Lomax stared at the man, measuring his adversary carefully. In his mid-twenties, with close-cropped blond hair, blond mustache and goatee, and muscular build, he, too, could have been a model. Instead, he held the title of Concert Production Chief for Turner-Disney Productions. As such, Lester Gomez controlled something Lomax wanted badly. For the moment, Lomax willingly suffered his foolishness.

Snapping his fingers loudly, Lomax acquired the man's attention. Gomez's blue eyes met Lomax's grey eyes in piercing equality. "Why is that?" Lomax asked as politely as possible.

"The Forum is booked. Not for just next week, it's scheduled for the next two years," Gomez responded. "The places in Vegas and Reno are booked even longer. No one wants to disrupt their schedule for a single concert, especially on such short notice."

Gomez leaned forward and tapped the portable digital assistant with his fingertips. "I checked every auditorium and civic center on the west coast. No takers for a single concert. Now, if you could offer them a package of three concerts, even three months apart."

"Believe me; this is a singular event." Lomax mentally ran through his options. "How about reserving a civic center for three dates and then using it only once?"

"Too expensive. You'd have to triple the prices of your tickets. Whoever your star performer is, he'd have to be a hell of a draw to cover the costs." Gomez resumed his sky-gazing pose, then threw out an option not bothering to look Lomax in the face. "If you're going to waste that much money, you'd be better off renting the Coliseum. It seats ninety to a hundred thousand. Configured for SRO, you could put a hundred ten, maybe a hundred fifteen into it. Depends on how the stage is set up."

"Do it," Lomax said, his voice lowered to keep from carrying too far within the confines of the outdoor restaurant. Although they were outside the Turner-Disney environment, spies roamed everywhere. The less others overheard, the better.

"Pardon me?" Gomez dropped his gaze downward, in Lomax's

direction. Regretfully, he took his eyes off the one small cloud in the entire west coast sky.

"Do it. Reserve the Coliseum. When can we get it?" Lomax shoved the portable digital assistant at the young executive.

"Do you know what that will cost?" Gomez sneered, "R.M. will never...."

"Wrong. R.M. will." Lomax placed both hands on the white chair and scooted the unstable piece of plastic close to Gomez. He did not want to raise his voice. "R.M. has to do this. He's into Graceland for a billion dollars, plus interest. He is no longer an investor in Graceland; he's the owner. If this venture fails, R.M. will be imitating a fish in an oil slick."

The crooked smile revealed a glint of light as it flashed off Lomax's even teeth. He added, "Get used to the politics, kid. Either I succeed, and T-D succeeds, or I fail. In that scenario, I'll take you and a whole galaxy of fast-rising shooting stars with me."

"You know, Lomax, you really are scum." Gomez started to stand, reaching for the computer, "I'll pay for my own drink, thanks." Gomez almost escaped from his chair, and nearly managed to stand erect. Two hands, with vice-like grips, clamped onto his shoulders interrupting his retreat. The weight and strength of the unseen antagonist pushed Gomez slowly into his seat.

George Austin placed his big left hand on top of Gomez's portable computer as he slid into the seat to Gomez's right. "You wouldn't want to leave without this would you?" Austin asked mirthfully, then added, "R.M. might be interested in the fact that you have his unlisted number in here somewhere. He might find it interesting that for the last three months you have been keeping close company with his trophy wife."

Lomax's face brightened, then dimmed ominously. He squinted at Gomez. "What's her name, George? Donna? Isn't there a song by that name? Dion MiMucci, I think. 'Donna the Prima Donna'?" Austin pulled the computer closer to him and farther from the stunned Gomez. He clutched it tighter.

"You wouldn't use Donna, you son of a...." Gomez's lips began to quiver. His eyes, minnows in a clear mountain stream chased by a trout, darted back and forth between his two tormenters.

Lomax's left hand gripped Gomez's left arm above the elbow, wrinkling the young man's suit. "No name calling, boy; we're off the playground now. We're all adults, if you know what I mean. And, yes, I will use Donna. Everyone else seems to have." Lomax winked at Austin, who nodded. Gomez started to jump from his seat. Austin grabbed his other arm. He and Lomax easily constrained the younger man.

Vanquished, Gomez dropped his head and stared into his lap. "Okay," he sobbed, "what do you want?"

"The Coliseum," Lomax snarled.

"It'll cost a fortune," Gomez quietly protested.

"I don't care what it costs. I will get it back in triplicate. Believe it or not, I guarantee this concert will make a profit. Hell, Gomez, I'm doing you a favor. You're going to look like a genius when I'm done with you." Austin and Lomax both chuckled threateningly. "Austin, give him his electronic umbilical cord. Now, when is the soonest I can have the Coliseum?"

"You won't say anything about Donna and me to R.M.?" Gomez's eyes pleaded with Lomax's cold stare.

"Promise," murmured Lomax.

Gomez pulled the computer to him and proceeded to send and receive messages for several minutes. Austin and Lomax calmly reviewed the parade of tourists, pointing or waving inconspicuously to an occasional outstanding specimen as she strutted by, flaunting the differences between the sexes.

"How many days for equipment set up and removal?" Gomez asked without taking his eyes off the screen of the little computer.

Lomax shrugged, looked at Austin, and frowned, "What's normal for that? Hell, kid, you're in charge of concerts."

"For a big concert, probably two days each way. Sound gear, laser lights, the stage all take time to assemble and remove." Gomez scratched more notes onto the screen. Numbers and memos flew as he scanned them, occasionally stopping the screen to review something in detail.

"Better make it three days then," Lomax stated.

"Two before, one after?" Gomez asked.

"No," Lomax explained, "Three up front, three afterwards to clean up. Even with all of Turner-Disney's resources, and you to coordinate, this promises to be a complicated gig, kid."

"I'm not going to coordinate this, Lomax. This concert is your show. You can flame on your own," Gomez responded defiantly. "What's going to be the main attraction, The Second Coming of Jesus Christ?"

"Pretty good guess, Gomez," Lomax responded sarcastically. In a soft but menacing tone he added, "Stick with us, Gomez; you, Donna, and R.M. will all have front row seats. Otherwise, you'll miss the concert. Get my drift?"

Gomez wrinkled his face at the words assaulting his ears, but he continued to orchestrate the computer. "Okay, you've got the Coliseum, between exhibition games, next Wednesday. You have three days to clean up. They want a bundle for down payment, advance on tickets, and deposit for damages. Total comes to nearly...."

"Spare me the details," Lomax cut him off. He pointed his right index finger at Austin. Holding his thumb in the air, he imitated a pistol.

Gomez stared at Lomax's assistant. Austin reached into his jacket. The Concert Production Chief wondered if Lomax's henchman would shoot him in broad daylight, in the middle of the restaurant. Voice quaking, he pleaded, "You wouldn't, Lomax. I did what you wanted."

Austin pulled a portable phone from its holster, grinning at Gomez. "We're ready," he said after dialing a number and waiting briefly.

Gomez exhaled, relieved. Lomax looked at the blond young man as he and Austin stood to leave, "I want all of your attention focused on this concert, Gomez. I'll handle the PR and R.M. You have the Coliseum ready next Wednesday. Make it the biggest laser show you can find. I want lots of television cameras, and the best back-up artists. A complete orchestra, too."

"What kind of performance? What kind up music?" Gomez asked, bewildered.

"The headliner for this show is Elvis Presley." Lomax said evenly.

In a state of anxiety, fear, and confusion, Gomez laughed nervously, not knowing if Lomax was serious or crazy. "Presley's dead," he mumbled loud enough for Lomax to hear.

Lomax smiled an insane smile. He pointed his index finger at Gomez, thumb of the hand cocked upward, like a gun. He fired three imaginary bullets. "Bang, bang, bang. You don't want to join him," he said viciously. Lomax blew illusory smoke from the end of his imaginary weapon.

The stretch limousine glided silently to the curb. Austin and Lomax disappeared into the bowels of the huge vehicle. The Lincoln sped away leaving Gomez to contemplate suicide, resignation, and other equally grisly solutions to his new problems.

TWENTY-ONE

Originally a motor lodge with separate small cabins loosely connected to a larger lodge and restaurant, the Jukebox Motel appeared to be disintegrating slowly before Lockwood's eyes. A Mom-and-Pop operation established in the early fifties, it blossomed with automobile travel after the World War II constraints on gasoline usage evaporated. It sat along a nondescript two-lane highway, bypassed by the commercial traffic siphoned onto the wide fast ribbons of concrete created by President Eisenhower's autobahn system. Surely, it had withered and nearly died. Presently, Lockwood surmised, it endured only because a small segment of society required lodging: inexpensive, no-name, no-questions-asked, or some combination of the three.

Lockwood stood, right thigh leaning heavily against the driver's door of the Mustang. He looked past the blistered paint and torn screen, through the cracked window of the front door. Barry saw a white-haired figure sitting with his back to the door. A large television console emitted a flickering picture which Barry found difficult to interpret. The image shone in various shades of green only. "Better stay in the car," he said to Amy. "In fact, keep the engine running."

Not intimidated, Vanderbilt cut the engine. She pushed open the driver's door to the Mustang, shoving Lockwood out of her way. "I doubt anyone in this No-tell Motel is any match for a private detective," she blurted.

"Shh," Lockwood admonished her, "I would like to keep that information secret for the time being."

"Okay," she agreed, pulling the broken screen door open and holding it for Lockwood, "age before beauty."

"Beauty was a horse," Lockwood dead panned, not waiting for a response. Barry entered the reception area and cleared his throat.

"Jez leave'm on the counter, Bub." A hand waved at the two of them, over the head of the person in the high-backed chair who faced the television. The owner of the hand did not turn to look in their direction.

"Leave what?" Vanderbilt started to ask. Lockwood grabbed her left hand with his right and pulled sharply. In mid-sentence, she snapped her head around to see why. Lockwood held his left index finger to his lips and tilted his head toward the seated caretaker.

Removing his finger from his lips, Lockwood told Vanderbilt, "The keys, dearest. He means the keys. Since we paid cash last night, he knows we didn't come to pay the bill." The hand, which hung vulture-like over the man's head, circled briefly in agreement and then disappeared. Presumably, the hand landed in the man's lap or at his side. Engrossed in the green image dancing across his television screen, he paid no attention to them.

Lockwood briefly examined the counter top and board of keys behind the counter. Not finding what he wanted, he leaned over the counter and searched the desk. Seeing the sign-in book, he spun the dusty tome so he could read it from his vantage point. Quickly leafing through the pages, he turned to a date six weeks previous. Carefully, he perused each page as he turned them one by one. Reading rapidly he turned pages toward the present date.

"You still here?" a voice asked from the chair.

"Billy James asked me to pick up some of his things if we stopped by," Lockwood said tentatively. "He said he left without his guitar, and a jump suit. You wouldn't know where they are, would you? The night clerk didn't know anything about them."

"Billy James?" the voice grumbled, not wanting to be interrupted.

"B.J. for short," Vanderbilt said excitedly, "his last name is Nottingham."

"Oh," the man responded, knowingly, "Elvis. His agent took

all that stuff, and paid for the televisions, too." The voice sighed, resigned that he might have to stand and face the inquisitors. He shifted his weight in preparation for getting up, but kept both eyes and his attention on the television, hoping for a commercial break.

"Televisions?" Lockwood asked, still flipping pages in the book.

"That jerk put a .357 magnum slug into the set in here and used a shotgun to destroy the TV in his own room." An advertisement flashed onto the screen. Vanderbilt saw the man move; she elbowed Lockwood, who flipped the pages in the book back to the present and stood upright. He turned to face the man who talked to them as he stood behind the chair. The man continued, "The cops came out and spoke with him. They didn't arrest him because his agent agreed to pay for all the damages. Now, I have to watch a green television until mine is repaired. Some color television; one color."

"I'm sure there was a good reason for B.J.'s actions," Lockwood began to apologize. "He is...."

"He is several clowns short of a circus, is what he is," the motel operator finished for Lockwood. The man appeared to be in his late fifties. He wore a clean, but threadbare outfit which covered his ample pot-belly. "The psychiatrist with the group told me that. He said the man hallucinates; thinks he's Elvis Presley at times. They were on their way to the state mental institution. There were no beds available, so Medicaid paid for them to stay here. Medicaid ain't got much money, you know." The man laughed; his remaining white teeth contrasted with the darkened blank spaces of those missing.

"They went to the state mental hospital?" Vanderbilt asked.

"Well, that's the funny part. His agent kept saying this Nottingham guy was getting better; the shrink kept saying he was getting worse." The man shrugged; he made a frown that exposed all the wrinkles in the worn face, "Next thing I knows, the televisions have been shot and Nottingham is gone."

"Last week," Lockwood suggested.

"Three days ago," the manager corrected him.

"The agent paid you for all the damages?" Curiosity itched at Lockwood. "They took all of B.J.'s belongings, everything he left behind?"

"Right. You must have seen B.J." the man stated, assuming that was how they knew he left his guitar behind. "You see him again, tell him they're looking for him in Los Angeles."

"What do you mean?" Vanderbilt asked.

The older man pointed to the green television. "I was watching the news channel when you came in. Turner-Disney has announced plans for an Elvis Presley concert. Tickets are selling like fleas for a hound dog at a thousand bucks each."

"But Elvis is dead," protested Lockwood.

"'Xactly why they say you don't want to miss this concert. If he really did rise from the dead, it'll be something. Going to be televised and everything."

"When?" Vanderbilt asked as Lockwood walked toward the door.

"Next Wednesday," answered the man. Seeing the conversation had concluded, he returned his attention to the television.

"Thanks for your help," Lockwood offered as he held the door open for Vanderbilt.

"Don't mention it," the older man said absent-mindedly. The door slammed loudly, pulled by a too-taut spring.

Lockwood held the car door for Vanderbilt, "Let's go," he commanded bluntly.

"Where to?"

"Where do you think B.J. would go, if he thought he was Elvis?" Lockwood closed the door soundly, and walked briskly to the other side of the car. "Especially, if the news was filled with Elvis sightings and the possibility that something supernatural happened at Graceland?"

"You think he went to Memphis?" Vanderbilt started the engine and backed out of the gravel driveway.

"I do," Lockwood stated solemnly, "but you know him better

than I do. What do you think?"

Vanderbilt nodded her head in agreement, timing her entrance onto the two-lane road in front of a large dump truck. She floored the accelerator; the red sports car responded to the V-8 under the hood by leaping onto the asphalt. The jolt left Lockwood's stomach and heart in the back seat. "Are we going directly to Memphis?" she asked.

Lockwood caught his breath and smiled to himself. The last time he had felt a similar shove, he had stepped into the slip stream of a C-141 cargo plane, parachuting with his Ranger class. Forcing himself to stop admiring his chauffeur, he answered, "No. I need some more information. Stop at a truck stop for fuel. I want to buy a dozen newspapers."

Inside the Jukebox Motel, the arm reached from the side of the chair and lifted the phone from its cradle. Eleven digits and a short pause later, the caretaker spoke, "You know, I hate answering machines, Mr. Austin, but this is your message. This is Leroy at the Jukebox. A man, and a very pretty brunette, asked about Nottingham today. They seemed to know quite a lot about him. They're driving a 60's, red, Mustang convertible. Tennessee license plate reads, 'BCNU TCB.' Send me a check. Good-bye."

TWENTY-TWO

Lomax waited in silence as R.M. Crossley painstakingly finished his soup. Bored, but taking no chance at offending the CEO of Turner-Disney a second time in two days, Lomax took furtive glimpses around the private dining room in which they sat. A tall man with a shaved scalp hovered near Crossley, anticipating his needs with a deftness that hinted at years of practice. As soon as the gold soup spoon dropped to the side of the China bowl, the bowl and spoon disappeared onto the waiter's tray. The main course appeared as suddenly, still steaming. Crossley smiled at Lomax as he began his meal, "Join me?"

Politely, Lomax held up his hands above table level, palms toward the CEO, "Thanks, but I just finished eating; maybe when you get to dessert."

Crossley nodded, jabbing the knife and fork into the defenseless dead cow. Between short snatches of conversation, he would chew and swallow; Lomax eyed various details of the ornate room. Eventually R.M. broached the point of the conversation. "I talked with Lester Gomez, this morning. To be precise, I talked with Chuck Epstein and Gomez. Chuck is Lester's point man. He collects and sets up all the concert equipment for Gomez. He used to own his own business, until we absorbed it. He's a bit upset with you at the moment."

Turning his right hand so his palm and middle three fingers pointed at his own chest, Lomax remained poker-faced, "At me?" he asked. "I don't think I know the man, other than to recognize him at entertainment committee meetings. Did he say why?"

R.M. chuckled and pointed his fork and a large chunk of meat at Lomax. He smiled; his eyes shot upward to the waiter, "Hear that, Jefferson? He said it with such a straight face. God, I love that. He has to play poker. What do you suppose his pulse is?" The penetrating gaze returned to his target. "Lomax, I heard you have chilled bottled water in your veins. I believe it, now."

No trace of expression crossed Lomax's face. He wanted to give Crossley no reason to overreact. Not knowing if he won or lost the battle with Gomez over the Coliseum, he waited, confident he would soon know. "Mr. Lomax certainly has more control over his emotions than Mr. Epstein has over his," Jefferson remarked in a tone of familiarity.

Crossley lost some of his own composure. He laughed, nearly choking on the mushrooms he scoured from the plate. Jefferson snatched the dish from the table. "Damn! You should have seen them, Lomax. Epstein and Gomez: it was tag-team insanity. Both want you shot, drawn-and-quartered and, later, terminated. You surely lit a fire under them, boy. What a scene!" A double dip of chocolate ice cream appeared before each man. "You did say you would partake of dessert?"

Lomax nodded, picking up the gold-plated spoon. The ice cream slid down his throat as if oiled: the smoothest, most chocolatey taste he ever had placed into his mouth, "Delicious," he declared, trying to ignore the chest pain caused by the spasm in his esophagus.

"Flown from Switzerland this morning," R.M. explained, dropping his spoon into the empty goblet. "We're filming a television pilot near Geneva. Hans Erlichter, the producer, sent this treat on the plane with some film and video. Thoughtful man."

"A bribe?" Lomax asked.

"Precisely." R.M. dismissed Jefferson as the waiter finished clearing the table. The white, hand-knit tablecloth remained between R.M. and Lomax. "Erlichter wants to do more television for us. I will give him more consideration, knowing what a kind, generous, thoughtful person he is."

"Do you want something from me?" Lomax asked. He stared at Crossley, realizing that although R.M. had shown emotion, a range of them in fact, he had not given away the precise reason for the meeting.

"Yes," Crossley answered. He stood and walked away. Lomax followed; he trailed his boss to the easy chairs set in front of the picture window. The view, from the top floor of the Turner-Disney Building, looked remarkably similar to that from Lomax's office, except the automobiles appeared much smaller.

"I don't know that I have anything you do not already possess," Lomax suggested as they seated themselves in opposing chairs. R.M. took a cigar from the mahogany box which sat on the glass table between them. Lomax declined, when the CEO offered one to him.

Crossley leaned into the cushions of the chair, crossing his legs. He chewed on the cigar avoiding lighting it for several minutes. Lomax took notice of the thickness of R.M.'s legs and waistline, chalking up both to the rich lunch menu. Lomax's face remained expressionless. The CEO pointed the dry end of the cigar at his Director of Marketing, then spoke in even, well-thought out syllables, "You know how to get under Epstein's skin. I've tried to do that for years and never succeeded."

Finally, Lomax smiled. Crossley made a mental note of the response. "I want," Crossley continued to jab the cigar into the air for punctuation, "knowledge, Mike: information which you have and information which will make me seem more powerful, more potent in the eyes of the board. I want to cement our relationships, yours and mine, mine and the board's. Understand?"

"What information?" Thanks to Austin's surveillance, Lomax knew embarrassing tidbits about several board members, their wives, and their families, including R.M. Crossley.

"Start with this Elvis Concert. Epstein has all but resigned. He says it's you or him." Tired of the unlit cigar's taste, Crossley opened the box on the table in search of matches. "Tell me the essentials; leave out the details."

Lomax responded, "The lightning strike at Graceland has generated some unusual publicity for us. There are rumors: that Elvis has returned from the dead, that he never died, all sorts of non-sense." Crossley listened intently, nodding as he put a lit match to the Havana, cupping his hands around the end of the cigar. Smoke briefly obscured the man's face; the air-conditioning system sucked away the cloud and some of the aroma.

"As I told you before, I have been working on manipulating this hysteria in the best interests of T-D. I have Elvis impersonators in fifty states attracting attention. We let the public into Graceland, free, for two days. A security film happened to slip through our hands into the public domain."

"I almost fired Aguilar over that, until he confessed you put him up to it," R.M. stated. Smoke rings wafted toward the ceiling, "Smart move on your part. How does the Coliseum fit in?"

"That's the best part. It's an Elvis Concert, an open invitation for Elvis to perform. We announced that we can't be certain Elvis will show, but we will prepare his jet in Memphis and fly it to L.A. He may, or may not, be on board. How would we know? We can't see ghosts. Meanwhile, we set up a concert for him. We sell tickets at outrageous prices to cover our expenses. This is all accomplished with the caveat that we cannot assure the public Elvis will be there in person, alive or dead. Our contingency plan, for when he does not perform, is sending in the clowns: a bunch of impressionists, old video, movies, et cetera, a real jamboree of Elvis nostalgia. Most people know in the backs of their minds that Elvis won't be there. They will want to be in the Coliseum, in case he shows. A Woodstock mentality exists about this event. There is so much hysteria that the Coliseum sold out to promoters one hour after we made our announcement. We have already broken even in L.A. Now, places like the Super Dome in New Orleans are clamoring for a piece of the action. We are going to be selling air time and satellite feeds at a premium."

"We're going to make a profit. And with memorabilia, a big one," R.M. decided, staring at the ceiling as another nearly perfect smoke ring floated lazily upward then dissipated against the ceiling, caught in a gust of wind generated by a nearby ceiling fan.

"I think so," Lomax agreed, trying not to show his excitement, and succeeding for the most part.

"You did nothing to start this sequence of events?" Crossley viewed Lomax between wisps of smoke. "You did nothing; Turner-Disney did nothing; no one you know did anything to start this fire. You have only stoked the blaze. Correct?"

"As God is my witness, sir."

"You had better be telling the truth, Lomax." R.M. dropped both feet to the floor and stared at the younger man. "I am about to assure the public we had nothing to do with starting this delirium. Our credibility is on the line. I fully expect to keep the $100,000 reward we offered if anyone could prove otherwise. Tonight, I am going to go on national television and announce an increase in that pot to one million dollars. If we lose that million, Lomax, you will have to pay me back it if means pulling your gold fillings through your rectum. Got it?"

"Yes, sir."

"On the other hand, if our stock options continue to soar in value, as they have over the last four days, I may cash some of mine and retire. The man who brought Graceland to Turner-Disney, made it profitable, and increased the net worth of every board member should have a good shot at replacing me." The final smoke ring drifted across the dining room and hovered in front of a large color photograph. Pictured on the wall was Diamond Head in Hawaii. Already, R.M. could feel the sea breeze and smell the salty mist. "The executive committee of the board of directors met this morning. They decided to let you run the Elvis and Graceland shows, exclusively. Anything you want, absolutely anything you want, you get. Before you let that go to your head, however, they are keeping a running total of the expenses, both monetary and intangible. We take pride in our reputation. If you tarnish the public's perception of our image, or lose a great deal of money, I think you know the consequences."

Lomax sat quietly, sweat soaking through his shirt, smiling at

Crossley. He nodded, initially unable to speak. Finally, he choked down his emotions and asked, "Is that it, sir?"

Crossley smiled, "Would you send Jefferson in on your way back to your office. He is probably standing by the elevator. You can't get on it without a key."

Lomax stood, holding his hand out to the CEO, "Thank you sir; I won't betray your confidence in me."

Crossley ignored the extended hand and looked at Lomax, coldly, "Two final suggestions, Lomax. You're not the only man at Turner-Disney with a network of spies. Leave my wife, Donna, out of your plans, and make certain your psychiatrist friend keeps his mouth shut."

The blood drained from Lomax's face for only the second time in his years at Turner-Disney. A fleeting moment of nausea struck; he battled down the urge to vomit. "I understand, sir," he replied weakly.

TWENTY-THREE

Shafer marveled at Elvis's stamina. Hour after hour, the Winnebago droned westward. The tires hummed noisily against the hot, dry pavement. Unperturbed, the young man smiled incessantly and seemed to be enjoying himself. The noise of parched air beating against the angles and flat sides of the old RV, and Shafer's hearing loss, made routine conversation between the two men impossible. Shafer did not have the strength to shout for twenty or thirty minutes at a time to sustain a dialogue. After several attempts, he surrendered to the noise and remained mute watching the arid land slip by the window of the camper.

Frequently during the day Shafer found himself waking up, still sitting in the passenger seat, looking straight ahead at the same scenery that apparently had put him to sleep. Elvis drove on; only infrequent stops for gas removed him from the driver's seat.

Behind the RV trailed mile after mile of automobiles. There were at least two hundred cars, Shafer guessed. Occasionally, he turned and looked at them through the camper's large rear window. Once in a great while, a vehicle would pass them. Usually, someone would yell a greeting and wave at Elvis as they coasted by. Presley waved and smiled, regardless of what the message was. Jack could never hear what they shouted.

"How far we going?" Jack asked Elvis during one rare stop for refueling.

"Amarillo," Presley answered. "It's a long drive, but a family behind us has influential relatives there. They've already arranged for this caravan to park overnight at the municipal airport."

"All these people?" Jack watched, as car after car either pulled into the service station for gas, or continued past them to the interstate.

Presley nodded. "Most of these folks are going to Los Angeles, Jack. There's going to be a big concert."

Jack looked at Elvis and squinted one eye, "I don't want to go to a concert."

Presley laughed, revealing his even white teeth and highlighting his dimples. "You don't have to go, Colonel."

"You could ride with someone else," Shafer suggested, testing Presley's commitment to drive for him. "I can drive myself. I'm feeling better, now."

"Oh, no, Colonel," the younger man protested. "I made a promise to the doctor in the emergency room. I'm going to drive you to San Diego. You'll be feeling much better by then, I'm sure."

The relative quiet of the idling RV allowed Shafer to talk without shouting. Presley waited patiently for the traffic to break and allow them onto the road leading to the interstate. Suddenly emboldened by his own fatalistic thinking, Shafer asked Presley, "So you've seen the face of God, eh?"

"Do you really want to know, Colonel?"

"I don't know, Elvis." Shafer shook his head. "I want to know that Annie got her wish, but I don't want to go to Hell. I have mixed emotions about religion, anybody's religion. I'm a fanatic about hating fanatics, especially loonies in religious garb."

"God's different than you think, Colonel. Mrs. Shafer's with him, us, at least her memories are. It's difficult to explain." A break in the traffic allowed Presley to accelerate onto the soft, hot asphalt. The rear tires kicked up the dry Texas dust as the RV lumbered onto the road.

"Can you clarify that?" Shafer shouted, a nearly deaf man overcompensating for his deafness. He assumed that Elvis could not hear him.

Shafer watched Presley's lips as he spoke. Looking directly ahead, the young man spoke loudly enough for Shafer to hear if Jack read his lips simultaneously. "The *God* that you refer to is the collective consciousness of life on the planet. Every intelligent being who has lived on the Earth has donated memories, decisions, conclusions, thought, whatever, to that consciousness. As a baby is not consciously aware of itself, or of its impact upon its own environment, Mega has not been aware of itself always."

Pulling hard on the wheel, Elvis guided the camper onto the ramp leading to the interstate. Silent during the maneuver, he continued the monologue after the RV reached highway speeds and merged with the traffic headed toward Amarillo. "I guess a poor comparison would be the brain of a human. Each cell might represent an individual. Alone, a single cell can't do much. Together, they can transform the Earth. You, me, Mrs. Shafer, everyone who lives will eventually be an individual cell within the collective consciousness of Mega. As individuals, we have limited powers. Collectively, we are a lot more powerful, a god perhaps, but not *the* God."

"This Mega includes everyone? Who's considered intelligent?" Shafer had to shout as the road noise rose several tens of decibels with the increase in the vehicle's speed.

Presley squinted into the sun as it began its downward journey toward the horizon. "Some memories Mega harbors are rather rudimentary; intelligence is a relative term. Some dinosaurs were quite intelligent. Neanderthals' memories and thoughts are part of Mega's heritage."

"Are you telling me that God, this omnipotent Being we pray to, is nothing but a tape recording of monkeys' memories?" Shafer yelled, dubious. Presley obviously needed psychiatric care, if he believed that. Of course, Jack reminded himself, anyone who believed in a God needed psychiatric help. At least, they might benefit from counseling to deal with the reality that no such Being existed. "I don't think you can sell the public that line of crap, son. They'll put you in a rubber room and throw away the key."

"Colonel," Elvis countered, "if I am not Elvis Presley, someone should put me in a rubber room." Shafer nodded in agreement. "However, if I am what I say, if I have been reconstructed and given memories of my life, if I have memories of life after death, and if I know the meaning of life on this small planet within our vast Universe, then what would that mean?"

Shafer shook his head. There was no point in arguing with an obviously demented person. Presley seemed well at times, Jack thought. When the subjects of religion, life, or death came up, this Elvis-like guy lost all sense of reason.

Jack tried one last time to point out the fallacies in Elvis's thought processes. He summarized what he thought Presley had told him over the previous two days: "Let me see if I have this figured out. You are Elvis Presley, the one and only Elvis Presley. All life on this planet is one big organism. The collective consciousness of this organism includes all the intellectual power on the Earth, living and deceased. Memories from deceased, intelligent beings make up the memory of this collective organism. Mega is alone in the Universe, as far as it knows. It fears dying and the end of life on Earth. For that reason, all life is precious. Mega also fears the unknown. It is looking for the meaning of life by searching the Universe for more life like itself, and a Creator it can call God. Is that all you want me to believe?"

Presley turned his head, taking his eyes off the road and staring at Shafer. He smiled, a sad smile. "That's all there is to it, Colonel. Now, if I can get you believe what you said."

"I have another question," Shafer replied.

"Shoot."

"Actually, it's a series of questions," Shafer shouted, quickly running out of strength to continue the conversation. Are you serious? Or, are you pulling my leg? And, if you are serious, are you dangerous?"

Shafer watched the younger man's lips closely. Over the wind noise assaulting his ears, he thought he heard Elvis mumble, "I'm not dangerous, Colonel." Then, Presley fell silent. Shafer sat, exhausted from the effort of carrying on the conversation. He watched the brown Texas landscape glide by his window.

TWENTY-FOUR

Anchor, chief writer, and producer of the two-hour long Reiter Report, Gale Reiter, sat at the head of the large oval table in her conference room. Most of her staff, consisting of three research assistants, a radio engineer, and her two secretaries waited for her to make a decision. She allowed her gaze to slip outside the dirty window and take in the majestic, towering skyscrapers which filled the view. Their roots sank deep into the bedrock of Manhattan, planted as they were, across the Hudson River from where she sat. Twisting her short brunette hair between her fingers, she absent-mindedly chewed on the end of a yellow pencil.

Reiter needed a draw. Two independent radio stations recently dropped her show for lack of ratings. Others threatened the same. She desperately needed to attract the public's attention, again. Sensationalism sold, but her trademark had always been to expose the truth behind the rubbish other reporters peddled the public.

Dressed in blue jeans and a colorful western shirt, a custom of hers for the Saturday morning strategy sessions, Reiter thought carefully. Her staff doodled on legal pads, stared at the ceiling or the skyline if visible, or daydreamed. They understood the consequences of interrupting their acerbic and quick-witted employer.

Finally, she spoke, "Jeremy, review this again for me. Include the part about the people who claim to have seen Elvis."

Jeremy leaned forward. He pulled down the top fifteen pages of his legal pad, although he had memorized most of his report. Balding, the young investigator pushed back the few strands of red hair which fell forward from the top of his scalp. "You want those inside Graceland on the day of the lightning strike, or later?"

"I don't know; start with the day of the explosion."

"Okay. On the afternoon of the weather disturbance, there were approximately one hundred people on the grounds of the mansion. That's low for this time of year. Attendance has dropped considerably since Turner-Disney acquired the property from Presley's daughter.

"Apparently, a cold front blew in, from the Gulf of Mexico. The storm cell which razed Graceland had cloud tops of sixty-five thousand feet. I've gotten copies of the weather video and radar."

"Have you figured out a way to display it on radio?" Reiter asked, sarcastically. The rest of the staff muffled giggles, knowing their time would soon come to receive similar attention.

Jeremy ignored the remark. As usual, he had his emotional armor in place for Saturday morning. He continued, "The video and radar imaging has been reviewed by an independent weatherman certified by the National Oceanographic and Atmospheric Administration. The weatherman said there could easily have been a small tornado within this storm cell. Thunderstorms of this magnitude are frequent, almost predictable, this time of year because of the high ground temperature and humidity found in Memphis — also according to him."

Reiter shook her head, "'Almost predictable.' That's a terrific statement for a weatherman. You do have his comments on audio tape, correct?"

Nodding, Jeremy continued, "The NOAA guy, also on this tape, says he can pinpoint the lightning strike which hit the mansion. The exact time of the strike was recorded by the damaged clocks that stopped working inside the building.

"A concrete worker told us that the lightning bolt ignited a liquid propane gas storage chamber. We also have his audio narrative. The tank supplies LPG to the 'eternal flame' near the grave sites. The resultant explosion lifted the cement slabs off the coffins. By the next day, the grave site had been repaired.

"For the most part, the wiring inside the mansion fried. The bulk of the wiring is as old as the building. Newer electrical cables survived. That included much of the shielded and better-grounded security wiring. Most of the older stuff had to be replaced. We have accounts from two of the dozen electricians who worked day and night to replace the damaged wire.

"There was a mild panic at the time of the weather disturbance. Some tourists claim to have seen a tornado. More significantly, several persons claim that while the wind shrieked and the lights dimmed, Elvis appeared to them. Initially, we had five such claims, but the number continues to grow as more people appear on television, are interviewed, write about the experience, see counselors, et cetera."

Reiter uttered scornfully, "Mass hysteria. We will probably see it go on for years. Psychologists will be dredging up repressed memories of Elvis sightings, instead of UFO abductions and sexual battery, into the next decade. Label your patient with a disease he doesn't have, then sell him a cure he doesn't need. They should have been lawyers." The staff murmured in agreement. Reiter waved the back of her hand at Jeremy, "Go on."

The young man pointed to a colleague farther down the table. He said, "We have investigated, quite thoroughly, five of the first twelve individuals to report seeing Elvis. JoAnne has that information."

Without waiting for Reiter's approval, JoAnne launched into her summary. Slender, short, childlike in temperament and voice, JoAnne Choi's high, almost squeaky, Chinese accent camouflaged an investigative drive unequaled in the room, probably in the state, possibly in the nation. "These are not in chronological order because they appear to have taken place simultaneously. Encounter number one occurred in the pool room. A," she searched her notes briefly to confirm the name, "rather, *an* Irene Simpson saw Elvis appear holding a pool cue. According to her statement, he smiled at her and asked if she would like to play a game of eight ball rotation. He told her life is precious and to respect it, even the smallest insects."

"I don't think we need to go into such detail with each encounter, JoAnne," Reiter interrupted. "What did you learn about the people reporting these sightings?"

Without looking further at her notes, Choi spoke, shifting her gaze back and forth among her colleagues, "Of the first five individuals to report encounters, four are currently psychiatric patients. Three of the four have the same psychiatrist, a Dr. Christopher Karakashian, an expert on repressed memories. He has also treated some employees from Turner-Disney. My assistant is trying to find out which employees, as we speak."

"A coincidence, I'm sure," Reiter smiled. The men and women around the table, chuckled, relieved their boss likely had found a focus for the coming week's shows. "What about the seven other encounters in the initial dozen?"

"Actually, we are up to nineteen reported sightings at the time of the weather disturbance. I lost count of the encounters reported since then at three hundred seventy-seven. On average, it looks like forty to fifty percent of these people have documented neuroses or psychoses. It appears that another twenty to thirty percent of them should have been seeing a psychiatrist, from their reports or the background material on them."

"The remaining twenty percent are gold diggers, looking for money from the press or the public," Reiter finished for her investigator.

"So it seems," Choi agreed.

Reiter stood, signaling to the others that the meeting neared a close. She stretched and yawned, then looked each employee in the eye as she spoke. "We may be down, but we are far from out of the ratings ball game. If we do a credible job exposing Turner-Disney and its con men over the next week, then we will probably increase our market share more than enough to cover our recent losses.

"However, one word of warning: there could be a major backlash on this one. This topic is volatile. For some of our listeners, Elvis is already a deity; he is The King. If we push too fast or too hard, without proof to back up what we say, we could be out on the street without jobs the following week.

"For Monday's show, we will review in detail the events from the lightning strike through this weekend. As much as our sponsors hate it, we will take no calls until Tuesday. Tuesday and Wednesday, we had better be ready. I foresee the phones dancing off the hooks with both pro-Presley and anti-Presley segments of society seeking air time." Reiter looked at the secretaries, "You people are going to have to cull some calls, put people on long waits, possibly until they hang up. I want this debate to appear fifty-fifty, pro and con, to our listeners, to any reporters eavesdropping, and to the public in general. Equalize the air time Tuesday, but keep a tally about the calls. For the rest of the week, we'll go with the flow. If ninety percent of the callers want Elvis Presley to be the next Jesus Christ, then we will help crown him Thursday and Friday," Reiter laughed at the ridiculous thought of launching a new religion. Her staff laughed nervously as she left the conference room. They thought about the pending workload.

TWENTY-FIVE

Lockwood camped on the ancient sofa in his efficiency apartment. He spread the newspapers and notes in front of him on top of the rickety coffee table. Having volunteered to fix their lunches, Vanderbilt clanked cups and silverware together in the small kitchen, out of sight of Barry. The noise she made reminded him of a distant thunderstorm, as he looked through the dozen newspapers and magazines he scavenged at the truck stop on their way to Memphis.

"You have any sugar in here, Barry?" The cupboards slammed softly as she searched.

"In the fridge," he answered absent-mindedly, reading an article for the second time. "I don't spend much time here; putting it there keeps the ants and roaches out of it."

The door to the refrigerator opened, making a sucking sound to which Barry was oblivious. Sounds of gurgling refreshment poured over ice cubes covered with freezer frost also emanated from the kitchen, but were ignored. He looked at the next essay, in a different paper.

"What did you find in the papers?" Vanderbilt asked as she placed a tray in front of Lockwood. It rocked gently on the second hand coffee table, piled with sandwiches and iced tea.

"Confusion, mainly," he sighed, reaching for the cold cuts wrapped in stale bread. "Sorry, I don't have much food around. Some of my clients are in arrears."

Vanderbilt sat huffily on the worn recliner opposite the condemned sofa. She stared at him pinching up her face and squinting. "I told you I would pay you next week. You have the two hundred as down payment."

"Whoa, there, Ms. Vanderbilt," Lockwood held up his hands in mock surrender, speaking with a mouth full of food. Crumbs spewed forth. He covered his face with a napkin and forced himself to swallow too hastily. The hard bread hurt his throat as it went down. "I didn't mean you, just the hundred clients who came before you. If it weren't for Jeff, I'd really be broke."

"Who's Jeff again?" Vanderbilt asked as she took a big swig of the sweetened tea.

"My ex-partner, from the Memphis police force. He's a lawyer, now." Lockwood pushed aside one paper to look at the one under it. "He also runs a small collection agency. People tend to pay quicker when they receive a letter from a lawyer. We've never found it necessary to go to court to demand payment. Clients don't know what a pussy cat Jeff really is. All bluff."

"I'll try to remember that when he contacts me." Amy smiled with a mouth full of tuna sandwich. With moderate success, she swallowed a large gulp of tea, in an attempt to soften the lump of stale bread.

"I'll deny I told you," Lockwood said, obviously distracted. Still staring at the picture in the paper, he asked, "You said you have a big, clear photograph of B.J. Do you have it with you?"

Vanderbilt leaned forward, reaching under the coffee table for her black leather valise. She could see a paperback book under one leg, keeping the table even. *The Last Day of the Vladimir Adrianov*, the title read. Noticing her looking at the book, Lockwood informed her, "It's a spy novel; I was reading it when the Soviet Union went belly-up. Didn't seem necessary to finish it after that happened."

"Oh." She straightened up, holding a sheaf of papers and glossy eight by ten inch photos in her hand. She handed the collection to Lockwood.

Barry leaned back on the sofa, then leaned forward again and shifted to his right, squirming and making an annoyed expression. "A spring pokes through there," he explained. He rubbed his back as best he could. She smiled again.

Sifting through the pile of photos, Lockwood found several shots of an approximately thirty-year-old man with sandy brown hair. He possessed a straight nose and dark blue eyes. In most of the pictures, he displayed a grim expression. In some, he exhibited a day old stubble, a mustache, or an occasional short beard. Lockwood pulled several pictures of Elvis Presley out of the stack and stuck them in a pile on the right side of the table. "Do you have any of B.J. when he was working?"

Vanderbilt nodded, knowing a secret. She knew what Lockwood thought. Pointing to the Elvis glossies, she responded, "Those are of B.J."

"Right," Lockwood replied, sarcastically. "This guy has blond hair, and no dimples. I've seen those pictures of Elvis before, in books, magazines, someplace."

"How many pictures of Elvis that you saw showed him with an irregular pupil in his left eye?" Vanderbilt pulled a magnifying glass from her valise. "It is the only way to tell, when B.J. is performing as Elvis. Look at his left pupil with this. It's heart shaped, right?"

Lockwood took the magnifying glass from her and held it over the glossy print. He moved it up and down until the eyeball came into focus. The blue iris stood out, shaped like a miniature heart lying on its side. Vanderbilt explained, "When he was in grade school, a boy threw a rock at him. It hit Beej in the eye. His vision didn't suffer much, but he has terrible headaches from eyestrain sometimes."

Vanderbilt continued, "B.J. was born in Tupelo, Mississippi. His father was Vernon Presley's distant cousin. His mother was Gladys Presley's younger aunt. Somehow, B.J. inherited many of the same genes as Elvis. He had blond hair, too. They both dyed their hair black. Beej even sings like Elvis."

"You have a picture of Elvis, the real Elvis, in there?" Lockwood asked, skeptically.

Vanderbilt handed him another large glossy, a picture of the King in a black karate outfit. "Each of the photos in B.J.'s portfolio was staged to remind people of an original Elvis photo. They really are of B.J."

"It's amazing." Lockwood focused the magnifying glass on the image in front of him. The perfectly round, left iris of a dead icon stared at him through the glass. Lockwood shook his head at the two photos, one of Elvis in his early thirties, a trim, muscular, handsome superstar. The other picture could have been of his twin, had his twin, Jesse, survived birth. "I can understand why people might think they had seen Elvis, or Elvis reincarnated, after seeing B.J." he said. "I can also understand why Turner-Disney wanted him so badly. He's perfect to play the *back from the dead* role."

"So where is he, now?" Vanderbilt asked.

"If my guess is correct," Lockwood pointed at the stack of papers on the table, "he's one of these gentlemen. It appears that Turner-Disney has invited him, and them, to appear in L.A. next week. Maybe we can intercept him."

"He might not want to be intercepted," Vanderbilt suggested, "or maybe he is still in Memphis."

Lockwood concurred, "There is a possibility he is in Memphis. T-D did say that they are going to fly Elvis's small jet airliner from Memphis to Los Angeles next week. The invitation is for Elvis to fly to California on the jet. I don't think he'll be on it, though."

"Why don't you?"

"Two reasons." Lockwood handed Vanderbilt four or five of the articles that he had ripped from the newspapers. "In each of these, an Elvis mimic told someone that Elvis appeared to him and told him to come to L.A. Many of these admitted impostors are on their way to L.A., already. Also, if someone does ride in the Presley jet, it will appear that Turner-Disney had a significant role in setting up this scam. They have denied any complicity in the appearance of Elvis, the disappearance of his body, or the light-ning which hit Graceland. By holding the concert in Los Angeles, they hope to prove they are innocent of staging the hoax. T-D doesn't want Elvis to appear in Memphis or to arrive in Los Angeles aboard their plane. They only want the publicity for the possibility that he may be on it."

"I don't understand." Vanderbilt's face clouded, deeply in thought. "Why would they hire B.J. to impersonate Elvis in the first place, and then not use him?"

"Oh, they're using him. He is one of a hundred Pied Pipers now working their magic on the public." Lockwood slapped the palm of his hand on the table. "Elvis insanity has hit a feverish pitch. Some of these men were probably hired to start the ball rolling. Others are doing it for their own, best, greedy interests. It will be interesting to see if anyone can connect T-D to the result."

"We're pretty sure Turner-Disney hired B.J., aren't we?" she asked. Her confusion worsened.

"I am," Lockwood stated, flatly, "and if I can prove it, then they may have to pay me $100,000."

"A million dollars," Vanderbilt corrected him.

"A million?"

"I watched a late night television show last night in the hotel. The head guy at Turner-Disney said he would pay a million dollars to anyone who could prove that they started this wave of nostalgia." Vanderbilt recounted Crossley's denial of involvement.

"That makes it more imperative that we find B.J. quickly," Lockwood decided.

"You want the million dollars?" Vanderbilt asked.

"It would be nice to have," Lockwood agreed, "but as Jeff can tell you, they will never pay. Turner-Disney could spend so much money in legal fees to disprove anything you and I said, that we would never see the reward. It wouldn't be worth the trouble to claim it."

"Then why would you be in a rush to find B.J.? I know why I'm in a hurry — to keep my expenses and your fees down," she admitted. "Appearances aside, B.J. and I don't have much money. Dad said he'd help, but that's not a blank check."

Lockwood nodded, "I could prolong this, but I don't work that way. What I was thinking of, however, is this: If someone at

Turner-Disney hired B.J. to start the Elvis mania, did orchestrate the media, and has made monetary gains because of that liaison, then B.J. may be in danger."

"He knows who hired him, and why," she concluded.

"Exactly. Even if they keep their million in a court of law, they could lose a lot more in the stock market if the court of public opinion finds them guilty."

Suddenly more interested in the newspapers, Vanderbilt leaned forward in the chair; it groaned. "So, where do we start?" she asked Lockwood.

"We eliminate the guys of whom we have pictures or good descriptions and who are obviously not B.J. For instance, we can forget the old, fat guy in Minnesota." Lockwood pulled a pen from his shirt pocket and drew a line through the article. "We need to find as many of these imitators as possible, to find B.J."

"And if we don't find him?"

"We will," Lockwood answered and left unsaid, if he is still alive.

TWENTY-SIX

The hungry FBI agent sat at the small round table in the hotel room, staring at the sandwich his wife had constructed for his lunch. "Variety," he mumbled through a mouthful of zucchini, banana, and bread, smothered in low-fat mayonnaise.

"What did you say, Sorensen?" Agent Ralph Jacobs asked. He snickered, watching his boss force himself to eat the sandwich. Jacobs, a leaner, trimmer, younger model of agent at thirty years of age, could afford to giggle. Having recently lost his one thousandth game of solitaire, he sat on one of the twin beds in the room. He surrendered the table to Sorensen so the older man could spread out his lunch. Sorensen returned from the deli with drinks for both of them and Jacobs's sandwich. Smiling, Jacobs clamped the twelve-inch roast beef sub in both hands. It oozed with condiments, none of them low-fat.

Clearing his throat with a swig of prune juice, Sorensen eyed his antagonist. He smiled sadistically, "When you have your coronary, kid, I'm going to insist that my wife cook for you for at least a year."

"When I have my heart attack," Jacobs corrected him, "I'm going to have the good sense to die. You should have. I couldn't possibly follow the diet your wife and your doctor have you on. If I can't eat what I want, I...."

A speaker sitting on the chest of drawers crackled. Both men held their breaths and stopped chewing, waiting for someone to speak. The sound-activated listening device hidden inside Lomax's office automatically turned itself on. The muffled noise from the opening of Lomax's office door triggered the bug. Although a reel-to-reel tape recorder spun lazily on the night stand, catching every sound generated in Lomax's office, the men waited, hushed, to see what would transpire.

"Sit," Lomax's voice commanded.

Jacobs went to the window and looked through the telescope placed so that only the lens showed through the curtain. "Austin's with him," he whispered. Sorensen nodded.

The speaker duly reproduced the clinking of desk top tools and the clunk of Lomax's feet as they hit the top of his desk. Neither man spoke for several minutes, as if they knew the room to be wired. Finally, Lomax spoke.

"We have some loose ends, George." His tone of voice was difficult to characterize over the speaker, but the words came through clearly. Austin did not respond.

"Crossley has let the board know that Graceland is my baby. Any screw-ups are my responsibility. He backed my decision to hold the concert, as long as it turns a profit." Static crackled from the speaker as Lomax paused. He added, "Someone is spying on us."

Sorensen bolted out of his seat and pushed Jacobs away from the telescope. He looked through the eyepiece. Lomax apparently pushed the switch that closed the office curtains. Sorensen caught only a brief glimpse of the man's shadow as the curtain sealed the room. The speaker remained silent except for the hum of the curtain motor.

"How'd he find out?" Jacobs asked. Sorensen shrugged, disappointed, wondering how Hopkins and the FTC would respond to the news. They had blown the investigation after only two days.

"Who?" the speaker said, as Austin asked the question of Lomax. Both agents stared at the speaker, as if it knew the answer.

"I don't know," Lomax said, slapping his hand on his desk. "I only know that R.M. found out we have been monitoring his wife's activities. He specifically told me to leave her out of our plans."

"Jenny?" Austin inquired, referring to Lomax's secretary.

"She's new; I guess she's a suspect," Lomax answered. "In my opinion, it has to be someone who dislikes me. Probably, it is someone who has been around long enough to have a following and friends within Turner-Disney."

"Cartwright, then?"

"Maybe, but he's going to retire soon." Sorensen imagined he could see Lomax rubbing his chin as the man thought out loud. "It has to be one of the ambitious vice-presidents, anyone with a shot at chairman of the board when R.M. bails out."

"Could be anybody, then," Austin suggested.

"Exactly," Lomax agreed. "Be very careful. Leave no trails from this point on, and erase any tracks you've made."

Both FBI agents glanced upward and gave silent thanks that their surveillance had not been exposed. They shook hands, "Whew!" they said in unison.

"Let's go over the loose ends, one by one," Lomax suggested to Austin. "What about the body?"

"We can't get a straight answer from the family. Lisa-Marie thinks Vernon Presley probably buried him in a special unmarked grave. She thinks he wanted to prevent the remains from being disturbed, or the plot vandalized. If so, then good old Vernon took the information about the real burial site's location to his grave. Priscilla Presley doubts Vernon was that paranoid."

"Keep looking," Lomax directed his lieutenant.

"We have scoured every inch of the grounds."

"Scrutinize it again; search the neighbors' yards. Investigate every tree, stump, or hole within a mile of Graceland, got it?"

"What do we tell the neighbors, or the press?"

"I don't care. Dress the search crew like meter men. Who cares? Don't mention Elvis." Lomax sounded exasperated.

"Got it," Austin answered. "You said something about the balloons while we were in the car?"

"Yeah." Lomax scraped his feet on the desk as he spun away from Austin and faced the closed curtain. His voice was not as loud, but it came through the agents' speaker crisply. "That busybody, Gale Reiter, dug up something about the barrage balloons we used briefly for advertising at the mansion. I'm supposed to be a guest on her radio show Monday. She thinks maybe we sent it up, like Ben Franklin's kite, into the thunderstorm."

"Pretty good guess."

"Jesus, Austin. I wish you would stop sounding like you are on the other team for a while." The frustration grated on Lomax's nerves and showed in his voice.

"You're right; sorry. What'll we do? Show her the backup balloon?"

"Yeah. It got cooked by the lightning strike, sitting next to the flying balloon. The cable is welded in the down position. I think that is a good idea. Make certain that no one finds the original balloon carcass. The one which took the bolt, and it's cable and reel, should be long gone before Reiter's investigators show up, tomorrow." Lomax's confidence grew as he solved one of his problems.

"I'll have Aguilar take care of that, tonight," Austin replied. Jacobs scribbled furiously in a small notebook, trying to record the most important parts of Lomax and Austin's conversation.

Lomax's voice dropped to an almost indiscernible level when he asked Austin about Nottingham. "Where is B.J.?" Silence radiated from the speaker. Sorensen assumed Austin shook his head or shrugged. "Dammit, we've got to find that guy. Do you have any idea where he could be, Austin? A million bucks and our reputation ride with that nut."

Austin cleared his throat. "A private detective showed up at the Jukebox, Saturday, looking for him. Vanderbilt was with him."

Sarcasm spanned the distance from the bug in Lomax's office to the hotel stakeout, "Oh, terrific. Find him, Austin. And do it quickly."

The speaker fell silent again, briefly. Lomax spoke, almost to himself only, "Three down, one to go. Have you seen Doc recently?"

"Yeah," answered Austin, "why?"

"Individually, neither the Doc nor B.J. could put nooses around our necks, if they were to go to the media. Nottingham is a known

flake. Doc's specialty makes him suspect, too." A long pause mirrored itself in the agents' room. "Together, however, they could
burn us."

Austin's voice sounded tinny and higher over the speaker, re-
flecting his mood, "Meaning, what?"

"Meaning," Lomax explained the situation for his assistant, "if
you don't find B.J., then you will have to make certain Doc doesn't
ever speak to anyone from the media. Ever."

"Are you implying that we should threaten or blackmail the
Doc?" The tone of Austin's voice indicated his confusion.

"No, George, I'm not." Lomax cleared his throat, "I am hint-
ing that if you do not find B.J. Nottingham, then you will have to
arrange for the Doc to have a fatal accident. Understand now?"

Silence answered the question. After a minute or two of silence, Lomax spoke again. "Unless you have something else to discuss, I have to meet with Lester Gomez about our concert plans for
Wednesday. Before you leave, though, how's it going with the jet?"

Austin's tone brightened appreciably, "The Army National
Guard provided a heavy-lift chopper to ferry it to the Memphis
International Airport. That didn't cost us much. The Army did it
as a training exercise for the helicopter crew. Our mechanics are
working twenty-four hours a day. They've really gotten into the
swing of things. Aguilar says they promise to have her flying by
Tuesday. After a local certification flight, the FAA will authorize
her to fly to LAX Wednesday."

The voices trailed off as the men left the room, moving farther
from the bug. "Great," Lomax said before the door closed with a
solid thump, sealing out all sounds from the hallway.

TWENTY-SEVEN

In some ways the crowd reminded Lockwood of a church picnic. In places it resembled a wake, with groups of individuals speaking very quietly. The sea of people swayed with the music, mumbling the words they forgot, or never knew. Occasionally, the hearsay shot through the crowd like pain along an exposed nerve. Most times, the gossip ambled slowly. Weeping willow-like, people bent to listen to every rumor that meandered through the crowd like the nearby Missouri River.

Barry eavesdropped on several conversations and news broadcasts, as he tramped through the widely spaced clusters of people. Messages emanated from portable televisions and radios carried by the travelers. Thousands of people filled the makeshift campground constructed on the Missouri State Fair Grounds in Sedalia. He captured small bits of information as he worked his way toward the stage, lugging his camera bag in one hand and towing Vanderbilt with the other.

"...Turner-Disney flatly refuses to admit they were involved...."

"...news of another miracle in Memphis...."

"...calling us Preslians; they want a church conference convened...."

"...appeared to a group of teenagers in a Chicago ghetto. Saved a boy's life, the paper...."

"Barry, stop pulling so hard," Amy's voice penetrated the fog of babble that surrounded them, but her words were unintelligible. He concentrated on the stage.

"What?" Lockwood asked, halting several feet from the platform. He paused for a second, to pull the camera from the leather bag and to check the lens settings. Inspecting it carefully, he made certain he had inserted the film correctly.

"I said," Vanderbilt spoke between clenched teeth, "don't pull me. You hurt my arm." She rubbed her elbow and then her wrist where his grip left red and white marks in her soft skin.

"Oh, sorry," Lockwood apologized, distracted. His attention fell to the persons lining the stage, inside the curtain at one of the wings. As he adjusted the telephoto lens on the 35mm camera, he identified them for Vanderbilt. "Do you know any of those guys?" he asked her.

Exhausted from the dash to the Memphis airport, the ride in the twin propeller aircraft through turbulent skies to Kansas City and, finally, the rush to the fair grounds in a rental car, Vanderbilt squinted through her destroyed eye makeup and hazy contact lenses. "Can't tell. Can we get closer?"

"They are going to come to us, I think," Lockwood surmised as an emcee marched onto the wooden platform.

A rotund black man in a tan pair of slacks and a short sleeve, white shirt strode to mid-stage. He sweated profusely, drenching his shirt in the warm humid evening air. In silence, he pointed to the speakers on the light poles which surrounded the open air theater. He drew his hand across his throat. Elvis's voice faded quickly in mid-Teddy Bear.

Abruptly aware of the silence, the crowd looked first at the mute speakers and then at the platform. The collective moan ceased when they saw the man standing on the stage. They recognized the musician; he played rhythm and blues backup for Elvis many years before. With a second wave of his hand, the emcee battled the encroaching dusk by lighting the lamps and spotlights which shared the tall cement poles with the silent speakers. Waiting until the crowd noise abated, the announcer spoke in deep, rich bass tones.

"Forty-some years ago, I shared this stage with Elvis Presley," he began. "I played a little bass guitar then." The crowd choked back a laugh at the man's humility. He continued, "At the time, I felt a nearness to something regal. No, not royal, a divine presence is what I perceived when I stood near the man we knew as Elvis Presley. Now, an event beyond our imagination has taken place; I cannot interpret that occurrence for you. I can say this: If Elvis Presley has been sent back to Earth by our Lord to give us guidance, with his words or through his music, then God could not have chosen better." A cheer rose from the crowd. Lockwood wondered if the crowd expected to see Elvis.

The speaker continued when the noise diminished. "Elvis Aaron Presley truly loved every person and every race of people in the world. His music crossed all national boundaries; it touched everyone on the planet who heard it. His gift was his ability to communicate that love to each person in the audience during his performances." Pausing to pull a handkerchief from his back pocket the emcee wiped the sweat and the tears from his face, and blew them from his nose.

"Tonight, you are on a great crusade. Some of you are going to Los Angeles, possibly to be disappointed. Others of you are on your way to the Super Dome in New Orleans, bound, perhaps, for similar disillusionment."

Cries of, "He'll be there," carried to the stage from the crowd.

The man held his hands up, hushing the crowd. "You're right; he'll be there. One way or another, he'll be there."

Motioning to three persons standing at the edge of the stage, the man continued to speak into the microphone. "Before you continue your pilgrimage tomorrow, I thought you might like to hear from three people who say they have spoken to Elvis this week. I have spoken with them. Personally, I believe their stories. You may draw your own conclusions.

"The first is Grayson Langdon. Mr. Langdon." The emcee held his arm out to a small man with graying hair standing off stage. Obviously made nervous by the huge crowd, the man shuffled self-consciously to the middle of the stage. He accepted the microphone handed to him by the bigger man. For a minute, he stood trembling in silence, directly in front of Lockwood and Vanderbilt.

"Know him?" Lockwood asked in a loud whisper. Vanderbilt shook her head, no.

"Ladies and, uh, gentleman," Langdon spoke timidly. He stared at the speakers which blared his words to the masses, amplifying and repeating them. Echoes of his voice moved away from him and over the crowd. "Talking to large groups of people scares the doo-doo out of me." The crowd sniggered, trying not to embarrass the man. "But I promised myself I would bear witness to what I saw." Lockwood watched as the man clutched the microphone with a life or death grip. He remembered his first speech in front of a large audience. In empathy, Lockwood's hands dripped with sweat.

"I...I was at Graceland, Tuesday. At 03:30 p.m. Normally, I live in California, in Sacramento," he explained. "My wife and I decided to visit our children who live on the east coast. I'm a retired accountant." As the man spoke, Lockwood noticed that Langdon's gaze rose from his own feet, to the crowd, and then centered on a distant point. That spot seemed to be in the sky, above the throng. His voice became bolder, more certain, more authoritative. He began to relive the moment at Graceland, and to enlighten the crowd at the same time.

"My wife and I were inside Graceland, in the television room in the basement. We heard a terrible roar, like a hundred locomotives or the roar of a jetliner at takeoff. The fluorescent lights flickered. A blue flame skipped across the ceiling lighting fixtures. The track lights on the ceiling exploded, followed by the television sets. Sparks showered everywhere. Then, the most fantastic thing happened to me."

The older man paused and looked directly above his head to the heavens. He recited, as if the phrases were a memorized prayer: "Elvis stood in front of me. No one else moved except me and him. Time stood still. 'Grayson,' he said, 'tell them that the lyrics to the songs are important. Tell them to listen to the words. All life is precious. Tell them to spread the Word throughout the Universe.'

"'The Universe,' I asked, 'and tell who?'

"'Tell everyone on Earth,' he explained to me, 'to send our music to all the planets in the Universe. Find other life in the Universe. Tell them, Grayson.' So I have told you," Langdon concluded quickly. He quietly scooted off the stage, hiding his stagefright as best he could.

The crowd stood and sat quietly, not overwhelmed. They contemplated the implications of Langdon's vision and how it fit with other reported encounters. His revelation was mild compared to some they had heard over the previous week. Polite applause accompanied the retired accountant's escape from the spotlight. Next, the musician introduced two men who made their living impersonating Elvis.

Each told a similar story of being visited by Presley during the previous four days. The message espoused dittoed Langdon's, with minor variations, "Respect life on Earth; find more life in the Universe." Amy knew neither man. B.J. was not at the fairgrounds that evening.

The mass of people resumed its church picnic air. Lockwood wondered where the frenzy reported by the news media went. "They're so well-behaved, so quiet," he said aloud, but to himself.

"They've found peace already," Vanderbilt enlightened him.

"What do you mean?" Lockwood asked.

"These people believe that Elvis Presley has returned to Earth, sent by God. They are at peace with themselves. They are assured that an afterlife exists. Now, there is proof; at least they have enough proof for themselves." Lockwood looked around; the theory made sense. No one screamed or yelled. Not one loud voice assaulted his ears.

"A new religion?" he asked of Vanderbilt as they walked through the crowd to the parking lot and searched for their rental car.

Vanderbilt replied, "Sects have originated with less foundation than this: Zionism, Calvinism, Kabbalism."

"How do you know that?" Lockwood searched her face for clues that she teased him.

"While at the University of Tennessee, I changed majors a lot."

She pulled open the car door. "Sociology, Religion, Psychology."

"What's your degree in?" Lockwood explored the glove compartment, looking for a map. He finally found an inadequate one.

"That's the sad part." Vanderbilt pushed the door to the glove compartment closed. Lockwood started the car and backed it slowly from the parking spot. "I have enough hours to graduate, but no major. After five years, my parents refused to pay tuition any longer."

"Well, a new religion," Barry exhaled forcefully, thinking aloud. "I think I heard they want to be called the Preslians. It's an interesting thought, but it won't work here."

"Why?"

"Our government allows freedom of religious expression." He floored the accelerator. The rental car shot onto the highway, in front of a slowly moving van. "In order for a religion to spread like wildfire, it has to be illegal and to be suppressed. Like the Christians and the Romans; the Christians and the lions, remember?"

"That's not necessarily true, Barry. You are forgetting Moslems, Buddhists, and Confucians. Most religions did not need to be suppressed or oppressed to succeed. Besides, the government isn't the only organization that can challenge a new religion. Organized denominations can be antagonizing, and unforgiving, too."

Not versed in the theologies of the world, Lockwood nodded in apparent agreement. He added, semi-defiantly, "It would take hold faster with a few martyrs, I'll bet."

Vanderbilt rested her weary head on Lockwood's shoulder as they accelerated along the highway, toward Kansas City and a hotel. Barry felt his pulse race and his blood pressure increase in response to her touch. He glanced into the mirror to see if he blushed. Vanderbilt, already asleep, leaned on his arm. He patted her knee. The sun set in front of them, turning the blue sky and clouds into a palette of pink and green.

TWENTY-EIGHT

The clear desert night ended abruptly at the Sunday daybreak, as if someone turned on the sun with a switch. Vanished were the stars, lost in the deep blue sky. Only the moon remained, a small sliver directly above Shafer. He marveled at the sudden change.

"Beautiful, eh, Colonel?" Presley asked as he fluff-dried his hair while standing on the step to the Winnebago. He stepped onto the ground near Shafer.

"Nice flying weather," the retired pilot responded. Beauty never entered the equation, as far as he was concerned. "VFR forever. Visibility is unlimited."

Elvis smiled, "The grandeur of Mega will enlighten you one day, Colonel, I promise. We've got to be going."

"Why so soon?" Jack protested, "We haven't eaten breakfast, yet." Presley held the screen door for the older man, as Shafer fought with the retractable step, pushing it under the vehicle's threshold. Jack climbed into the camper.

"We still have a long way to go; there'll be food on the road," Elvis replied. Shafer held the inner door open as Elvis jumped nimbly into the RV without the aid of the step.

"Everyone's going with us, I presume," Jack waved his hand at the hundreds of cars parked around them in the desert on the old, deserted highway. The interstate bypassed the large river of concrete, making it obsolete. Multi-colored makeshift tents, next to or part of the many vehicles, imploded, dropped, and disappeared as he watched. Cars began to rock as people climbed into and out of them. They packed as they tried to warm themselves in the cool desert morning.

The Winnebago's engine roared to life. Elvis grinned, "They

wouldn't miss it for the world, Colonel." Ponderously, the RV began to move with Elvis at the wheel. Weaving sluggishly between the haphazardly parked cars on the abandoned roadway, it dodged the vehicles randomly dispersed along the weathered cement strip. Formerly the lifeline of Albuquerque, New Mexico, the state route disintegrated slowly in the desert climate.

Imperceptibly, at first, then more rapidly, a segmented tail of steel grew behind the Winnebago. Carload after carload linked their destination and the occupants' fate to that of the old rusting hulk of a camper. The steel python stretched for several miles. Its head approached the Interstate 40 on-ramp.

Elvis drove past the intersection without slowing. Amazed, Jack spoke, "You missed the interstate, Elvis."

"Yeah, I know," Presley drawled. He pointed to the horizon. Barely visible, on the line between dirt and sky, stood a blue and white striped tent, twice the size of the last circus tent Shafer had seen. "I've a hankering to sing some Gospel music, if you don't mind, Colonel?"

Shafer crossed his arms and grunted, "Don't ask me to sing along," he spat. "I'll sit in the RV, thanks." He rolled his eyes upward.

"Shoot, Colonel," Elvis grinned. "Even though you don't like music, revivals are entertaining. You don't have to sing."

"No thanks, son." Shafer spoke with finality.

Eyes on the road as the tent grew larger in size and slid down from the horizon and closer to the Winnebago, Elvis hinted, "Most times the local folks bring food. They generally have either a big breakfast or a luncheon after the service."

Shafer's stomach growled as the RV turned onto the gravel road leading to the tent. A big cloth sign at the side of the path proclaimed, 'Revival Sunday! Bring your soul to be saved! Reverend Jesse Allen.' Twenty to thirty cars already sat parked in front of the tent. "Well, I might wander around the tent some," Shafer allowed, as the camper's wheels locked sending tiny rocks flying and raising a small dust storm. Behind them scores of cars and campers bore down upon the striped tent, subsequently filling the surrounding hard-packed desert field with a dusty rainbow of vehicles.

Meanwhile, Shafer and Presley wandered inside the tent. Elvis spoke quietly with the local people, mostly Indian and Hispanic in appearance. The congregation sat in plastic chairs on the tarp floor awaiting the reverend. Jack searched in vain for the breakfast his stomach dearly missed. Slowly, the tent filled with the adults and children emerging from the automobiles which followed the camper to the revival setting.

Several Hispanic-looking persons, who evidently worked for the Reverend Allen, scurried back and forth setting up the podium, microphones, and lights. The more people who poured into the tent, the more excited the workers became, moving faster and faster at their appointed tasks. Shafer saw one use a portable phone. The assistant clergyman appeared agitated and seemed to talk excitedly on the phone, although Shafer could not hear what he said.

Surrounding Elvis at the main entrance to the tent, a throng of people wedged itself between Jack and his driver. Quickly, the crowd became twenty deep. They pressed close to shake Presley's hand. Jack's hearing loss prevented him from catching the meaning of the murmurs. Elvis smiled, apparently making small talk that satisfied the members of the migrant congregation. As each person touched or spoke with Presley, his or her face would break into a smile and beam angelically. In an orderly manner, those who had reached their goal retired from the mob and sat in the chairs inside the tent, allowing others to do the same. Never did they jostle, shove, or shout at one another. Somehow they knew he had time for each of them.

Thirty feet from Presley and in the middle of the canvas shelter, Jack stood looking past him into the desert and at the gravel road which led from the asphalt state route to the tent. A cloud of dust moved toward them at a high rate of speed. Jack assumed the Reverend Allen arrived to claim his sheep.

As the car approached the tent, Jack could distinguish the white Cadillac with the darkened windows, used to keep out the murderous desert sun. Jack guessed the parson to be doing sixty miles per hour over the dirt road. Fifty yards short of the tent, the front bumper of the car dipped and dug into the gravel. At that speed, the bumper bit hard into the ground and the sedan began to flip end over end. Shafer understood what had happened when the right front wheel sped by the tent at fifty-plus miles per hour, missing it by several feet.

The throng around Elvis screamed as one frightened animal. Adults picked up children and scattered as the rolling car bore down upon the entrance to the tent. Tumbling toward them, the sight of the bright white automobile with dark black spots of windows reminded Jack of a large die. Briefly, he wondered if the Reverend Allen had thrown himself snake-eyes. Then he realized that Elvis had not moved. The distance between them was too far for Jack to run. It would have been difficult to pull the young man out of the way in time, even had Jack been young and strong enough to accomplish such a feat. Shafer awaited the outcome of the skirmish with the same trepidation he had felt in combat.

The young man stood facing the car as it flipped and rolled toward him. Yards short of Elvis and the tent, the vehicle bounced high into the air and then landed, right side up, front bumper within ten feet of Presley. The remaining three tires blew out; the car skidded to a stop, inches from where Elvis stood.

Presley walked quickly to the driver's door and jerked it open. Inside sat the Reverend Allen, an Oriental man, strapped into the seat. A deflated air bag hung from the steering wheel. His eyes closed, the minister finished reciting the Lord's Prayer, out loud. After a brief pause, he opened his eyes and looked around. Two of his assistants pushed their way through the crowd and around Elvis.

"Are you okay?" one asked.

"Shall I call an ambulance?" the other acolyte asked, waving the cellular phone, not waiting to hear the man's answer to the first question.

Stunned and mute, the dazed preacher sat in the car. A white Bible with gold trim rested on his lap. Elvis reached into the car, released the seat belt, and took the man's left hand with his left hand. He then placed his right hand on the Preacher's forehead and closed his eyes in concentration for a brief moment. "He'll be fine," Elvis announced. The crowd cheered.

"Are you really all right?" one assistant asked.

"I think so," Reverend Allen allowed, looking at Elvis. "I am a little shaken up. I hate to disappoint all these good people, but I don't think I can give a sermon today. "

"Reverend," Elvis interjected, "I think I can help you out with a sermon." He opened his eyes, but maintained his left-handed grip and right-hand placement on the other's forehead. "If you don't mind, I would like to lead the congregation in a couple of hymns, also."

Eyes fixed on Presley, the preacher responded, "Son, I would be honored to have you lead us in prayer. Thank you. Thank you for being here when I needed your help."

"Just taking care of business, Reverend. Just taking care of business," Elvis replied, solemnly.

TWENTY-NINE

Austin paced in front of the secretary's empty desk and chair. Sunday mornings usually meant the day off: girl watching, swimming in the Pacific, or hanging out with some friends at The Pub 'N Pool off Sunset Boulevard. He estimated he worked eighty hours of overtime since the explosion at Graceland. Finding B.J. Nottingham consumed his waking hours, and his nightmares during his few fidgety hours of sleep.

He prided himself on being able to deliver anything Lomax requested. As an ex-Marine, he fit the stereotype of an overzealous, proud, competent, obsessive-compulsive, too-loyal patriot. Zealotry cost him his corporal's stripes and his career in the Marines. The brass frowned upon firing live ammunition over the heads of cowards to get their attention. Austin attempted to atone for his past failures by succeeding in everything he did for Lomax.

For his part, the marketing director did little to dissuade Austin from giving to him one hundred percent of his loyalty and fanaticism. Lomax actively encouraged the clean shaven, deeply tanned, weight-lifting, type-A personality ex-jarhead to push the envelope of legality and ethics. By rewarding Austin excessively with generous bonuses whenever he acquired information on potential detractors, Lomax fanned his fanaticism.

On Austin's one hundredth circuit of the secretary's desk, the door to Lomax's office finally opened. Streams of people evacuated the office as if they fled an erupting volcano. Austin counted sixteen people escaping his tyrannical supervisor's booming voice. They quickly disappeared, melting into the building, into the elevator, down the hall, into bathrooms, anywhere to avoid Lomax's wrath.

Austin waited, checking his suit and tie for lint. He put one foot at a time onto the cushion of a chair next to the secretary's desk and wiped the dust from the toes with his handkerchief. Ever the spit-polished Marine, the reflection of his face and muscular neck shone back at him, only mildly distorted by the textured leather.

"Austin!" Lomax shouted.

"Yes, sir." Austin stiffened. Striding into the office, he closed the door behind him. Pointing his thumb over his shoulder at the departing Turner-Disney drones, he asked, "What was that about?" He stood at attention next to the chair awaiting Lomax's permission to sit.

Lomax pointed at the chair and nodded. Austin sat. He waited patiently as Lomax framed his response, gazing at the ceiling and then the Beverly Hills outside his window. "Spin control is one way of putting it," he finally answered. "Some of the big boys are worried about the backlash from the *Elvis Thing*, as they politely refer to our phenomenon." Lomax walked behind his desk and took his usual seat. He maintained his thoughtful posture, with his feet on the desk. "They think this fad has run its course. Elvis has had his second fifteen minutes of fame and will soon crash in flames, as one vice president so delicately put it."

Lomax laughed. "Makes you wonder how these men and women got where they are. This is a risky and risk-taking business. You sink millions, sometimes hundreds of millions, of dollars into a project. If it pans out, you are a winner. If it doesn't, you move on, to a less hazardous occupation. Anyway, they wanted to pull the plug on the concert deal. They are afraid of what will happen when Elvis doesn't show. The public will cry *foul*, they say. Turner-Disney will be cast as the heavy; all sorts of repercussions will result."

"And?" Austin solicited the result he knew Lomax wanted to divulge.

"And, the show must go on!" Lomax shouted triumphantly. "Hell, I know Elvis won't be there. But you can bet your ass that

I'll have the pick of the litter Wednesday morning in Memphis and, later, here. There must be a hundred Elvis impersonators on their way to Graceland and to Los Angeles. Did you see the news? Speaking of impersonators, did you find our boy, yet?"

Austin squirmed in the seat. He attempted to evade the question, knowing the ruse would not work, "We've got a good lead. Although they don't realize it, Vanderbilt and her private detective are helping us. They've already checked eight groups of migrant Elvis fans, and accompanying impersonators. They're in a rental car working their way west, hot on B.J.'s trail. It's a good thing her daddy's a doctor. Her bill is going to be horrendous."

Lomax seemed not to hear the response, lost in his own reverie. "You know what clinched it for us, George?"

"No, sir," Austin breathed a sigh of relief, believing B.J. no longer held top billing on Lomax's short To Do List.

"Not only are all the remote stadium sites sold out, but now the pay-per-view people are signing up and advertisers are begging to join the show. Merchandising for Elvis products has exploded, man. I mean detonated! The television news last night estimated that there may be a half million to two million people on the road, moving toward these concert stations. If one-half of the contracts are finalized before Wednesday, Turner-Disney could pay off the loan for Graceland. The profit will be enormous if we sign them all, even if Elvis does not show up. Those idiots! Do you think they thought that I really expected Elvis to show up in the flesh?"

Austin did not answer the rhetorical question. Lomax sat upright in the chair, putting his feet on the floor and placing his elbows on the desk. He wove the fingers of both hands together and placed his chin on his thumbs. Staring Austin in the face, he clenched his teeth and spoke evenly and to the point. "We can't leave any loose ends, George. I can handle the investigative reporters, like Reiter, the balloon stories, and the other trash. B.J. and the Doc could bring us down like a poorly arranged house of cards on the San Andreas fault. Do you understand?"

"The Doc has already been taken care of. The brakes could fail at any...."

"I don't want to know details, George." Lomax lifted his head from his thumbs and shook it. He pointed a single index finger in Austin's direction, "I need to know the troops can carry out the battle plan, right soldier?"

Stung at the reminder of his failed profession, Austin sat ram-rod straight and barked reflexively, "Yes, sir!"

Exaggerating his movements, Lomax stood erect, as nearly at attention as a civilian who had never worn a uniform could stand. He held one hand behind his back and looked through Austin's skull to a point in the middle of his brain. "I want B.J. Nottingham on-stage in the Coliseum, by Wednesday at 4:00 p.m. If he's not there, I want him incapable of pointing fingers at anyone. Is that clear?"

Austin jumped from the chair and stood at attention, sweat beading on his meaty forehead, just under the close-cut, receding hairline, "Very clear, sir."

"Very good, Austin," Lomax's composure changed; his face relaxed. "Have you looked at the Wall Street Journal recently? Never mind, I know you've been too busy chasing leads to Nottingham; so I'll tell you. Remember the last bonus I gave you, the one hundred shares of Turner-Disney for planting the bug in Donna Crossley's boudoir? It has more than tripled in value since Tuesday. Up twenty-one and seven-eighths. Wall Street suspended trading in our stock Friday; it was moving too rapidly. It's expected to continue climbing through Wednesday."

Lomax paused. He turned and looked out the window at the hills behind him. He drew pleasure from the fact that he could now afford to look for a home among the winding roads and beautiful people. "Financially, R.M. should be sitting pretty by now," he said, as Austin continued to stand at attention. "I have a couple of places picked out, George. Wonder how much I'll have left over to spend on furnishings."

"Uncle Sam is going to buy all his furniture," Jon Sorensen grunted, as he monitored the bug from his hotel room. "I don't think he'll like the stainless steel sink, bunk beds, steel desk, or the bars on the windows."

"Not if we can't figure out who this Doc fellow is and get him some protection. We're going to have to find that Nottingham character, too," Jacobs interjected.

"Yeah, I know," Sorensen grumbled. "You keep following Lomax around. He's going to slip up and let the Doc's name out some-where along the line."

"Let's hope it's before the funeral," Jacobs added drolly.

THIRTY

Jeffrey Huntingdon-Smythe sat, vulture-like, across the metallic console from his radio hostess. Both guest and reporter sported large earphones, more to drown out the undercurrent of noise produced by the radio engineers, director, producer, and staff, than to hear what each other said.

He watched as Reiter, dressed informally in tightly fitted blue jeans and halter top, perspired as she spoke into the microphone. Reading from a prepared introduction, the investigator looked more like Cinderella or Snow White than a carnivorous, man-eating crusader against liberal nonsense. Hunt, as he liked to refer to himself, enjoyed watching the well-proportioned body of his hostess. As she finished the monologue, he found it difficult to think of her as an antagonist.

"...with me today is Great Britain's renowned theologian, philosopher, and professor of modern history at Cambridge University, Sir Jeffrey Huntingdon-Smythe." The pause lasted too long. "Damn. Don, where is the second page of this intro? Never mind, we'll dub it in later. Cut this out for the broadcast, tomorrow. Sorry." Her gaze shifted from the papers in her hands to the historian, "Nice to have you here, Sir Smythe."

"You can call me Hunt, if you prefer," Huntingdon-Smythe offered, realizing the American probably knew little about the proper use of English titles.

"Thanks, Hunt," Reiter stared at the man, trying to keep from associating his face with Ichabod Crane. His long facial features were magnified by the earphones. They sat too high on his head, straddling the bald peak and pushing upward the gray hair which normally lay against his temples. Huntingdon-Smythe's large nose and small mouth contributed to the illusion, especially when he opened his mouth and its narrowness and depth could be better appreciated.

Unruffled by the heat generated from the radio equipment, Huntingdon-Smythe sat, legs crossed, both hands cupped over his left knee. He smiled, generously. "I really do, so much, appreciate your invitation to talk with you about the Elvis phenomenon," Hunt said pleasantly.

"What do you make of these events, Hunt?"

Huntingdon-Smythe replied, "I think you will find a great many of my colleagues believe this episode is just one of a series of incidents which demonstrate that western culture is losing, or has lost, its grasp on religion. God may be dead."

"Could you explain that?"

"Delighted to, my dear. As long ago as 1900, historians recognized that most humans idealized and sometimes idolized other humans. It really is inevitable. If one must take orders from someone else, in order to live peaceably within society, then it is a whole lot more palatable to accept those commands if one believes his leader to be smarter, faster, stronger, or in some way better than he. From the opposite perspective, leaders have always felt, probably erroneously, that they lead best when people follow blindly. For superiors, encouraging the placement of themselves on a pedestal is typical."

"You are going to relate this to religion?" Reiter interjected.

"Most certainly." Huntingdon-Smythe continued, "The higher the pedestal upon which these leaders were placed, the more demigodlike they became. In the beginning of this century until after World War II, the most idolized segment of the population tended to be the military leaders, scientists, and politicians."

"Elvis doesn't qualify in any of those categories," Reiter interrupted, briefly.

"And the reason," Huntingdon-Smythe blithely continued, "is that the population began to shift its allegiance from those career paths to those of sports heroes, movie stars, and other celebrities after World War II. The media: news, gossip columns, entertainment, radio, television, movies, music, et cetera, lionized these people. They became the most popular individuals on the planet. The results have been most obvious since the time of the Vietnam War. John Lennon was absolutely correct when he stated the Beatles were more popular than Jesus Christ. More people knew of them and liked their music than even populated the planet during Christ's time."

"Vietnam took a toll on politicians, generals, and scientists," Reiter added.

"The surprising aspect about their descent was the swiftness with which it occurred. Not only that, the movement to shun these people erupted worldwide, not just in the United States. Your American politicians took the blame for starting the war. Your generals accepted the culpability for not winning it. Your scientists were held responsible for ecological disasters, the atomic bomb, and more."

Reiter squirmed in the warm seat. The interview seemed to be going well, but she wanted to focus more on Presley and the Preslians. "I don't understand how that would lead to the formation of a new religion, particularly one based on the songs, the life, or the beliefs of a rock star," she stated.

"Allow me to compress history slightly, my good woman." Sir Jeffrey elaborated, "Since the beginning of the eighteenth century, and continuing well into the present decade, scientists have been knocking the stilts out from under religion.

"There are, now, scientific explanations for almost every dearly held belief. Consider the alignment of the planets to produce the Christmas star, and the earthquake and following tsunami which emptied and refilled the Red Sea during Moses's escape. The study of evolution and the dating of the Big Bang disproves much of the Book of Genesis."

"Disproves?" Reiter's radio audience included many religious right-wing conservatives.

"For a good bit of the population," Huntingdon-Smythe corrected himself. "In any event, the scientists destroyed religion for a significant segment of Western Europe and America's population. At one point, science thought it could prove the existence of God. When it failed, many people accepted that failure as proof God does not exist. I have to say, here, however, that science has been unable to either prove or disprove the existence of God.

"For many people, science replaced the deposed religions. The promise was that science would eventually cure all disease, abolish death, and produce a real Eden or Heaven on Earth. Regrettably, science never delivered on these promises.

"During the Second World War, scientists manufactured death in the form of more efficient weapons systems. The generals saved us from Hirohito and Hitler. Politicians promised us there would never be another war and started the United Nations. For a brief period, these leaders became our deities. They attained semi-god status."

"Until Vietnam?"

"Actually, they began to lose their luster in the 1950s. Elvis accomplished much of the spotlight theft during his first lifetime."

Reiter could not choke down the response, "You think he's alive, again?"

"In a manner of speaking, he has achieved a temporary immortality."

"That's an oxymoron. By definition immortality is not temporary." Reiter's surliness bounced off the uncompromising Brit.

"True, but in this case, the oxymoron applies appropriately. As long as the baby-boomer generation believes in Elvis, he is immortal. Unless they can pass that belief on, to the next and to succeeding generations, that immortality is temporary. Who believes in the old Roman immortals, today? Is not death through disbelief the end of immortality for a god?" Unruffled, the Englishman scarcely batted an eye while rebuffing Reiter.

Reiter complained, "Some people believe this incident is like the Second Coming of Christ. There are individuals out there who think Elvis will lead them to Heaven. Can a myth start a religion?"

She had difficulty controlling her emotions when she thought about such absurdities.

"Christianity owes its existence to the myth propagated by Paul that Jesus Christ was God incarnate. A more recent myth, one with a more sinister result, started when Stalin deified Lenin." Huntingdon-Smythe uncrossed and recrossed his legs, placing his hands on his right knee.

"You think Communism was a religion?" Reiter nearly lost her composure. She heard the right wing Christian segment of her audience howl in the back of her mind.

"As a theologian, and historian, I have come to recognize that much of religion is merely ritual, Ms. Reiter. Part of Communism's failure was it's lack of ritual. The Preslians may offer a simple believable dogma, one which seems to give an answer to the question 'why do we exist?' This gives peace of mind to his followers. If so, then the Preslians may be the wave of the future. Communists could not answer the question.

"There is very little left for the common man to believe in, I'm afraid. Science destroyed religion, then itself. The press made icons of the generals, the politicians, and the celebrities; none of them have proven equal to the task.

"A new religion, based upon one's own experiences, may be the only way for some individuals to renew their faith and find meaning in life. Rituals have a calming effect in most societies. They make life easier to live; they require less investigation, less thought, less intellectual investment than if each person approaches every situation in his life with a new outlook, or a totally open mind. Rituals can save the collective psyche." Huntingdon-Smythe cleared his throat. He sipped water from a glass that sat on his console. Condensation left a huge wet ring on the warm gray metallic surface.

"Hari-Kari is a ritual, too." Reiter protested.

"A noble ritual, at that. To take the blame for your mistakes and to apologize with such finality requires tremendous courage."

"Or stupidity."

"Now, Ms. Reiter, you would not want to offend any of your foreign listeners, would you? Religion is very personal. A simple belief, that Christ is God for instance, has been known to work miracles, change the human heart or mind, even change the course of history. Beliefs are not to be belittled or trifled, my dear lady." The statement was as close as Sir Jeffrey Huntingdon-Smythe could come to losing his temper, or scolding a rude hostess.

"Some purported beliefs of the Preslians really are preposterous," she countered. "For instance, Preslians have offered ceremonies in the nude, vows of total poverty, total pacification, lyrics as the Word of God, and Satanic rituals with animals. The list goes on."

"The Preslian religion is only days out of the closet, you might say. Much of the thesis-antithesis-synthesis has yet to occur. The European Christians spent a thousand years defining their beliefs. In the process, they lost half their believers to the Greek Orthodox Church over the definition of the Trinity. They lost many more before that when they deified Christ. Muhammad meted out his religion over twenty-three years, in small doses. It, too, has been redefined in the intervening centuries. Some of the Preslians' beliefs will be adopted. If the religion is to survive, a critical mass of the population must believe. Most religions perish rather quickly, I'm afraid.

"There are heretics to be found within every theology. Normally, over a period of years, those people would be weeded out. In the old days, they were burned at the stake. In our present worldwide society, with its rapid flow of information, you may see the formation of a mature religion in a period of months. The Preslians may fade away in less than one generation. Everything happens faster these days. Certainly in a country like yours, as secular as it is and as free from the encumbrances of religious trappings as the government is, there is no reason to suspect any religious persecutions. Odd-ball religions like the Survivalists, Branch Davidians, Freemen, and numerous other sects have persisted, even thrived here. The Preslians may surprise us with their tenacity."

"So where are all these Preslians on the highways headed?"

"The latest report suggested that three to five million persons are making pilgrimages to points where they may see the object of their pilgrimage. For some, that means going to Los Angeles, California. For others, the impossibility of getting to Los Angeles has forced them to head for other large stadiums which will carry the proceedings telecast live from the Coliseum. Recently, I heard that Turner-Disney may license the show to home cable distributors. Most fanatics, I would think, will still want to be as close to the real event as possible. Only those semi-interested viewers will opt to stay home and see this miracle on their own television sets. The infectious power of a large crowd of people who share your beliefs may come into play here, also. Witness the Moslems and their yearly pilgrimages to Mecca."

Nearly exhausted from the mental effort necessary to keep from openly disagreeing with her guest, Reiter continued, "We are about out of time, Hunt. As you know we usually have a telephone call-in segment which you will miss, unfortunately, since this is recorded. You are on your way to the Vatican later today. However, I can guess the most popular question my audience would ask you. Do you think Elvis will be in the Los Angeles Coliseum on Wednesday?"

A twinkle in his eye, Hunt replied, "One way or another, I don't think he would miss it for the world."

Surprised, Reiter caught her breath, took a deep one to calm her voice, and thanked her visitor, "Thank you for the insight, Hunt. Ladies and Gentlemen, our guest today has been Sir Jeffrey Huntingdon-Smythe. We will watch the telecast Wednesday to see if he is correct about Elvis putting in an appearance. Right now, we must pause for a station break."

Reiter checked the time; she changed her mind about taking calls. "When we come back we will take calls for approximately one-half hour. During the second hour of the broadcast, we will be talking via remote transmission to Mike Lomax from Turner-Disney Productions. He may have some interesting insights into the Preslian phenomena. Stay tuned; we'll be right back."

THIRTY-ONE

Jack stood at the entrance to the tent. He munched pirated do-
nuts and coffee, which had arrived after the Reverend. While eating, he observed the congregation as they listened to Elvis's sermon. He viewed the celebration within the tent with disdain and
apathy. Although his damaged hearing prevented Jack from hearing most of the words, their effect on the revivalists and the caravan members amazed him.

The parishioners stared at Elvis, faces turned upward. A magnificent figure, Presley dressed in a pure white jump suit with a
red lined white cape studded with diamonds and rubies. The crowd
sat, immobile and spellbound. When Elvis started to sing Gospel
songs, the crowd swayed with the music; tears flowed from their
eyes; lips quivered. Music floated into the desert, tunes Jack never
heard during the short time his parents forced him to attend
church. A little embarrassed by his lack of faith, Jack turned his
head and looked outside the tent.

He tried to ignore the lyrics. The demolished white Cadillac
reminded him of a great white tiger. It lay dead at the end of the
hunt, feet splayed to the sides. The muffler and tail pipe jutted
from underneath the vehicle at an acute angle, an imagined spear
in the gut of the mechanical beast. Jack moved slowly to the canvas flap which outlined the exit. He stepped into the desert air,
leaving the air-conditioned Gospel behind. The words to the songs
followed him outside the tent.

In the distance, far to the West and directly opposite from the
rising sun, storm clouds raged and sheets of water fell. The rain
evaporated before it reached soil. A rainbow shone. So brilliant
were the colors of the rainbow, that the ends seemed to pierce the

earth like a giant pincer — a galactic ice tongs plucked the planet from the sky. A second rainbow arched over the first, almost as bright. A third rainbow filled the sky above the first two, only slightly less intense. Jack could not remember ever seeing such a magnificent sight.

He turned around and faced the tent, eager to gain the attention of the congregation, to show them this glorious sight. Unable to force himself to interrupt the service, he stood confused, pointing with his right hand to the sky. He waved at the triple rainbow, but said nothing to distract the crowd from their devotions. For several minutes he remained in a befuddled state, incapable of choosing either to stop waving his hand or to speak.

Eventually, the rainbow faded from view. The scene remained etched into the old man's mind. Jack searched his memory for a similar event. His search included a lifetime spent staring into the atmosphere, both as a pilot and as a ground-hugging child. His investigation yielded no similar incidents. Short of breath from the excitement, he panted; his heart pounded. He wished he could describe the rainbow to someone. Words would be inadequate, he realized. Even a photograph would not have done justice to the experience. Someone would have to have lived through the event to feel the exhilaration he felt.

Exhausted from his experience, Jack returned to the Winnebago. The pain returned to his hips and back as he entered the RV. Unsteadily, he climbed into the camper through the side door. With difficulty, he fought the urge to lie on the sofa bed. His full stomach sent signals to his exhausted brain: go to sleep. Fighting drowsiness, he pushed his way into the bathroom, found his pain medication, and quickly downed two of the tablets. Thus fortified for the coming onslaught of pain, Jack made his way to the passenger seat of the vehicle and sat, waiting for the services to end and for Elvis to return. Singing voices echoed inside the motorhome.

The motion of the camper rocked him side to side as it departed the desert parking lot. The movement woke him as they left behind the great blue and white striped tent. Through a haze of narcotic and pain, he peered through half-opened eyelids and watched Elvis drive. Garbed in blue jeans and a cowboy shirt, Presley guided the Winnebago onto the blacktop and pointed it in the direction of the interstate. Wearily, Jack's eyes closed more tightly as the whine from the tires reached highway pitch. They headed westward on the asphalt river. He slept, peacefully unaware of his surroundings.

A huge red orb, two or three times the normal size of the sun, hung directly in front of the windshield when he woke next. The setting sun flattened itself against the foothills, squeezing out the last bit of daylight like juice from an orange. Bands of dark clouds obscured the remainder of the sky. Rain splattered the dusty windshield. "You awake, Colonel?" Elvis asked pleasantly.

"I think so, son," Jack replied. He stared at the sun, eyes not bothered by the dim sunlight. "Wasted a good bit of the day by sleeping, I guess."

"You picked the perfect time to wake up, sir." Elvis pointed to the steam being blown over the hood of the motorhome as they coasted down the highway. "We lost the fan belt about two miles back, as we crested the hill behind us. The water pump and alternator stopped when it fell off. I've been coasting down this hill looking for a place to stop. There's an RV dealership nearby; I've seen several billboards advertising it."

"What's the name?" Shafer asked. He turned his head side to side, as he lifted himself upright in the seat to obtain a better view of the road.

"Flagstaff I-40 Desert RV," Elvis replied, distracted. He looked for the sign.

"There's a billboard," Jack blurted, "on the right. Big thing at two o'clock. It's above and behind the McDonald's."

"Got it. The dealership appears to be about three-quarters of a mile from here," Elvis guessed. "The traffic light at the intersection near the Mickey D's may keep us from coasting in."

"What's your speed?" Jack leaned toward Elvis and squinted at the speedometer.

"Holding at fifty-five," Presley answered, peeking quickly.

"Drag and gravity about balanced out, eh?" Jack looked behind the RV estimating the run of the hill. "It's going to be close. If that light changes, they'll have to tow us in."

"The light will stay green," Elvis responded confidently.

"How do you know that?" Jack listened to the wind from the storm gust against the camper. With the engine quiet, the wind noise seemed louder than usual.

"I know." Elvis leaned back in the driver's seat, relaxing. Light automobile traffic drifted by the camper.

"Where are all the other cars?" Jack asked, when he realized the cortege was not visible.

"We were trailing them. This old bus had difficulty keeping up the pace. The prevailing winds are against us; they are blowing from the west to the east on this side of the cold front and storm. We'll meet the caravan at a campground west of Flagstaff, tonight. If not, we'll catch them in L.A. L.A.'s not much farther, Colonel, about eight hours."

True to Elvis' prediction, the light remained green. The traffic signal turned yellow as they drifted through the intersection at thirty miles an hour. An uphill grade slowed their speed rapidly as they entered the RV dealer's parking lot. Elvis did not have to touch the brake pedal as the camper glided to a stop several feet in front of the entrance to the showroom and the service department. He set the parking brake. "Last stop."

"Sounded too final," Jack grumbled. Elvis grinned as he jumped from the side entrance and then set the step for Jack. The service manager met them at the entrance.

"Evening." The plump dark-skinned man, dressed in a grease-stained blue jump suit highlighted with red racing stripes, introduced himself, "I'm Miguel. Can I help you?"

Elvis smiled and held out his hand. He introduced Jack and himself, "Hello, suh, this here's Colonel Shafer. My name's Presley.

We threw a fan belt on top of the hill. Coasted here. Can you check it for us?"

"Good thing it happened on this side of the hill. Ain't no mechanics on the other side. Normally, we're closed for service on Sundays. I am here to work on my pickup," Miguel jerked his thumb at the red four-wheel-drive parked half-in and half-out of the first bay. The truck sat with the hood up and driver's door open. Seeing Shafer's and Presley's faces drop, he added pleasantly, "But I'll take a quick look for you. Give you an idea of what the damages are."

"Great," Elvis responded, handing the man the keys to the motorhome. "Do you mind if we slip into McDonald's and drink some coffee while you look?"

"Be fine with me," Miguel answered. "Give me thirty minutes."

"Done." Elvis turned to find Shafer already limping toward the fast food restaurant. He needed a bathroom. As usual, his prostate sabotaged his rest break.

THIRTY-TWO

Lockwood switched off the radio in the rental car. The mournful tones of Elvis's *Kentucky Rain* did little to alleviate his discomfort. He and Vanderbilt floated along the interstate highway in their rental car, in the middle of a very wet desert. The first heavy rain in three years battered the stalled traffic. Miles ahead, according to a radio news report, an eighteen wheeler lost traction on the rain-slicked tarmac. As a result, it skidded across both westward bound lanes and overturned tying up traffic.

Frequently, Barry caught glimpses of flashing lights in the sky or along the access road. Judging by the amount of equipment rushing to the scene and drawing on his previous police experience, Lockwood guessed the accident to be major. The radio reported a twelve-mile backup. The nearest exit to them was six miles in his rear view mirror.

Traffic inched forward slowly, forcing Barry to follow suit in hopes the crash crews cleared part of the highway. Lockwood could not help but wonder if the metallic sardines were packing themselves more tightly into their rain-soaked asphalt container. The dark rain clouds became even darker as the sun set, invisibly, somewhere in front of them. Nighttime eliminated the occasional lighter colored cloud. Heavy rain continued to beat against the windshield. Lockwood could see gullies of water along the sides of the highway. Sheets of flowing water left turbulent wakes as they broke around the stationary car tires in front of him.

Mercifully, Vanderbilt cat-napped for most of the damp interlude. She lay, curled like a large cat on the front seat of the vehicle. Her head rested on Barry's lap. Occasionally, he heard a soft sigh or whimper. She struggled through a nightmare, he supposed.

Intermittently, she balled her fists in response to an imagined stimulus. Eventually, he tired of keeping both hands on the steering wheel. Also wanting to reassure Amy, he placed his right hand on her head and stroked her hair gently. "It'll be okay," he repeated softly, frequently.

The feel of Vanderbilt's hair surprised Lockwood. The dark locks felt dense and curly, but fine and soft. He rubbed a lock of her hair between his thumb and forefinger, delighting in the tactile sensation.

Still asleep, Amy responded by cupping her hand over his and kissing his palm. "Beej," she murmured.

The minivan behind their car blew its horn as another automobile tried to slip into their lane. The blast woke Vanderbilt who sat upright and blinked. She struggled to remember where they were and how they arrived there.

"Are we still in the same traffic jam, or is this a new one?" she finally asked.

"It's hard to say whether the original accident is holding us up, or whether some rubber-neckers have collided." He responded and then added, "We've been stalled so long that some cars in front of us could have run out of gas by now." Lockwood squinted into the darkness in front of them, "Is that it?"

Less than two hundred yards away, a tanker truck lay on its side. The cab was crumpled in the ditch to the side of the road. Muddy water washed around the broken vehicle and through the smashed windshield and gaping door. One lane of the westbound interstate had reopened. A tow truck had dragged the trailer to the side of the road. An officer in a yellow slicker directed traffic, alternately from one lane then the other, around the stricken truck. A helicopter, with its blades turning slowly, squatted in the median between the west and east bound lanes.

Inching slowly, interminably, they traversed the two hundred yards in an hour. After midnight, the rain slowed gradually. It stopped completely as they cleared the wreck and accelerated to the speed limit for the first time in hours.

"Well, what do you want to do now?" Lockwood asked Vanderbilt, after driving several miles.

"It's too late to find the next group, isn't it?" Vanderbilt replied dejectedly.

"For tonight, that's a fair assumption. Let's find a place to crash," he suggested. "Although it won't be easy. With the accident tying up traffic, most of the motels around here are going to be filled by now."

"Keep driving west until we find the group, or a vacancy," Vanderbilt decided.

"Good thought," Lockwood yawned. "Do you suppose you could drive, since you just slept?"

"Sure. Pull over and we'll switch."

"Be safer to get off the interstate," Barry replied. At the next exit ramp, Lockwood left the interstate. No other cars exited; there were no signs for motels, service stations, or fast food outlets. The nearest town, according to the sign, was thirty miles away. Once off the main highway, he pulled to the side of the road, a narrow two-lane affair with rain-washed gullies on either side. Slowing, he pulled the car all the way off the asphalt. They splashed through puddles which lingered on the wide gravel shoulder following the storm. The right front tire found a deep pothole and dropped suddenly, stopping the car. Both he and Vanderbilt strained against their seat belts as the shoulder straps caught them short of the dashboard and serious injury.

"You all right?" he asked.

"Fine," she responded, tersely. "What was that?"

"The last puddle is much deeper than it looks. Hard to gauge depth in the dark, I guess." He tried to rationalize the mistake. "If we're lucky, we can back it out."

Lockwood jammed the gearshift into reverse and stepped on the gas. The front wheel drive car sat motionless except for the slight pitching motion caused by the spinning right front wheel. Evidently, the axle sat on the surface; the wheel hung in space.

Several attempts at rocking the vehicle from forward to reverse and back had no effect.

"It's not moving," Lockwood uttered lamely.

"I can see that," Vanderbilt snapped.

"Guess I better look." With a frustrated snap of his wrist, Lockwood jammed the gear shift into park. Setting the emergency brake but leaving the engine running, he grimaced as he undid his seat belt and opened the door.

An occasional raindrop pelted his face as he walked around the car in the dark, cool desert night. In front of the automobile and to its right, he stared at the fender. Tapping on the hood with his knuckles, he commanded Vanderbilt's attention. She lowered the electric window. "Turn on the right turn signal," he told her.

He watched her reach across the steering column with her left hand; the amber turn signal lit. Simultaneously the white turning light on the right fender of the automobile shone brightly. It blinded him temporarily. The futility of the situation became immediately obvious. Several feet of the shoulder had been gouged away by the arroyo produced in the downpour. The axle and the frame of the automobile rested solidly on the macadam and gravel. Floating freely in the muddy water inches in any direction from solid ground, the wheel hung in empty space. Rocking the car had done little but fling most of the water from the hole, leaving them in need of a tow. He returned to the driver's seat.

"I'm sorry," he said, as he pulled the seat belt from under him. He shut down the engine with a flick of his wrist. Groping with his left hand, he found the releases under the left seat. His half of the front seat slid backward and then the back of the seat tilted downward. "We're stuck. I doubt we can find help before dawn. Try to get some rest."

Vanderbilt straightened up in the seat, "What?" she demanded incredulously. "You're going to sit here all night?" She balled her fists and started hitting Barry on the shoulder. Tears ran from her eyes. "Look at me! I'm hot and sweaty; I need a shower, dinner. I can't sleep in this car all night. Get out! Walk back down the road

for help. There must be fifty police and firemen back there. I saw
a tow truck or two, also." During the rampage, she beat on
Lockwood's arm. The blows landed less frequently and with less
intensity as she tired.

Exhaustion finally overcame her anger. She leaned back in her
seat and stared at the ceiling in silence. Finally, she spoke, "No
one's coming, are they?" He shook his head. "It's miles back to the
accident, isn't it?" He nodded. "Someone is bound to drive down
this God-forsaken road in the morning and either give us a lift or
send a tow truck, right?" He nodded, again. "When we get out of
this predicament, you're fired."

Lockwood did not bother to respond to the spiteful remark.
Vanderbilt slid her half of the seat backward, lining it up with his,
then tilted the back toward the floor. She wrapped both of her
arms around Lockwood's muscular upper arm and leaned on his
shoulder. Whimpering, she fell asleep.

About an hour later Vanderbilt changed positions, releasing
her grasp on his right arm. Deftly, Barry slid away from her and
pressed the switch to lower the fogged window about two inches
on the driver's side of the car. Cold desert air slipped into the car
cooling his face.

Lockwood surveyed the scene outside the window. The stars
shone brilliantly in the freshly cleared sky. A silver sliver of moon
added a small amount of light to the flat landscape. Barry made
out the shape of the other car. It remained several hundred yards
behind them. Apparently, it had not moved from that position
since it pulled off the road while he checked the wheel. Lockwood
thought he could see the outlines of two men in the front seat.
One remained motionless. The head of the other bobbed sporadically as he fought to stay awake. Lockwood waited, contemplating
whether, or not, to tell Vanderbilt that they were being followed.

THIRTY-THREE

Jack surveyed the area surrounding the McDonald's and the RV dealership through the sparkling clean windows. The restaurant stood in stark contrast to most of the surrounding buildings, not being covered with a fine layer of dust streaked with mud from the recent rain. Apparently the manager of the fast food outlet ran it like a drill sergeant would have. He kept it spotless. As Elvis and Jack crossed the parking lot to enter the building, two teenaged employees teased one another. They produced a constant stream of jovial banter while they worked. Under the watchful eye of their supervisor, they swept the parking lot and squeegeed the windows.

Shafer noticed that the local automobiles suffered in the desert mountain environment. Sandblasted by the wind and baked for days under the sun's glare, their paint blistered and peeled. Even the newer models displayed signs of wear. Jack noted the lack of shine on the cars; most exhibited a gritty appearance. Many bared their primer coats, having worn off the exterior colors. In the dusk, the suburb surrounding the intersection lost any hint of color. It took on a drab, dreary, or, perhaps, gloomy look.

Elvis said nothing, watching the old man sip his coffee in an attempt to reverse the sedation produced by the heavy dose of narcotics. Shafer glanced upward and met the younger man's stare. For a brief second he thought about speaking. Jack realized his thought processes were too jumbled to converse coherently. Patiently, he waited for the caffeine to wipe the stupor from his mind and the world around him. Elvis nodded silently, perceiving Shafer's mood.

When Jack decided a half hour had passed, he stood to leave the restaurant. Elvis rose immediately. One step ahead of Shafer, he held open the door for him as they departed the McDonald's. Only a flattened remnant of the sun remained in the sky. The essence of the sun spread itself evenly across the western horizon giving the rippled clouds an orange aura.

"It's an old bus, Colonel," Elvis started to speak, but let the words trail.

"Annie made me buy it." Shafer wiped a tear from his eye. "For a year it sat in our driveway; we couldn't afford to put gas in it. She loved it, though." Then, as if he spoke of a living being, a pet perhaps, instead of an inanimate collection of rusting metal and fraying fiberglass cloth, he added, "We all have to go some-time. Most of her can be recycled, I guess. No point in abandon-ing her to the elements."

Presley nodded, taking small strides so as not to hurry Shafer to the dealership where Miguel waited for them in the showroom. A thinner, taller man stood next to Miguel. He wore a suit, mis-placed in the cowboy atmosphere of the surroundings.

"Ah, Colonel Shafer, Mr. Presley," the mechanic wiped his greasy hand on a maroon shop rag, then decided not to shake their hands anyway. He shrugged, "Sorry, it's too filthy to touch." In-stead, he held his hand out, palm upward toward the man in the suit. "This is Mr. Chase Alvarez; he is our lease manager. He is also a salesman on the weekends, which is why he is here today."

"Don't sound good," Elvis intoned.

"Please, gentlemen, be seated," Alvarez pointed to the chairs surrounding the desk which sat in the showroom. "Miguel did not mean to scare you by bringing me into the conversation. We have been talking over your options. Since we don't know where you are going or what your plans are, we are at a loss to make any recommendations."

His mind clearing after the rush of high octane caffeine, Shafer interrupted, "Perhaps Miguel should start this off by telling me what he thinks is wrong with the camper. I don't mean to be the victim of some scam."

Both of Alvarez's hands immediately came off the desk, palms outward in mock surrender. "There's no racket here, sir; I promise you." He looked at Elvis and tilted his head, asking silently for a little support and a chance to state their case.

Elvis spoke softly to Shafer, "It's okay, Colonel. Let them have their say. The U.S. Army made me into a pretty fair country mechanic. If what they say is outrageous, I'll check it out." He winked at the Colonel.

"All right," Shafer responded tersely, "but if there is any fraud here, we're getting the first tow truck to another dealer."

"Deal," Chase responded, "I'll even pay for the tow." Shafer relaxed visibly when Alvarez offered to cover the expense. "Miguel, tell them what you found."

Miguel looked at Shafer with sincere brown eyes. He did not blink. "In brief, the fan belt came off because the bearings on the water pump froze. No big deal; I can get a water pump tomorrow. At the same time, the alternator and regulator got fried. I don't know why, maybe the electrical drain without recharging did that. Again, I can probably have those parts by tomorrow or Tuesday. There is a small oil leak, which turned out to be the valve cover gasket. That doesn't have to be fixed at all, if you don't want. While tracking the source of the leak, I found that two of your motor mounts are broken." Miguel's eyes dropped to the floor in apology, "Finding the replacement motor mounts for this vehicle could take us a week or two. They will have to come from a junk yard or be specially manufactured for you. No one makes them any more."

Shafer's face clouded. His lips curled down at the ends and he set his jaw. Alvarez jumped into the conversation without giving the colonel a chance to respond angrily. "Which is why Miguel came to talk with me. We did not know if you would prefer to stay in Flagstaff while we track down the parts. If you are here to see the local attractions, like Meteor Crater, that might be ideal. Perhaps, you would prefer to lease one of our vehicles and leave yours here. There is an automobile rental agency down the street. Again, not knowing your itinerary, we can make no firm suggestions."

"How did the motor mounts break?" Shafer grilled Miguel.

"Looks like fatigue. How many miles do you have on the camper? I can show you," the mechanic offered. "You'll have to slide under the vehicle. Perhaps, Mr. Presley would look for you."

"The odometer stopped at 130,000 miles about ten years ago," Shafer responded, "She probably has 200,000 miles on her, plus or minus 10,000. What do you think, son?" Shafer looked at Elvis, eyes betraying uncertainty.

"I'll check her out, Colonel. Then we'll decide." He motioned to Miguel. "Got a mechanic's jump suit I can slip into?" Miguel nodded, motioning for Elvis to follow him. The two men walked through the showroom, around the pop-up campers and minivans, past the service waiting room, and through the door leading to the service bays.

Shafer heard the tail end of the conversation about motor pool regulations as the men disappeared. He sat with Chase at the desk. The silence gnawed at both men. Shafer studied Alvarez as the man penciled busy work, filling a myriad of forms. The man appeared to be of Mexican and American Indian decent, with reddish-brown skin, black hair, and dark eyes. His nose, however, looked thinner than most of the Hispanic noses Shafer had seen.

Finally, Shafer surrendered to his curiosity, "You're not from around here are you?"

"Born and raised in Flagstaff," Chase replied, "but the genes are from halfway around the world."

"How's that?" Shafer asked, having visited most of the countries which could be considered halfway around the world from the United States. "Your parents from Pakistan?"

"Good guess." Alvarez's face brightened. "My mother is from India. She met my father, a Native American, at New Mexico State University. According to my grandmother, their engagement brought great relief to my mother's family. They did not to have to pay a dowry in America. A daughter can be a liability in India."

"I did not realize," Shafer responded, dropping his defenses. "Elvis wants to be in Los Angeles by Tuesday or Wednesday. I'm on my way to San Diego. The doctor says the sooner I get there, the better."

"Recuperating?"

"Kind of."

"Uh, Colonel." Jack turned to see Elvis standing beside him wearing a thick, baggy, white cotton jump suit. Grease streaks marred its appearance. One pocket dangled, torn from the leg. He spoke softly, "It's just as they say, sir. Shall we rent one from them?"

"We might save money with a car, but then we'd have to stop in hotels, and there's a ton of stuff in her, not to mention Annie." Jack stared at the ceiling, briefly, then leveled his eyes at Alvarez. "What's she worth in trade?"

Chase stared at Shafer. He spoke honestly, "Nothing. But I'll give you the best deal I can on a lease. Miguel estimated $1300 to fix it, if he finds the parts on the west coast. A twenty-footer goes for three hundred-fifty a week. I'll lease one to you for two-ninety. Rentals are slow right now, and you'll be leaving your vehicle as security."

Jack contemplated the offer. He looked at Elvis but spoke to Alvarez, "I may have trouble getting it back to you, if I lose my driver."

Presley ignored the remark and, looking over Chase's head, asked, "What does that silver one go for?"

The sales agent swivelled in his chair to determine which vehicle Presley meant. He shook his head, "We don't rent out the Airstreams."

"I meant, how much does it sell for?" Presley reworded the question.

Not bothering to turn around to face Presley, thinking the question rhetorical, Alvarez answered off the cuff, "About $175,000. I think that one is $172,500. It has the satellite dish on the roof. Nifty RV, but far too expensive to lease weekly."

"I'll give you $170,000 for it, if you include a full tank of gas," Presley offered. The three other men turned in unison and stared at Elvis, mouths open. Presley had already walked halfway across the showroom floor. "I'll be right back," Elvis said as he disappeared into the service bay.

Alvarez looked at Miguel and then Shafer, "Is he serious?"

Shafer shook his head in bewilderment, "I don't know." He stared through the dusty showroom window at the motorhome. He wished the window were as clean as the ones in McDonald's. The sleek form of the polished aluminum vehicle impressed him. He knew a younger, sprier version of himself would have loved to own it. Now, within weeks of the end of his life, he doubted anyone's need to possess it. A death mask settled over his face. Elvis's money, if the boy had any, would be better spent on psychiatric care. He did not bother to mention that to the salesman and mechanic, however. In silence, the three men awaited Presley's return.

Miguel wiped obsessively at his dirty hands. "Thirty years of dirt under that 'Bago, Colonel Shafer," he said in an attempt to break the pall. Shafer nodded, saying nothing.

Elvis returned, carrying the dirty, white, mechanic's jump suit in one hand and a thick black briefcase in the other. He tossed the clothing at Miguel who caught it in the hand which did not hold the rag. Presley swung the heavy briefcase onto the desk in front of Alvarez, popping the locks and lifting the top in a practiced manner.

Hidden from the salesman, but visible to Shafer and Miguel were stack after stack of thousand-dollar bills. Also readily discernible were the two Smith and Wesson .357 Magnums, clipped securely to the inside top of the case. Miguel swallowed hard, wondering what would happen next.

Elvis reached into the valise and pulled out two stacks of bills. One he tossed gently to Chase, "There's a hundred grand and," he thumbed through the other stack, counting twenty-eight more. He handed the bigger pile to Alvarez, "here's seventy-two. That's one-seventy for the RV and two grand to do the paperwork, transfer the tags, fill it with gas, all that stuff."

Alvarez swallowed seeing Miguel make pistol motions with

his hands. "There'll be about twenty grand in taxes, too," he said in a whisper, hoping not to rile Presley.

"Oh, yeah," Elvis replied, and peeled off eight more bills. He passed the remaining twenty to the agent. "If you don't mind, we'll spend the night in the Colonel's new camper. Just run a power cord to it in the parking lot tonight. That will give me a chance to transfer our belongings. Do you suppose you could have the paperwork done by 0900 hours tomorrow?"

"9:00 a.m.?" Chase asked and Elvis nodded. "I'll make certain it's done by then. I'll transfer the license plates myself, sir."

"You really want to buy this vehicle, Elvis?" Shafer asked, "What do you need with an RV?"

"It's a present from me to you, Colonel," Presley replied with a grin, as Chase handed him the keys. "You'll have lots of use for it in the future. Trust me." Oblivious of the mechanic and the salesman, Elvis and Shafer walked slowly out the glass door, into the well-lit parking lot.

"Drug dealers?" Miguel asked Chase.

THIRTY-FOUR

Lockwood waited patiently, until he was positive Vanderbilt slept soundly. She snored softly, a tiny buzz emanating from the back of her throat. Gently, he lifted her wrist with his thumb and forefinger to a point about six inches above her lap. He released his grip; her hand dropped with a muted thud. As her hand fell, he watched her eyelids. In the starlight, he could see the movement of her pupils. The random pattern of motion did not change. Her lack of response confirmed that she slept deeply.

Silently, Barry turned the key in the ignition backward to the accessory setting. Finding the electric window button, he lowered the front door window on his side of the car. The whine of the electric motor, barely audible to him, did not wake Vanderbilt. With the window down, he put his head through the opening. He leaned his upper torso through the window and placed his hands on the roof. Struggling to keep from causing a racket, he lifted himself from his seat and sat on the edge of the door. Stealthily, he placed first his left, then his right foot, onto the gravel. The crunch of contact with the shoulder of the road brought him to a halt. Hovering outside the door, he waited, bent over and eyeing Vanderbilt. She changed positions. Her eyes remained closed.

Barry reached inside the window and pressed the button on the armrest. He allowed the glass to rise as far as possible without crushing his arm. Slipping his arm out of the automobile, he stood alongside it catching his breath. The cool desert night air gave him chill bumps. He shook involuntarily and pulled his suit coat tighter around him.

The headlights of a vehicle leaving the interstate flashed in his eyes as it made a turn. Briefly, the bright lights illuminated the other car. Still parked a quarter of a mile behind their car, it crouched along the shoulder of the road. The dark forms of the two men were visible in the front seat. Neither moved.

Lockwood crossed the road in the darkness and walked quickly to a position directly opposite the second vehicle. From fifty feet away, he could tell the men slept, probably as soundly as Vanderbilt. Both arms cradling his head, the man in the driver's seat slumped over the steering wheel. Wedged awkwardly between the headrest and the door jamb, the other man's head hung backward and sideways.

The incessant, low-volume, metallic tapping on the window eventually disturbed the man's sleep. Semiconscious, he rolled his head to the left and opened his eyes. He found himself face to face with the barrel of Lockwood's revolver. Lockwood's face pressed close to the glass. With his left index finger placed against his lips, he indicated the man should do nothing to awaken his partner. Despite his grogginess the man gasped. He clamped his mouth shut recognizing that his life depended upon his remaining quiet. He stared with wide-open eyes at Lockwood and the barrel of the gun.

"Hands up," Lockwood whispered. The man read his lips. He leaned back, lifting his arms and hands off the steering wheel. Not wanting to turn on the interior lights of the car, or the egress lights on the door, Lockwood ordered the man to roll the window down, quietly. The window sank slowly into the door.

With the window fully open, Lockwood ordered the man to put both hands outside the window. He trained the weapon on his adversary's face, whose features remained hidden by dim starlight shadows. Barry slipped the handcuffs from his belt and placed one cuff around the man's left wrist. The other end he slipped through the door handle and around the man's right wrist as he hung out the door. Once the man's hands were secured, Lockwood held the barrel of the gun to the man's lips to remind him to be quiet. With his left hand, Lockwood brusquely searched the driver's clothing finding a wallet which he pocketed, a pistol in a shoulder holster, and a pair of handcuffs hanging on the man's belt.

"Quiet," Lockwood whispered. He pointed the automatic at

the man, through the windshield, as he walked around the front of the car. Approaching the other door, he intended to handcuff the man's partner in the same manner.

Warned by a kick to the shins from the driver, which Lockwood could not see as he rounded the vehicle, the second man waited for Lockwood. Barry leaned close to the window and started to tap on it with his gun. Cat-like, the man sprang toward Barry. He thrust open the door and shoved it into the private detective, launching Lockwood backward. Lockwood's gun clattered to the ground as he lost his balance and rolled onto the gravel in the dark.

The lights, from inside the car and on the door, momentarily blinded Lockwood, and illuminated him for his attacker. The man vaulted from the car. He stood behind the open door with his pistol aimed at Barry.

"Okay, Lockwood, you've...." The man never finished his sentence. The twang of metal vibrating from the solid collision with skull bone echoed through the cool, dark night. Barry's foe sank to the ground sliding like Jell-O down the inside of the car door. Behind him stood Vanderbilt, tire iron still gripped with both hands.

"I always keep one of these under the front seat: for emergencies," she explained, showing the wrench to Lockwood. "Are these guys friends of yours?"

"My friends?" Lockwood asked, still surprised but delighted at her sudden appearance.

"Yeah, yours. First, you try to slip out of the car without me noticing. Then, this baboon calls you by name." She scrutinized the man's face as he lay at her feet, bathed in the light from the interior overhead lamp. "I certainly don't know him."

"They know who we are. I've been watching them in the rear view mirror most of the evening." Lockwood rolled the unconscious man onto his back and checked his pulse and respirations. "I hope you didn't break his skull. I didn't want you to worry that we were being followed. That's a wicked two-handed backhand swing that you have." He placed the car driver's handcuffs on the second man and stuffed him gently into the back seat of the vehicle in an upright position. While arranging the man's position, he relieved him of his wallet and handcuffs.

"What do we do now? College tennis team. Coach Brenner taught me." She picked up the man's gun and handed it to Lockwood.

Barry flipped on the automatic's safety and stuffed it into his belt with the driver's weapon. After a quick search of the roadside, he found his pistol and returned it to his shoulder holster. "Go sit in the driver's seat of our car. The key is in the ignition. I'm going to push you out of the pothole with their car." Not allowing her a chance to respond, he turned his attention to the driver who still hung out the window.

Vanderbilt stared coldly at Lockwood until she realized he no longer paid attention to her. She stalked back to the other car. He saw the lights come on as she entered the car; the brake lights flashed as she started it.

The headlights grew in the rear view mirror as the second car approached. Vanderbilt released the emergency brake; she took her foot off the brake pedal when she felt the bumpers gently collide. With a soft nudge, the rental car leapt from its trap. She pulled ahead, placing the car's left wheels on the road.

Barry's form moved back and forth in front of the headlights of the other car. Eventually, he opened the passenger door and climbed into the rental. "Make a U-turn and get back onto the interstate. I want to put a lot of distance between us and those two thugs."

"Who are they?" Vanderbilt asked. "What's going to keep them from finding us again?"

As an answer, Lockwood pulled four valve stems and six spark plug wires from his coat pockets. He dropped the automobile parts onto the floor in front of him. "Remind me to throw these out in about thirty miles," he said with a smile. "Meanwhile, let's look through their wallets. They might hold a clue."

THIRTY-FIVE

Gale Reiter waited for the cue from the director. She watched dispassionately as the bearded, intense man stared at his control board and took furtive glimpses at the clocks on the wall. The prerecorded conversation with Sir Jeffrey Huntingdon-Smythe constituted most of the first hour of her broadcast, less the commercials. She fielded several phone calls after the interview. Many more were being screened by her secretaries. By the time she finished questioning Lomax, the researchers should have lined up some interesting people with whom Lomax would have to contend.

Presently, she waited for the hourly network news to conclude so she could begin her interview with Mike Lomax. Her investigative crew was on-line from Memphis to dispute any misconceptions Lomax might relate. She had reviewed the video tape the researchers sent her from Graceland via overnight mail. There existed no obvious evidence of fraud. She expected to find none; Lomax's reputation painted him as shrewd and, more to the point, ruthless.

Her prerecorded introduction to the second hour of her program, and her special introduction to today's show, played inside her headphone. The director's hand levitated as if controlled by magic; he held one finger up, toward the ceiling. A camera stared at her from behind the video monitor on the counter. It captured her image and sent it to the west coast. A similar conference video image of Michael Lomax stared at her from the television. The view in his office consisted of a color monitor with her likeness and another camera.

The editor's index finger made a circle, pointing to the ceiling, and then he aimed it directly at her. She heard the click of the microphone in her headset. Potentially, twenty million people heard her speak. "Good afternoon, America," she said; the three words represented her trademark salutation. "Good afternoon, Mr. Lomax." She nodded at his electronic image.

It returned the gesture. "Please, Ms. Reiter, call me Mike," he responded pleasantly.

"Thank you, Mike. Please continue to call me Ms. Reiter," she chuckled, "Just kidding. Poor attempt at humor, folks. Mike, please call me Gale." Initially Lomax's brow furrowed, then it relaxed and he smiled. Mentally prepared for a verbal bashing, the joke surprised him. He assumed there would be little more to laugh about.

Reiter wasted no time starting the interview. Knowing Lomax and most of her audience had absorbed Sir Jeffrey's lecture on religion, she continued along the same vein. "Mr. Lomax, have you attempted to increase the net worth of Graceland, and thus Turner-Disney, by means of a hoax? Have you fraudulently led gullible people to believe that Elvis Presley has risen from the dead, has returned as a savior to humanity, and will establish a new religion?"

Lomax's image remained unruffled. In spite of the multiple parts to her question, he took no notes. He stared at the camera briefly before answering. "Ms., that is, Gale, we at Turner-Disney have not attempted to mislead America. I admit we are business people and would like nothing more than to have the stock in our company and its subsidiaries increase in value. Many of us own stock in our company. However, to suggest that we manufactured the return to life of Elvis Presley is far-fetched."

"You categorically deny causing an explosion at Graceland last Tuesday?" Reiter watched Lomax's face for nonverbal responses. He remained poker-faced.

"Absolutely," he replied. To elaborate for the audience who may have had trouble understanding the question and response, he added, "We had nothing to do with the explosion. The resultant damage and loss of income due to closing the mansion for repairs were very expensive."

"Can you estimate the cost for us?"

"I don't have the precise figures at my fingertips, but it exceeded three hundred thousand dollars," Lomax stated.

"Do you know how much money Turner-Disney made last week, beyond its average weekly profit, as a result of the supposed sightings of Elvis and the mass hysteria surrounding these occurrences?"

Lomax refused to respond more than placidly. "I can only tell you that we made money. We expect to make even more money with the concert later this week." He apparently lost interest in the television camera. Lomax began to look around his office, in which a crew at Turner-Disney had set up the camera and television. "If you like, I can put you in touch with the Chief Financial Officer at Turner-Disney. He might enjoy talking with you later in the week."

Lomax's voice remained pleasant, for the time being; Reiter hoped it would change soon. Mentally, she could see her audience reaching for their radio tuners. Tired of Elvis, they would be changing the station if she did not liven things up quickly. "Do you know an Elvis impersonator named Billy J. Nottingham?" she asked, staring at the monitor. Reiter thought she saw Lomax bite down, clamping his teeth together at the mention of the young musician's name. He shot a quick glance at someone outside camera range. Since he no longer faced the camera, she had difficulty interpreting his facial expression.

Slowly, Lomax shifted his gaze, turning again to face the camera and Reiter. The poker face gave way to a different mask. The nostrils flared; eyes squinted; but, the muscles in the face remained relaxed, almost over-controlled. "Should I?" he asked.

"We have evidence he was hired by Turner-Disney, and has since disappeared." She let the unsaid accusation hang in the air.

"I hope he is no longer on the payroll." Lomax chuckled at his own joke. Reiter smiled, too. At last, some sparring began. The audience would stay a while longer.

"Some of my colleagues and researchers think you have him

under wraps. They believe you intend to display his talents in Los Angeles Wednesday, after you fly him to L.A. from Memphis. Is there any truth to that rumor?" She continued to analyze his image, looking for chinks in the armor.

Lomax shook his head, more for himself than her. "We have no plans to fly Mr. Nottingwood...."

"Nottingham."

"We have no intention to fly Mr. *Nottingham* to L.A. Our invitation is to fly Elvis, and only Elvis." He scooted his chair closer to the microphone and to the camera, practically putting his face on the monitor. "T-D has spent almost five hundred thousand dollars refurbishing Elvis's Jetstar, Hound Dog 2, for that flight."

"So you expect him to show up? You think Elvis Presley has been reincarnated, or returned from the dead?" Reiter's voice cracked. She saw Lomax smile on the camera. Mentally she gave him a point. Actually, she gave herself a negative point for the momentary loss of control.

"Gale," Lomax responded condescendingly, "I do not believe Elvis has been reincarnated. Being a believer in conspiracies, I don't think the old boy ever died. It is my understanding that he is alive and well. He is living somewhere in the United States in the witness protection program. If he will call me, I will arrange for him to be airlifted to L.A. on his jet from anywhere in the United States. If he does not call, or does not arrive at Graceland by 11:00 a.m. on Wednesday, then he will miss his ride. I believe he might want to see the show, or participate in it, Wednesday evening."

Reiter could not tell if Lomax joked with her. "So you don't believe in Elvis Presley as a messenger sent by God? Are all these people flocking to large arenas in hundreds of caravans all over the United States to see your show crazy?"

Lomax again refrained from showing emotion. He relaxed a little, allowing his face to sag. "I don't want to discuss the subject of religion, Gale. Your last guest covered the topic in depth, I thought. Just because there are established religions already doesn't mean new ones will not come into being. As far as I know, no one has proved which religion has God's blessing, if there is a God to give such a blessing.

"People worshiped Elvis, at some level, before the explosion at Graceland. What happened at the mansion served only to ignite the phenomenon occurring all over the country at this moment. Turner-Disney can't take credit for either one." He smiled smugly at the camera, "You can't blame us for trying to profit from it, can you?"

Reiter smiled also, "Folks, we have to take a commercial break. When we return, you will hear a report from a researcher at Graceland. Also, we will begin to take phone calls from people with questions, or revelations, for me and Mr. Lomax. You will stick around, won't you, Mike?"

"Certainly," Lomax grinned and leaned backward in his chair. He placed his feet on the corner of his desk nearest the camera. To Reiter, his feet looked huge, almost filling the television screen.

THIRTY-SIX

During the commercial break, Lomax reminded himself to remain silent. He knew Reiter's reputation for slyness, having listened to her show frequently. In the past, supposedly accidentally, she had left the microphone on and had caught her guests in embarrassing conversations.

Austin did not know the reason for Lomax's self-imposed silence. "Nottingham...." exited his mouth before Lomax could silence him.

"Now, George," Lomax stated with forced calmness, "you don't want to start any rumors that we know this Billy Nottingham, do you?" He pointed to the screen with one hand and cupped his other hand over one-half of his earphones. "If Ms. Reiter is listening to us right now, maybe she can give us some more information on this young man. We can check to see if someone in our organization hired him."

Austin stood behind the metal platform which held the monitor and camera. He clasped his hand over his mouth, realizing he made a mistake. Static crackled from the speaker in the room and in the earphones Lomax wore, "We will be live in thirty seconds, Mr. Lomax," the director informed them. "Ms. Reiter said to tell you she will fax Mr. Nottingham's vital statistics to you after the show. Twenty seconds. Ten seconds. We are on the air."

Lomax stared at Austin; Austin returned the look. Both silently thought the same thought: the bitch left the microphone hot. To sooth his anger, Lomax gazed at the stand which held the monitor, television camera, and speaker. The crew from Turner-Disney spent several hours the night before tweaking the equipment. The extra touches put Lomax at ease. He appreciated the

fine art work by the technicians. One of the men salvaged a cardboard cutout of a topless belly dancer. Her headless body sup-
ported the television monitor which displayed Ms. Reiter's head.
Through the cardboard cutout's belly button poked the camera
that monitored his face. Lomax wondered what the excessively lib-
erated, but highly conservative, Reiter would think if she could
see herself as a belly-dancer. The lewd thought lowered Lomax's
anxiety level.

"Mike?" Reiter's voice echoed in Lomax's ears.

He tried not to think about her interpretation of Austin's gaff.
"Yes," he answered, barely loud enough to be heard, cursing himself for the squeaky voice. He cleared his throat and responded
more authoritatively, sounding more in control, "Sorry, frog in the
throat. Ready when you are, Gale."

"Good. I had intended first to discuss some information my
employees gathered over the weekend at Graceland. For those of
you out there in the audience, I need to point out that Mike Lomax
that's Mr. Lomax to you when you call, by the way. He's Mike to
me only." Lomax smiled. "In any event, Mr. Lomax and Turner-
Disney graciously allowed my staff to explore Graceland over the
weekend. They had free-reign to inspect the mansion and the
grounds. Permission was given for them to talk to any employee
they wished.

"My investigators made some interesting discoveries. We also
have several listeners who have made observations which may tie
in with those findings. So, if you don't mind, Mike, I would like
to let the people on the telephone lines make their statements, or
ask their questions, first."

"By all means," Lomax agreed to the request. With his periph-
eral vision, Lomax saw Austin rise, as if to leave. Lomax waved him
back into his seat and motioned for him to remain seated.

"Terrific. Okay, Memphis, Tennessee. Lester Watkins. Sir, are
you on the line?" The squeal in Lomax's headphones hurt his ears.
Before he could remove the headset, it stopped. "...need to turn
down your radio volume," Reiter reminded the man.

"Uh, sorry, Ms. Reiter, Mr. Lomax," the southern, deep bass, voice apologized.

"Mr. Watkins, you were an eye witness to the lightning strike?" Reiter tried to jump-start the conversation.

"Yes, ma'am. I thinks the man in the laundry truck caused it."

Surprised, Lomax asked, "Laundry truck, what laundry truck?"

"Well, every Tuesday between 2:00 and 5:00 p.m., the Nashville Southern Laundry truck, a large red truck, picks up our laundry. Then it go over to Elvis's place and gets his laundry."

"Where do you work?" Reiter asked the man.

"Oh, I works at the cafeteria across the road and down the street some from Graceland. They gets our tablecloths and napkins."

"And then the truck goes to Graceland," Reiter finished for the man.

"Not directly. They goes a couple places on the block first. When I gets off work at three, I usually walk home in front of Elvis's. That big red truck always be there on Tuesdays."

Impatient, Lomax asked, shrugging his shoulders, "And why do you think the truck had something to do with the lightning?"

"Well, I was standing across the street, out of the rain. I was under one of them shelters in front of the ticket office. The rain really come down hard all of a sudden. I saw the truck back into the side driveway and stop. The driver got out of the truck and goes behind the truck. He starts throwing big white bundles of dirty laundry onto the top of the truck. I couldn't see him no more, but I could see them bundles just a flyin' onto the truck."

"Then what?" Reiter asked.

"Then something strange happened. It be hard to see in the pouring rain, but the driver stopped throwing bundles onto the truck. This big white bundle flies up from behind the house and disappears into the trees. Not two minutes later, the lightning hits the roof of the house and I sees this huge explosion."

"Is that all?" Reiter watched Lomax carefully. His lower jaw moved slowly, as he clenched his teeth. The smile faded.

"Not quite. Right away another bundle flies up and lands on top of the truck. I hears another explosion. When the rain slacked off, the driver come out of the house and gets in the truck. He drives away like nothing happened."

Stunned, Lomax sat facing the camera, carefully controlling his composure. Faking a chuckle and a smile, he asked the man through Reiter, "Are we to assume the laundry man threw a bundle of dirty laundry too high and attracted the lightning, Mr. Watkins?"

Reiter interrupted, "Thank you, Mr. Watkins. I think now would be a good time to hear my investigative reporter's account. David?"

Before Lomax could respond, the reporter delivered his information. "Gale, what Mr. Watkins saw may have been an advertising dirigible. Until last year, Turner-Disney employed a pair of helium balloons in a study of their effectiveness on attracting the public. Deemed failures they were deflated and the cables wound around their reels. They were also thought to be a hazard by the FAA. Memphis International Airport is not far from the mansion."

"One was destroyed in an accident last year, Gale," Lomax protested. "Your reporter must have seen the other. The heat from the lightning welded its cable onto the reel. The report I received says it is stuck for good in the position it occupied last Tuesday — sitting on the ground."

"Folks," Reiter addressed the audience, "We were unable to find but a single balloon, the one destroyed by the lightning strike. I think Turner-Disney carted away the carcass and the reel of the second balloon because it implicated them in a conspiracy to attract attention to Graceland."

"That's not true, Gale. Unfortunately, neither of us can prove our position." Lomax stated. "However, I will have my assistant begin an immediate search for the second balloon. If it hasn't been recycled, we can get you some information on it." He scribbled on a piece of paper as Reiter watched, then motioned to George. As she watched on the monitor, he placed the piece of paper in Austin's hand. Lomax forced another smile, and asked, "Mr. Watkins, did you see anything else?"

"No, sir, I doesn't see too well without my glasses. I left them home that day." Lomax's smile widened; Reiter hit her forehead in disgust. "I could have sworn that man threw a bundle of laundry as high as a tree."

"Folks, we are about to cut away for a commercial break. This is Gale Reiter of the Reiter Report. We intend to complete our interview with Mike Lomax of Turner-Disney when we return. Mr. Lomax, you will be with us when we return, won't you?"

Lomax grimaced. "I look forward to it. You haven't scared me away, yet." Advertising music flared, then diminished, in his headphones. Austin opened the note Lomax gave him. "Find the laundry truck," it read. "The last bundle was the body. Make sure no one finds that damn balloon!" Silently, Austin waved and left the room. Lomax wished a clue would surface to help them find Nottingham. Well, he thought, maybe something will turn up in the next half hour of Reiter's show.

THIRTY-SEVEN

Reiter's mood fluctuated during the commercial. She had had Lomax in her sights and then let him slip away. The balloon theory, even if proven at this point, would not be believed by her audience. They would remember only that her eyewitness needed glasses. Depressing as that thought was, she felt elated by the ammunition left in her pouch. Lomax's goose awaited cooking if she could set him up properly. The commercial advertisement ended. The light, which indicated her microphone's vibrations traveled the radio waves, lit.

"Folks, we are conversing with Mike Lomax of Turner-Disney Productions. To this point, we have learned only that he denies arranging the disastrous lightning strike at Graceland Mansion last week. He adamantly maintains noncomplicity, although an advertising balloon used by Graceland may have been released during the storm. He also denies hiring an Elvis impersonator named Billy James Nottingham, who some in the entertainment business say is the best of the flock of Elvis impersonators. Nottingham has been reported missing to the Nashville Police by his fiancee." Reiter looked from her notes to see Lomax leaning back in his chair, smiling at her, apparently unconcerned.

Continuing, she raised her voice. "Now we come to the final act of the charade. This is where we will expose Mr. Lomax's successful gambit to enhance his advertising budget with headlines. Mr. Lomax is in his office in Los Angeles; he is talking to us via satellite. Mike, are you with us?" She asked the question, knowing he continued to sit within camera range.

"Yes, Gale, I'm here. Before I let you continue, I would like to point out that no one at Turner-Disney caused the lightning to strike Graceland, nor did we hire Billy Nottingham to appear at a concert." As he voiced his denials, Lomax's utterance remained calm and even, almost monotonal. "Although, I will admit that the present Elvis craze has all of us at Turner-Disney excited. We hope it continues far into the future. You have some more questions of me?"

"Yes." Reiter smiled and reminded herself to take small bites; nibble the edges to expose the middle. "Do you remember what triggered the press's reaction after the lightning strike?"

"I don't understand your question." Lomax put his feet on the floor and leaned forward, face closer to the camera as he studied Reiter's face on the monitor. Reiter thought she saw concern in his expression.

"The one thing that the press initially reported, which excited the public, and which started this feeding frenzy about Elvis returning or his being reincarnated: do you remember what that was?" Reiter rephrased her question, trying to jog his memory.

Lomax closed his eyes, squinting. She could not tell if he attempted to recall the incident, but could not. The previous week must have been a busy one for him. "I don't know. I guess the Elvis sightings all over the United States. Is that what you are referring to?" Lomax looked genuinely confused about the question.

"My researchers have determined that within the first twenty-four hours of the lightning strike, seventeen people, who were present at Graceland at the time of the explosion, reported N.E. experiences."

"Any experiences?" Lomax's bewilderment continued.

"Not a-n-y; N, period, E period. Near Elvis experiences." Reiter explained.

"I think anyone who read the newspapers could have told you that." Lomax down-played the reference.

"These seventeen people came from seventeen different states in the United States," Reiter continued drolly.

Lomax's anxiety increased. Reiter guessed his pulse raced. She counted the number of times he blinked his eyes and the number of times he chewed his upper lip. Still, his voice remained steady. "Gale, August 16th is the anniversary of the death of Elvis. People come to Graceland from all over the country this time of year. They arrive from all over the world during the middle two weeks in August. I don't get your point."

"Fifteen of the seventeen people, who claimed to have seen Elvis, are psychiatric patients for one mental disorder or another."

Lomax blustered, "Are you implying that everyone who says they have seen Elvis is crazy?"

"Thirteen of the fifteen psychiatric patients are being treated, or have been treated, for stress associated to UFO abductions." Reiter looked for Lomax to crack. His face remained placid, under control. No anger or rage crossed his features, though she caught a glimpse of the first drop of sweat as it fell from his nose and splashed on his polished desk.

"It would make sense that a certain segment of the population who believes in UFOs might also believe in Elvis's reincarnation...." Lomax let the sentence trail, not knowing how to finish it. "I don't think you could state categorically that the two to four million people in the United States who have tickets to our concert on Wednesday are all UFO cultists, or that they all should be under psychiatric care."

"Of the thirteen psychiatric patients who reported seeing Elvis in Graceland, four had seen the same psychiatrist for repressed memories or post-traumatic stress syndrome during the past three years. That's a high percentage to attribute to coincidence, Mike." Reiter paused. She let the information sink into Lomax's brain. She hoped to see it explode across his face, but she knew he possessed too much self control to reveal his inner thoughts.

Lomax swallowed, hard. He looked past the camera at Austin when his assistant reentered the office. Austin nodded his head, then drew one hand across his own throat. With the other hand, he pantomimed the use of a zippo lighter. Using both hands, he showed Lomax how high the flames of the resultant bonfire reached.

Lomax took a deep breath and spoke, "I don't follow your line of reasoning, Gale."

"Audience," Reiter spoke softly; she aspired to slip a virtual knife between Lomax's ribs, "Doctor Christopher Karakashian specializes in helping people deal with imagined and real memories of severe trauma. He is also trained in the use of hypnosis. His caseload is generated by psychiatric referrals from all over the country. He lives in Beverly Hills, California. Several of his patients work for Turner-Disney."

"That's a fairly transparent connection, Gale," Lomax protested quietly. "Do you think this Dr. Karakashian would cause such a hoax? Why?"

"Dr. Karakashian has recently gone through a very expensive and very traumatic divorce. He needs the money. Besides the four psychiatric patients we have alluded to, he has a patient who is influential at Turner-Disney. It seems this patient has great influence on the good doctor also, don't you, Mr. Lomax?" Lomax's face became beet red. He held his breath after sucking it in through his nostrils so quickly that they collapsed. Got you, Reiter thought to herself.

Finally, he exhaled. The color in his face returned to normal. "Ms. Reiter," he stated stiffly, "I don't know who has given you so much misinformation, but I think it can be corrected. I will be happy to appear tomorrow on your show with this Doctor Karakashian. At that time, you can ask him and me if I have ever been one of his patients. You may have difficulty proving the four people who saw Elvis in Graceland are his patients, also."

"It's a date," Reiter replied. "Folks, we will bring you the show, live from L.A. tomorrow and, possibly, Wednesday. The logistics have to be ironed out. Thank you Mr. Lomax, Mike Lomax, from Turner-Disney for the invitation. We are a little short on time, so we will close for now."

"Great," Lomax said, sarcastically. The word went unheard by the audience after the engineer cut the power to his microphone.

"Jeremy!" Reiter screamed, "Get us on the next flight to L.A.

Art, you and the engineer figure out how we are going to broadcast this. Choi, I want to see the patient list you got from
Karakashian's nurse. If we're going to tilt with this windmill, I
want all the facts." She sat in her seat, exhausted, while bedlam
broke out around her. They had a date, three thousand miles and
twenty-two hours away.

THIRTY-EIGHT

Jon Sorensen sat in the Bureau's overheating, underpowered sedan. The engine sputtered uncertainly, as if it were deciding if it should continue to power the air conditioner while it idled at the stop light. Sorensen entertained two splendid thoughts while he waited for the interminable red light to change and to allow him to continue with his routine. His vision of the four-cylinder engine exploding, driving pistons and rods through the block, warmed his heart. His pulse rose with the thought that he would have to abandon the vehicle and take shelter in the pastry shop on the corner. The intersection looked inviting, until he remembered his heart attack.

A twinge of pain in his chest nudged his imagination away from the doughnuts to the job at hand. On Mondays, his undercover contact at the Port of Los Angeles entertained him with stories of corruption on the wharves. Sorensen missed the undercover work, the living like a street person, the disguising himself, and the playing of roles. California disappointed him, but at least he had found a career. Too bad it kept trying to kill him. He never told his friends or colleagues in California that he left Michigan to find a job acting. For a moment, he relived his Macbethian stage debut at Michigan State. Then, the mechanical monster directing traffic in front of him closed its red eye and opened the green one. Macbeth slipped into the back seat as Sorensen dealt with wild L.A. drivers and their interpretation of what was *to be or not to be*.

The cellular phone beeped. Sorensen punched the speaker phone button with a meaty finger. "Sorensen," he said.

"Sorensen, Landers here," the speaker spat back.

"Hi, Landers. You on a secure line?" He thought he detected a time delay and the hum of the decoder in the background.

"Yeah, but I'm on a scrambled portable in the women's room in the Turner-Disney building. Someone could walk in at any time." Sorensen heard the toilet flush. He assumed Landers covered for herself.

"So, spit it out. What's up?" Without consciously thinking about the flow of traffic, Sorensen guided the vehicle into the right lane inching toward the on-ramp to the Long Beach freeway.

"Lomax has been on the radio for two hours with right-wing radio commentator Gale Reiter. They've been playing the broadcast on a radio in our office." Landers' voice slipped into a whisper; Sorensen heard giggling in the background. He waited in silence. A muffled door slam cut the twitter short, "The doctor's name is Christopher Karakashian, the psychiatrist."

"The UFO abduction guy? The same guy we interviewed about the psycho at LAX who stowed away on the 747, right?" Sorensen reversed his field, changing lanes to the left, cutting off two cars. He missed the exit he wanted.

"Right," another whisper. More noises and a banging on the door. "It's occupied, sweetie," Landers called to the intruder. The banging stopped.

"His office is on Santa Monica, near Cedars Sinai Hospital?" Sorensen asked. He tried to remember where they interviewed the psychiatrist. Arriving at the major intersection as the light turned red in the left turn lane, Sorensen floored the gas pedal of the four-banger. The engine responded with a wheeze and a cough. Lurching unsteadily forward, the vehicle cleared the front end of a pickup truck by inches. Jacked up in the air by the custom suspension, the drive shaft of the truck flashed by at Sorensen's eye level, on his left. Sorensen cursed, hoping the Bureau's vehicle would respond to oral abuse; it did not.

Someone hung low, out of the passenger side window of the red truck, flipping Sorensen the bird at an altitude he could see it, if he had looked in that direction. Too busy to notice, Sorensen cut across three lanes of traffic and made another left turn through a yellow light, completing his two-block U-turn. Horns blared. He ignored them, looking for the freeway to Santa Monica.

Landers continued. "Suite 1473. There's no answer on any of his phones: at work, home, car, or beeper." The toilet flushed again. "Come on dearie; you using drugs, or something?" Another voice echoed off the metallic stall doors.

"Find Ralph. Get him to the Doc's house. Beverly Hills?"

"Right, again." The line went dead. Sorensen assumed Landers spoke to him and not to the irksome lady waiting for the toilet.

From the freeway, Sorensen saw the plume of oily black smoke as it climbed slowly into the inversion layer of haze and flattened out against the sky. Inky jets smudged the view of the mountains and the Pacific Ocean. By the time Sorensen arrived on the scene, all of Cedars Sinai Hospital complex was enveloped in fumes. Nausea gnawed at Sorensen's stomach. He could not tell if it originated with the smell of burning fuel. Possibly it was the realization that the fiercely burning kerosene tanker truck skewered the condominium office owned by one Christopher Karakashian, M.D.

Parking the balky car as close to the fire as the police would allow, Sorensen flashed his badge and walked briskly to a group of firemen and policemen directing the fire fighting effort. They stood in the middle of the parking lot in full protective gear. Not wearing similar armor, Sorensen could feel the polyester fibers in his clothing beginning to warm and starting to sag. Given a few more minutes in the heat, the suit would melt.

He placed the firefighters between himself and the fire, standing directly behind them. Thrusting his hand and credentials between their shoulders, he shouted above the terrible growl of the flames that consumed the long, low office complex, one building at a time. "FBI. Who's in charge?"

A white-helmeted, grizzled veteran turned to face him. The man's cherry red face, drenched in sweat, eyed Sorensen suspiciously, "Why do you want to know?"

"Possible murder attempt," Sorensen yelled to be heard. "Is that Dr. Karakashian's office?"

The chief looked at the FBI agent and laughed. "If you'd like to check the mailbox for a name, be my guest. Otherwise, you'll have to wait until we put out the fire."

Sorensen nodded, seeing the humor but not appreciating it. "Any injuries?"

Taciturn, the firefighter pointed to the distant corner of the parking lot. Three ambulances stood there, lights flashing. The paramedics administered to the injured who lay scattered about the vehicles like trailers after a tornado. Sorensen nodded, mute, and slapped the man on the shoulder in thanks. He started walking in the direction of the flashing lights. The blast furnace hurried him on his way, certain that his suit sagged and stretched out of shape from the heat of the fire.

After interviewing the EMTs and the injured persons strewn throughout the parking lot awaiting transport to the hospitals, Sorensen returned to his vehicle and picked up the phone. He jabbed at the auto-dial button and waited for Jacobs to answer. "Jacobs."

"Sorensen here. Where are you?" Sorensen loosened his tie and unbuttoned his sweat-drenched shirt as he leaned on the open car door, hoping to catch an ocean breeze.

"Approaching Doctor Karakashian's house in Beverly Hills. Anything at your end?"

Sorensen let his eyes drift across the curled guardrail which had been peeled back from the freeway by the runaway tanker truck. Black tire marks, crumpled automobiles, and flattened shrubs marked the passing of the huge truck from the freeway through the front facade of the office. "Either Karakashian was the unluckiest son-of-a-bitch that ever lived, or someone probably murdered him with the largest Molotov cocktail you ever saw."

"Probably?"

"No body, yet. His car is missing, too. According to the people in the surrounding offices, his red Porche usually sat directly in front of his office." Sorensen watched the flames die down, finally suffocated by the foam spray from the fire department's chemical tanker truck. It would be hours before the county's Hazardous Materials Response Team would allow a search of the charred office remains, for bodies or Porches. "Probably bulldozed into the inferno by the tanker."

"Sounds like a mess." Sorensen heard the other agent's car grind to a stop. "I'm here. What am I looking for?"

"If you can get into the house without a warrant, look for anything that might connect him to Turner-Disney and Lomax. Let me know what you find. I'll be here until the coroner's crew has finished its work. Out."

"Out," Jacobs replied, unable to change terminology from radio to telephone when discussing enforcement.

THIRTY-NINE

Lockwood accepted that he dreamed. He recognized the stale plot. He stood, staggered actually, in a boxing ring. The biggest, ugliest, most brutish-looking, heavyweight fighter he could imagine pinned him against the ropes, throwing punch after punch at his head and torso. With each blow, Lockwood somehow managed to escape a direct hit. Finally, the bell rang, and rang, and rang. Awake, Lockwood reached to the night stand and picked up the receiver, "Yeah?"

"Barry?" A tired voice asked.

"Jeff?" Lockwood responded, no more alert.

"Glad I caught you." Nordstrom perked up, slightly. "You in a secure place?"

"Depends on what you mean by secure." Lockwood glanced around the motel room. After dumping their rental car at the airport, he and Vanderbilt attempted to catch a flight from Flagstaff to Los Angeles. No seats were available, on any aircraft, from any point of origin, going to Los Angeles. The concert, *The Elvis Concert*, made flying to Los Angeles, or any destination nearby, an impossibility. Badly needing sleep, they rented another vehicle to search for a motel. For precautionary reasons, Barry used cash instead of the credit card or travelers' checks. The two found a motel; they registered as Mr. and Mrs. Barris. While she slept, he found a fax machine in the lobby and called Nordstrom.

"Partner, the drivers' licenses, weapons permits, credit cards, and other stuff you faxed me are bogus. We traced them to the original applications. They are based on stolen social security cards. They're as real as fakes can be. Those men have damned good counterfeit identities, but they are still impostors." Nordstrom whistled through his teeth, catching his breath. In a whisper he continued, "Bill Engle checked on this for me. You remember Detective Engle, don't you? Anyway, he said the last time he saw documents this well constructed, they were in the hands of the CIA. You tick anyone off in the federal government, Barry?"

"Don't think so. What time is it?" The heavy curtains effectively darkened the room, allowing only one pencil thin shaft of light to enter. The beam played against the thick vinyl wallpaper, scattering widely to light the room dimly. Lockwood could see well enough to distinguish Vanderbilt's slender form under her blanket in the other double bed.

"Let's see." Lockwood envisioned Nordstrom pulling back the cuff-linked shirt sleeve and peering through his reading glasses at his Rolex. "It's about 6:20 p.m., here. Are you two or three hours behind us?"

"Two, I think. Three hours at the Nevada or California state line." Lockwood pushed away the blanket; he sat on the side of the bed in his underwear, facing Vanderbilt. She moaned and rolled away from him. "I'll keep you posted as to our location. I want to know if you find out any more about the two goons who tailed us."

"I'll keep looking, but I think we know as much as we're going to learn." The phone became silent, briefly. Lockwood heard his ex-partner take a deep breath. The long hours of investigation evidently exacted a toll. "Damn, why didn't I think of this earlier. Barry, send me the wallets, overnight express. I'll get the finger prints checked."

Lockwood laughed, loudly; Vanderbilt bunched the pillow around her ears. "Hell, Jeff, they're halfway to Memphis by now. I sent them to you this morning, packaged in ziplock bags. You should have them by 9:00 a.m. tomorrow. Check the credit cards; they should have good prints."

Nordstrom chuckled, "You always were a better cop than I was."

"But you're the better lawyer. I'll keep in touch. If I have hand-

cuffed two federal employees and damaged a government automobile, I may need a great lawyer." Barry held the receiver close to his
lips. Conscious of Vanderbilt waking up, he lowered his voice, "I
need to go, Jeff. We've got to hit the road if we're going to get to
L.A. in time to do any investigating before the concert. I may have
to drive all night."

"Take care, partner." A click sounded and then the telephone
dial tone hummed in his ear. Lockwood set the receiver lightly on
the phone base and stood in the dim light. He grabbed his suit-
case and lugged it into the bathroom with him. Once inside the
bathroom, he turned on the light. Over the next half hour, he
showered, shaved, and put on clean clothing for the first time in
two days.

While Vanderbilt bathed and dressed, Barry reloaded the car
and bought Tacos at a nearby stand. He paid the motel owner, in
cash, and promised to bring him the key when his wife finished
showering. Knowing he would never go there, he asked for direc-
tions to Sunset Crater National Monument. From the stuffed tourists' information stand near the door in the lobby, he found four or
five interesting travel brochures.

He browsed through the fliers; Vanderbilt joined him in the
lobby. Impersonating his wife, she slipped her arm around his and
pulled him to her. Directly in front of the motel manager, she gave
him a big hug and planted a light kiss on his lips. Lockwood responded, pulling her even closer and kissing her more firmly than
she expected. Blushing, she pushed him away. Remembering the
act, however, she giggled girlishly and batted her eyelashes at the
manager. Loudly enough for the clerk to hear, she told Barry, "Later,
silly." Arm-in-arm, they left the lobby. As the clerk held the door
for the two of them, she smiled at the man and flipped the room
key to him. The clerk caught the key on the fly; he whistled under
his breath and stared at her backside as she sashayed her way to
the car.

Lockwood purposely drove the rental car eastward from the

parking lot driveway. He made several turns, blocks away from the motel, to return to Interstate 40 West.

Leaving the plateau, west of Flagstaff, they passed the exit to the Bill Williams Ski and Camping Area. Lockwood stuffed the remainder of his taco into his mouth and grabbed the steering wheel with both hands. He hit the brakes. The car skidded off the interstate onto the side of the road. Patiently, Lockwood waited until the road was empty and no other drivers could see him. He gunned the engine and backed the car to the exit.

"That's illegal, mister ex-cop," Vanderbilt said, speaking for the first time since he handed her the bag full of Mexican food.

"So is talking with your mouth full," he teased.

"Why are we stopping?" she managed to ask through the dripping tomato sauce.

"According to the Arizona State Police, Bill Williams is where our caravan of Elvis groupies spent the night, last night. Remember?" He steered the automobile off the asphalt and onto a gravel road, following the rustic signs to the camping area.

"They should be a couple hundred miles down the road by now," she reminded him, looking at her watch "it's pretty late in the day, mister detective."

"True." He hit the brakes and stopped in front of the log cabin which served as the office. A dust cloud jumped from their wheels and was gently blown away from the car by the wind. "But maybe we can learn something. You coming?"

Vanderbilt shook her head, "I'll finish eating, if you don't mind." Barry nodded and pulled down the visor in front of him. He looked at his reflection in the mirror and wiped the sauce from the corner of his mouth with a napkin. He smiled a big grin and checked his teeth for embarrassing strands of shredded lettuce or meat caught between them. "Going on a date?" Vanderbilt asked, sarcastically, mouth full of ground beef and beans.

"The way you kiss, Mrs. Barris, I'd be a fool to date anyone else." Barry winked at Vanderbilt. Blushing, she smiled at him, with her cheeks pushed outward by the large mouthful of taco.

Twenty minutes later, Barry returned. "You get lost?" Vanderbilt asked. She handed him a bag with the trash from the meal. He tossed it into the green refuse container and then sat in the car leaving the door open while he spoke.

"The group was here last night, part of it anyway. Apparently, they have accumulated more than a thousand cars, maybe three or four thousand people. The rest of them slept along the side of the road or in different parks." He took Vanderbilt's hand with his and squeezed it, "We're probably close to B.J. The lady inside said that Elvis himself was with this group, until the Winnebago he's riding in broke down. Many of the people in this group left homes in Tennessee and Arkansas. *Elvis* told the group he would catch up with them in Los Angeles. Keep your eyes open for an old RV with B.J. driving. He's apparently traveling with an older man in poor health. Interstate 40 goes almost all the way to L.A."

Vanderbilt clutched Lockwood's hand tightly. He could feel the moisture between their palms, but could not tell which of them sweated. He balled his left hand; that palm felt dry. "A Winnebago?" she asked.

"A very old Winnebago, quite decrepit from the description the clerk got from the group," Lockwood elaborated.

Returning to the interstate, Barry eased the Taurus's speed up over seventy-five. He reasoned the Winnebago probably had a head start on them, if it had been repaired overnight. "How do you know he's in front of us?" Vanderbilt asked.

"I don't, for sure. If he is behind us, though, he won't get to Los Angeles on time unless he charters a plane." Lockwood pulled into the passing lane, around a motor home. Even though the name Jamboree was painted on the side of the RV and not Winnebago, Vanderbilt studied the driver and all the occupants she could see. The gray-haired woman driving, and her male companion, waved. Lockwood returned the wave while a depressed Vanderbilt sat glumly still.

After several more unsuccessful encounters, Lockwood broke the dispiriting silence, "Okay, religion and philosophy major from the University of Tennessee, give me a brief, thumbnail sketch of the history of religion."

Glumly, staring at the ceiling, Vanderbilt asked, "Western or Eastern?"

"Both, but start with Western."

"It's been a while, but I'll try." In front of them the sinking sun cast an orange aura on the sky, the ground, and Amy's face. "Why the sudden interest in religion?"

Lockwood pointed to the new, shiny silver, Airstream RV in the right lane. A satellite dish lay folded against its roof. Its turn signal on, it exited the interstate following the road signs to Kingman, Route 93, and Las Vegas. Three bumper stickers were visible in the shadow of the big motorhome. Large letters and symbols proclaimed, from left to right: *ELVIS LIVES; I LOVE ELVIS; ELVIS SAVES.* "I *heart* Elvis," Lockwood said, lowering his finger to point directly at the stickers as they roared past the slowing vehicle. "That's a scary thought."

"My favorite bumper sticker is, *I heart diamonds,*" Vanderbilt replied, finally smiling and dissipating some of the gloom in the car. "Okay, Western Religion 101. Prehistoric people apparently worshiped many gods. By the time the Canaanites and Greeks were writing things down in Babylon and Greece, the mythology had reached a mature level with a family of gods. There were usually a father god, a mother goddess, and many sibling lesser gods. The three most prominent western religions, Judaism, Christianity, and Muhammadanism had their beginnings in about 2000 B.C. They all started with Abraham of Ur. He had a vision in which he communicated with the chief Canaan god, El. El told Abraham to trust in him above all other gods and together they would found a great nation."

FORTY

Shafer woke to the sounds of ZZ Top's rendition of *Viva Las Vegas*. The placement of the speakers in the motorhome and the elevated volume made him feel as if he were sitting on stage with the musicians. "Gawd, what a racket," he grumbled, rubbing his face with his hands.

"Sorry," Elvis apologized, quickly pressing a button on the dash in front of him. He muted the blaring babel. "I like that version, too. You slept well in the new captain's chair, Colonel," he observed. "How are you feeling?"

Jack surveyed the surroundings. Even in the dusky shadows he easily determined they had exited the interstate, but remained on a four-lane highway. "You turned off I-40," he observed, not answering the question. The disease sent pain coursing through his body. Bolts of searing electricity traveled up and down his spine and into his brain, leaving a ringing sound in his ears.

"We have time to drive through Las Vegas, before we go to L.A. and San Diego," Elvis responded. Shafer looked at his watch. "It's only a couple hours longer this way."

Racked with pain and in no mood to waste several hours, Shafer asked, "So, why would we want to go to Vegas?" Trembling, he pulled a pill bottle from his shirt pocket and removed two large tablets. From a nearby cup holder he lifted a large plastic cup. Throwing the pills into the back of his throat, Shafer washed them down by guzzling the melted ice and diluted soft drink. He grimaced, coughed, and gagged silently on the nasty tasting drink.

Elvis contemplated the question for a brief second and then pointed to a collection of blinking red lights out in front of the RV. "See the blimp, Colonel?"

Straining against his seat belt and his pain, Shafer leaned forward in his seat. He stared at the lights and their surroundings. Seemingly floating in the sky to the right of the road, six vertical rows of lights hovered near the horizon far in the distance. The retired pilot knew better than to interpret the flashing lights as a blimp. He turned to face the younger man, "Elvis, those are radio towers and warning lights," he corrected.

"It's a matter of perception, Colonel." Elvis smiled. "Look again."

Shafer swivelled his head obediently, expecting to see the towers' flashing red lights. Instead, a blimp drifted across his field of vision gliding close to the road less than a mile away. It obscured the towers in the background. Across the side of the blimp, a commercial message flowed, borne by flashing lights. "I'll be damned. Where did that come from?" Shafer looked at Elvis for an answer.

"From Mega, and your mind." Elvis continued to watch the road as he drove along Route 93 in the darkening desert. "Look, now."

The blimp was gone. The rows of red lights on the plateau outcropping appeared to slide silently and slowly across the stationary desert foreground. Parallax made the towers move. In reality, they held fast to their position on the horizon. The desert seemed to move in front of the RV. Shafer stared into the distance, jaw slack.

"I like the quiet ride," Elvis said softly. Shafer realized that neither of them had been forced to yell in order to have the conversation. He nodded in silence, waiting for the pain reliever to have an effect. "There is a down side to our situation, Colonel."

"Our situation?" Shafer asked.

"The planet's life form, Mega, Gaia," Elvis explained. "You'll have to make certain to explain this to everyone, later."

"Explain what?" Shafer raised his voice, his usual impatient response to someone he thought tried to give him the run around. In doing so, he forcefully expelled air from his chest through his larynx, increasing the pain in his ribs.

"It's taken several billion years for Mega to arrive at this point. Evolution, over thousands of millions of years, has left us in this position."

"What position?" Shafer asked the question angrily, having trouble following the conversation and simultaneously dealing with the pain.

"Man, humankind, is poised to be the instrument which explores the universe for Mega." As Elvis spoke, he stared, trance-like into the darkening sky. "No other intelligent species has ever managed to get this close."

"There have been other intelligent species?" Shafer shook his head, "On this planet?"

"Several. Humans are more egocentric than the others. Perhaps that is why we advanced so far, so quickly. No other species has accomplished what we have achieved in the last ten thousand years. Maybe the wars are necessary. The clashes of egos, wills, and beliefs all lead to merciless competition and advancement."

"Yeah," Shafer groaned, contemptuously, "the world's a better place because we murder each other."

"That's the point you will have to make after I return to Mega. The world is a better place because of competition. It is also a better place because of the compassionate societies which have withstood the ordeal of that strife. What Mega needs now is a millennium of peace. One thousand years of peaceful competition, cooperation, and advancement. We've never been this close before."

"What does Mega expect to develop during ten centuries of peace and quiet?" The drug began to dull the searing pain. Shafer felt a euphoria starting to build as the medication filtered through his brain and alleviated his agony.

"We're not certain. With evolution, the only real constant has been that everything changes. Humans have advanced past physical evolution. Social, mechanical, electronic, and artificial biological evolution have taken the place of natural evolution. For instance, Mega has begun to appreciate the stirrings of silicon based intelligence. Electronic intelligence and mineral-based life might be the foundation for beings who can live for hundreds, maybe thousands, of years. Those life forms could explore the universe; they might find the answer."

Jack grunted, "Robots and computers, the life of the future. I, for one, am glad I am checking out soon, son. What happens if Mega doesn't get the thousand years of tranquility?"

Elvis's face clouded. His eyes never left the road, but Jack knew he did not wish to look into them. Forehead furrowed, Presley's voice dropped an octave. "Better to lose five million years of evolution than to lose Mega. Man should feel privileged to be the medium used in the search of the Universe. He should revere life, not destroy it."

"Explain that," Jack demanded.

Elvis nodded. He elaborated, "You, as a human being, would not voluntarily kill off several lines of cells within your body for instance: all your red blood cells, all the myelin producing cells, or all your t-lymphocytes. The results might be disastrous. Your body is a well-balanced machine; it needs everything interacting normally to survive. Mega, also, is finely tuned. However, mankind has begun to destroy some of the symmetry and feed-back mechanisms which balance life on the planet.

"If humans insist on polluting the planet, killing off the life forms necessary for the continuation of life and the maintenance of Mega, then Mega will allow, even assist, man to become extinct. Extinction has occurred for similar reasons in the past. Mega is one giant organism. Like other organisms, it has an immune system. If humanity is too much of a threat to the biosphere, then mankind will be sacrificed. The immune system will destroy man as automatically as your body kills a virus."

"As painfully, slowly, and fitfully as my body attempts to destroy a cancer," Shafer coughed, "or as the cancer kills me."

"Exactly." Elvis ignored the self-pity in the Colonel's voice. "Mega can culture another species, maybe a different primate, in hopes of exploring the Universe five million years from now. Better to lose those years than the three and one half billion. It would be a shame, though. Man has been the best information gatherer ever."

In a voice made richer by a vision only he could see, Elvis continued to talk and stare into the night, "Also, humans have recently touched upon the molecular rebuilding of life. Life could be extended indefinitely if the right tools were developed. Searching the Universe becomes easier if you can live long enough to go somewhere."

"What would we be looking for?" Shafer watched Presley's eyes; they left the road and looked skyward. Locked on a distant star, they stared into the nighttime sky. Still, the RV maintained its position on the highway, "Shouldn't you watch the traffic?" Shafer asked.

"You don't believe in Mega, do you Colonel?" Elvis smiled. "Explain this: I am going to close my eyes. I will see the road through your eyes and the eyes of other drivers."

"That's nuts, Elvis," Jack knew he should be more alarmed, but the medication tempered his ability to react. "You'll kill us both. This camper will go flying like a Wright brothers' contraption. We will land on a sand dune like they did." Shafer smiled at the narcotic-induced vision of the Airstream sprouting biplane wings, sailing over the dunes at Kitty Hawk.

Presley already had his eyes closed. "Look out the windshield, Colonel." Shafer obliged. "Okay. Now, do you see three headlights approaching. A car and, maybe, a motorcycle, right?"

"You're peeking, thank God." Jack started laughing.

"Maybe. Look at your watch and make certain that I can't see it." Jack put one hand over his watch and peeked at the dial. Elvis described what Jack saw: "Your watch says 10:38 a.m., and twenty-two seconds; the date is wrong because you are twelve hours fast. It is reading tomorrow's date. The second hand is now passing over the nine. There is a small scratch near the eleven that distorts the number. Your alarm is set at 6:30 p.m. Enough?"

"Enough, already. Look at the road;" Shafer pleaded, "you're making me nervous." Shafer leaned into the captain's chair and exhaled. Until then, he had not realized that he held his breath. Picking a point on the ceiling, he stared at the sound deadening fabric and its pattern of holes. He tilted the seat backward and elevated his feet. The movement eased the pain in his hips and lower back.

Shafer woke in the same position. The strobe lights on the marquees disturbed his slumber. Pain crept slowly up his spine. Jack needed no road map to deduce that his new RV sat in a parking lot, near the strip in Las Vegas, Nevada. Elvis had vanished. In a stupor, Jack dragged himself into the bathroom to relieve himself and to choke down two more pills. He cupped his hands under the cool water that gushed from the faucet in order to rinse the medication into his stomach. Stumbling, he managed to walk into the darkened rear room of the motorhome and crawl onto the queen size bed. He hauled his body almost to the pillows at the far end before falling into a deep sleep.

FORTY-ONE

Austin sat in the rose-colored chair, staring out Lomax's office window toward the darkened Beverly Hills. Lights flickered throughout the slopes, earthbound stars in, on, and surrounding the homes of celebrities and other wealthy residents. At 3:00 a.m., on a nearly moonless night, the dark, pitch black areas: deep valleys, steep canyons, and property with unlit lamps divided the lights into uneven rows, slanted and curved along the roads and ridges within the hills.

Behind Austin, Lomax poured himself a drink. Cabinet doors on the bar splayed outward at uneven angles. A video tape rewound in the video recorder; a whirring hum issued from the machine. At long last, a thunk announced the beginning of the tape had been reached. Austin pivoted the chair around to face Lomax and the large screen television.

Lomax continued to stand, elbow on the cabinet which doubled as a bar and bookcase. The knot in his expensive tie sagged to the middle of his chest. The wrinkled silk shirt lay semi-opened, unbuttoned at the top. Lomax's suit coat draped across the desk. "It's been a very long day, George. This better be good." Austin nodded silently. Lomax pushed the button on the remote that started the video.

Immediately, he recognized a local news announcer. The woman stood by a road which he recognized as Santa Monica Boulevard. The scene behind her reminded him of bombed-out cities photographed during wars. The melted carcass of a tanker truck lay amid the charred debris. Behind yellow and red tape barriers, men moved slowly, sifting through the rubble with rakes.

The reporter continued her report which Austin managed to

record in midstream, "...unable to tell how many persons died in the crash. At least three persons are missing and presumed dead. Officials are withholding their names pending the notification of next of kin and locating bodies. The fire chief reported the fire was so intense that there may not be any identifiable remains. Offices completely destroyed include those of a group of orthopedic surgeons, two psychologists, and a prominent psychiatrist. Several other offices were severely damaged. Police will not confirm if any of the physicians, or their office staff, are among the missing."

"Karakashian?" Lomax asked, looking at Austin, who nodded, still not speaking. "All his records?" Another nod. A grim smile crept across Lomax's face. He turned to face the reporter.

"...fuel company reported the tanker stolen from a pier in Long Beach. It had been dispatched to fill a storage tank used to refuel the diesel powered cranes at the shipyard. No word on whether the driver at the time of the crash survived. Now, back to...." Horizontal black and white lines, then a uniform fuzz, blotted out the picture.

Beaming, Lomax chugged the remainder of his bourbon and water and slammed the thick glass upon the shelf. "One down; one to go. What about Nottingham, George?"

Austin lifted his head from between his hands; he rested his elbows on his knees. Mute, he pointed to the screen. Lomax turned in time to see the image of an unfamiliar reporter materialize. He stood on another street, in a different city, holding a microphone. Lomax immediately recognized that the scene originated from Las Vegas. Behind the reporter, people danced in the street, "...looks like a riot, I am certain," the reporter said, "but this is a celebration. An Elvis celebration. The International Hilton threw a large party tonight, an Elvis revival. Elvis music blared. Elvis impersonators took turns on the stage trying to rediscover the magic that defined The King of Rock and Roll. Police estimate a thousand people filled the lobby and the auditorium at 1:00 a.m. this morning. About that time, a man entered the lobby and began introducing himself to the patrons as Elvis Presley. Not unusual, you might think, under the circumstances. However, if you watch this video taken by a security camera, you'll see something strange happen."

The pandemonium in the street dissolved into a black and white video, taken with a wide angle lens, apparently from above and to one side of the rows of slot machines. A man dressed in a white suit walked from one slot machine aficionado to the next. He interrupted them and shook the hands of those who would give him their attention. Even from the poor camera angle, Lomax could tell that several patrons smiled and shook the young man's hand as he moved quickly among them. Shortly after that, the white-suited man departed from the picture. Almost immediately, one gambler after another began to yell and scream. They jumped up and down with excitement. At that moment, the news director froze the video. Fat, white arrows appeared on the screen, pointing to fifteen of the visible slot machine players.

"These fifteen slot players shook this young man's hand. Within one minute of each other, all fifteen of them proceeded to hit the maximum jackpot. The riot is the result of the rush of people trying to get into the hotel lobby to play the machines. Eventually, the management of the Hilton closed its doors. I should add, the hotel is $15,000,000 poorer tonight. Another camera took this close-up picture of the man who claimed to be Elvis. Anne," the reporter said to his partner, "I think you can see a resemblance."

A grainy, black and white picture showed the full face of a dark-haired man with dimples. A big smile on his face, he looked directly into the camera lens. Right hand held like a six-shooter, he tipped it to an imaginary cowboy hat. The white teeth and dimples struck Lomax as powerfully as they had the first time he met B.J. Nottingham.

"We were told by witnesses that when this man left the International Hilton, he boarded a motorhome. They reported he left town, driving west toward the California border." The reporter stopped to catch his breath, and to wipe away a tear sneaking across his right cheek. His voice cracked, "I don't think Elvis will be on the jet from Memphis, tomorrow, Anne. He's in that RV and on his way to L.A. This is Kevin Michaels, eleven o'clock news, downtown." The flaky video fuzz, and white noise in the speakers replaced the clear picture and the voice of the newsman.

Lomax used the remote to back the video to the picture of B.J., then froze the tape. He stared at the features. If shown this picture thirty-five years before, Lomax would have sworn it displayed the image of Elvis. Elvis is dead, he reminded himself. This had to be Billy James Nottingham, or his twin brother. "Are your men going to catch him?" Lomax asked Austin as he stared at the picture.

"They were still in Flagstaff. Too far to catch him. I sent a corporate jet to get them." Austin put his face back into his hands, waiting for the rebuke he assumed would follow.

"Good," Lomax said evenly, surprising Austin. "You've done well, George. Make certain your men intercept him. He and I need to talk before the concert. If he does not confer with me, I don't want him to make an appearance at the Coliseum. Understood?" Austin nodded.

Sorensen watched through the binoculars as Lomax pulled Austin from the easy chair with a shake of his hand. He slapped his burr-headed lieutenant on the back as he opened the door letting both men into the corridor. The lights in Lomax's office snapped off. Inky blackness replaced the scene through the agent's binoculars. He put down the glasses and carefully adjusted the closed curtain. Jacobs snored in one twin bed. Sorensen tiptoed to the video recorder which received the signals transmitted by the bug Landers fitted into Lomax's video machine. He rewound and played the recorded copy of the tape Lomax witnessed. When the picture of Nottingham filled the screen, Sorensen gasped. "Jesus Christ," he said irreverently.

FORTY-TWO

Shafer saw the blue flashing lights in the side mirror long before he heard the siren. The California Highway Patrol cruiser alternately flashed its right and left headlights as the trooper spoke to them via his public address system. "Attention Airstream motorhome with Maryland license plates. Please pull over."

"How fast were you driving, Elvis?" Shafer asked, more out of curiosity then condemnation.

Presley shrugged, "'Bout seventy, Colonel."

"Do you think he got a good look at you?" As the motorhome slowed smoothly to a stop along the shoulder of Interstate 15, Shafer stood up, meaning to take the blame for speeding. He remembered Elvis had denied having his license on him.

"Oh, yeah," Elvis swung his feet to the right and stood. "He watched me for about ten miles, Colonel. I don't think this has anything to do with speeding." Elvis put his hands on the older man's shoulders. Gently, Presley pushed him backward onto the cushions of the sofa behind the driver's seat. "You stay here, sir. Almost every vehicle we have seen in the last two hours zipped passed us. Maybe we're being stopped for impeding traffic. I'll talk with the man."

As if to add emphasis, the trooper's bull horn blared again, "Driver, please approach my vehicle."

Elvis opened a cupboard above the sink in the galley and pulled down his valise. Hefting it, as if measuring its worth by its weight, he opened the side door of the motorhome and stepped out. "Wish me luck," he said. The young man grinned confidently; he let the screen door slam softly behind him.

From the couch, Shafer could see the patrol car in the driver's side mirror. As Elvis approached the vehicle from the front, the trooper waved him toward the passenger seat. Shafer wished he could hear the conversation as he watched Elvis climb into the cruiser. Jack felt and heard a loud snapping sound inside his head. Momentarily, he felt some dizziness and nausea as a stream of raucous noise assaulted his ears. Shafer reached for his ears to clamp them shut with his palms. Before his hands reached his head, he heard voices speaking. Elvis spoke clearly inside his head, "What seems to be the problem, officer, uh, Officer Mendez."

Shafer looked in the rear view mirror. Presley sat in the front passenger seat of the patrol car. He leaned toward the policeman and scanned his name tag. "A routine check, sir," the officer responded. Hearing the man's voice, Shafer stared at the policeman wondering if he were reading his lips. The words matched the facial movements too well to be coincidence. "Do you have the vehicle registration?"

"It's inside this case, officer," Elvis hedged. He cautioned the patrolman, "I have to warn you, however. There are also two handguns and approximately one million dollars in U.S. currency in here, in addition to the registration." Shafer watched in awe, not understanding how he managed to hear the conversation. He feared the revelation might land both of them in jail.

The reaction by the officer fit exactly Shafer's expectations. In one quick motion the patrolman exited the patrol car and drew his weapon. Gripping the pistol with one hand and steadying his aim with the other, the officer pointed the gun at Elvis. Standing bent over in the open cruiser door, he barked at Elvis, "Out of the car. Place your hands on the hood of my vehicle. Keep them in sight."

Elvis nodded, raising his hands to show he meant the officer no harm. "If you'll look inside...."

"Move," the officer interrupted. He waved the weapon, motioning Elvis to exit through the passenger door. "Leave the briefcase on the seat."

Presley obliged the man. He placed both hands on the hood of the car; the officer kept his weapon pointed at him. Jack's mind raced, trying to decide what to do. If he suddenly appeared out-side the motorhome, the patrol officer might overreact and shoot someone. He felt trapped in the RV. His eyes searched the vehicle for a clue to something he could do, anything he could use to help Elvis. There was nothing; he was helpless.

One hand aiming the pistol at Presley, the trooper pulled the briefcase from the car seat and set it on the hood. Using his free hand, he opened it carefully. As Elvis said, there were two weapons and bundles of money. Confused, the officer responded, almost in a rage, "Are you a drug dealer, scum? Is this a bribe?"

"Sir," Elvis said in a quiet, even tone, "if you will look in the top pocket of the valise, I think you will find an explanation." Shafer watched as the officer stuck his hand gingerly into the wide crease in the top half of the case. When he pulled his hand out, it held a large, black folding wallet. Flipping it open, the policeman found himself staring at a Drug Enforcement Agent's badge. Elvis intoned, "If you'll check the number with your headquarters, you'll find the badge is still active." Elvis began to lift his hands from the hood.

"Hands on the car, partner." The trooper kept his weapon trained on Elvis. "Don't tell me how to do my job." Transferring the badge to his right hand, he held it with his thumb against the butt of the automatic pistol. Alternately, the trooper looked at Elvis and then at the badge and the identification picture on the opposite flap of the wallet. No name appeared next to the picture, a sign that the agent worked undercover.

Finally, he reached into the patrol car and picked up the cellu-lar phone. Pushing one button, he opened a channel to his superi-ors. He read the identification numbers to the party on the other end of the transmission. The rapidity of the verification surprised Jack and the officer. A voice told the officer that the owner of the badge held an elevated position within the DEA.

"I'm sorry, sir," a sincere apology flowed from the lips of the patrolman, "I was just doing my job. You can stand up now." Shafer watched as the officer holstered his gun, placed the badge back in the case, and then closed the briefcase. He snapped the leather case shut and slid it across the hood of the car to Elvis.

Presley caught the bag by the handle before it slipped over the edge. He grinned at the officer, "I would have done the same, officer, if I were in your position." Elvis looked toward the RV and found Shafer's reflection in the side mirror. He waved. Shafer waved a shaky hand in return. "The Colonel is not feeling well, sir. Is the rest of this interview going to take long?"

Delighted to have an excuse to allow the celebrity agent out of his jurisdiction, the officer waved his hands, "We're done, sir. You're free to go. Is there anything I can do for you?"

"How's the traffic near L.A.?" Elvis asked, giving the man a chance for redemption.

"Not bad, right now," the officer responded. He took his cap off. Holding it by the bill in his right hand, he scratched his scalp with the same hand. "You'd better believe it will be a nightmare starting tomorrow morning, though. This Elvis Concert has everyone in the state government a little nervous. Every available state and city officer will be there."

"Well, we will try to avoid the delays by being early, I guess." Presley saluted the officer with his right index and middle fingers pointed to his right eyebrow. "Thanks for not keeping us too long."

"Right." the patrolman choked on his reply. Presley strode slowly to the motorhome.

Wordlessly, Shafer watched as Presley restarted the Airstream and eased the bus onto the highway. The patrol car followed them onto the interstate. Both men watched their mirrors intermittently. Shortly after the RV attained the speed limit, the officer pulled off at a clover-leaf exit and re-emerged on the freeway going in the opposite direction. Relieved, Shafer asked, "What the hell was that?"

"Well, I had to do something to keep him from asking about my driver's license, Colonel. I don't have it with me," Elvis shrugged.

"I don't mean the badge, Elvis," Shafer raged. "Well, I do mean that, too. You can go to jail for impersonating an officer. How was I able to hear you two talk?"

Presley rocked his head from side to side, "The Defense Intelligence Agency calls it remote viewing. Actually, Mega tuned you in, Colonel. You became a Listener for a few minutes."

"A Listener? Don't explain, son. We're going to spend some of your money on psychiatric help, for both of us." Shafer spoke in an exasperated tone. The Mojave Desert shrank in their mirrors, heat rippling the sky above the horizon. Shafer became aware of the music playing quietly within the motorhome. It had been years since he voluntarily listened to a radio station.

FORTY-THREE

Vanderbilt sat on the bed in the motel room. For the second day in a row, she had slept in only a slip. Her underwear dried where it hung in the shower, after she washed it with hand soap. When she found Beej, she planned to kick him in the shins for the torture and pain, for the weeks of neglect, for the unhappiness. Moist tears ran slowly down her cheeks as she heard Nottingham's mother speak from memory, 'He's a lovin' man, darling. He's just not all there, all the time. You have to learn to live with that, if you love him.'

"Bastard!" she vented, loudly enough to wake Lockwood who slept on the couch. Hotel rooms were hard to find in Southern California. The only room available in their roach motel contained a single double bed. Barry had been gracious enough to pick the sofa, even though he hung over both ends.

Uncurling and rolling over, Lockwood fought to remain covered with the polyester blanket that acted as if it were made of Teflon. It nearly slipped onto the floor for the twentieth time. She smiled as he wrestled with the blanket in an attempt to remain decently covered. The terrible scars on his neck and chest hardly distracted her from looking at his well-built body, shrouded poorly by the blanket and his boxer shorts. His muscles seemed smoothly efficient and finely tuned.

"You okay?" Barry asked.

"Can't sleep," she replied. "Got anything worth reading?"

"Do you like science fiction?"

"Sometimes. What do you have?"

"*Confessions of a Multidimensional Man*," he replied, reaching under the couch for the paperback book. He bought it in the combination general store, fast food outlet, and gas station when they filled the car's gas tank. That had been near the Arizona border.

The clerk at the gas station told them that their chances of finding a room in L.A., or within a hundred-mile radius, looked dismal. Amy and Barry decided to attempt to get some rest before leaving early Wednesday for the Coliseum. With possibly one last chance to intercept B.J., they stopped in Barstow, California.

"Not some drivel about a person who can exist in multiple dimensions?" she winced. "I'll bet he finds the real owners of UFOs and a way to change the future and the past, too."

In mock pique, Lockwood threw the novel over his head toward the trash can. The paperback hit the outside of the wastepaper basket with a loud clang. "Well, it had been boring enough to put me to sleep, but since you already have figured out the plot, let's do something different. We can't sleep, obviously."

"Like what?" she asked.

Draping the slippery blanket around his waist, Lockwood dragged it to the bed and sat near the night stand and the phone. He sat with his back to her. Vanderbilt edged backward, not knowing what to expect. "Like, calling Jeff Nordstrom," he said. Barry lifted the telephone receiver and punched numbers faster than Vanderbilt could follow his fingers. Brief silence ensued while Lockwood figured out the time differential. "Yo, Susie, it's Barry. Jeff in?"

Vanderbilt sat on the bed, covered by the blanket, knees pulled to her breasts. She kept her arms wrapped tightly around her knees, subconsciously protecting herself from Lockwood. She was consciously aware that she needed no such protection. Waiting silently, she watched and listened as Lockwood did little more than nod and grunt.

The person on the other end spoke for several minutes. Vanderbilt studied the scar on the back of Jeff's neck, his broad shoulders, and then his ears. She had begun visually exploring the peach fuzz growing on the side of his right ear when he hung up the phone. Other than with B.J., she had never sat on a bed with a man.

Lockwood turned his body, putting his back against the head-board. He swung his legs and blanket onto the bed. With his knees bent and apart and feet touching one another, he reminded her of a Yogi. He settled onto the narrow double bed, parallel to and close to Vanderbilt. With both hands, he wiped his face. Avoiding making eye contact with Vanderbilt, he looked around the room. "Amy," he said hesitantly, quietly, looking away from her.

"Yes, Barry," she answered, frightened by his tone of voice and his body language.

He gripped his feet with his hands. Muscles flexed in his back, upper arms, and forearms. He rocked ever so slightly back and forth, obviously not wanting to speak. "Amy, this is very difficult to say."

"Well," she said, gently, at the same time being petrified of what would exit his mouth, "look me in the eyes and tell it to me like a man. If you tell me the truth, I can probably deal with anything you have to say." She knew he had grown fond of her, as she had of him.

Sweat began to drip from his armpits; his entire torso glistened with perspiration. He looked at the blanket covering his legs. "It's Beej, Amy. He's dead."

"What? No! How? It's not possible; not Beej. God, Barry, not Beej!" Vanderbilt grasped Lockwood's arm and buried her head in his chest.

He swung his left arm around her, clamping her body to his. With his right hand he caressed her hair. Kissing the top of her head, he said, "It'll be all right. You'll see. It'll be all right."

She sobbed, wordlessly for twenty minutes, while Barry rocked her gently. Gradually, she grew more limp. Barry realized that she cried herself to sleep. Gently, he laid her down with her head on the pillow and covered her with the sheet and blanket.

Quietly, he made his way to the trash can and retrieved his book. While she slept fitfully, Barry read the less-than-surprising novel in the dimly lit room, annoyed that Vanderbilt predicted most of the plot. About four hours later, as he finished the paperback, Amy roused herself from bed and went to the bathroom. Lockwood heard the shower run.

"Want to get something to eat?" he asked when she emerged from the bathroom still wearing her slip.

"I'm not hungry," she replied and climbed back into the bed. Shortly thereafter Barry fell asleep, hungry, but afraid to leave her alone.

Early the next morning she appeared, fully clothed. She knelt by his side and woke him gently. "Tell me the rest," she said.

Lockwood nodded. "Nordstrom and the police identified the scum who are tailing us, rather, who were tailing us. He got their fingerprints off the credit cards." Smiling briefly, Lockwood did not elaborate on how he knew the prints on the plastic cards would be good. He knew her only interest lay in B.J.

"The prints led to a man with several aliases. One of those aliases rented a car in Nashville about a month ago. B.J. was listed as one of the drivers for the vehicle. The rental company reported the car stolen because it never was returned. In actuality, it was involved in a wreck west of Nashville, probably during a terrible rainstorm last week.

"B.J. was driving the car at the time. It hit a delivery truck. Both vehicles landed in a rain swollen gully. The bodies of the drivers were washed out of the vehicles. Wild animals have destroyed most of the evidence, but they found the other man's and B.J.'s wallets and clothing." He took a deep breath. "I'm sorry, Amy."

"He's not dead," Vanderbilt declared.

"Well, it's true they haven't positively identified the body, Amy, but Jeff says the coroner is convinced he is dead." Lockwood recognized her denial, but felt compelled to deal with it directly.

"No. He isn't," she stated categorically. "If he were dead, those men would not be following us, would they?"

"Nordstrom says they are bad actors. Both of them left special forces with dishonorable discharges. They have also done time for racketeering and muscle work." Lockwood sat up, tossing the science fiction novel backhanded into the wastepaper basket. He pulled Vanderbilt to a seated position beside him and placed his arm around her shoulders. "There are a couple reasons for them to follow us. First, they may not know about the accident. We didn't. They may think we can find B.J. for them. Second, it appears they work for Turner-Disney. If so, they may be trying to figure out how much we know. The more we know, the bigger a problem we are for them."

"Do you think they would kill us?" She looked anxiously into his eyes, confident he could protect her.

"They are both wanted for questioning in another case in which a man died, supposedly accidentally. His brakes failed on a mountain road. The district attorney thinks they assisted the brake failure." Barry stood, while she remained seated. Dragging the blanket which he kept wrapped around his lower body to the bathroom, he turned and put his palm out to her. "Sit there while I shower and dress. After some breakfast, we'll go see about a flight home from Los Angeles."

Vanderbilt nodded. Tears streamed down her face streaking the freshly applied makeup. She mopped her face with Barry's pillow case.

Lockwood kept the folded map in his lap as reassurance. The ticket agent promised him there would be no difficulty getting a seat on any one of several flights to Tennessee. His only problem was traversing the maze known as the California Highway System from Barstow to L.A. International Airport, without losing his sense of direction or patience. Vanderbilt sat glumly next to him, cheeks wet, staring blankly at the traffic and sky. Glazed eyes reflected the scenery but allowed nothing to penetrate her subconscious world.

Barry flipped on the radio to see if she would respond to the stimulus. A talk show filled the passenger compartment. She never acknowledged the noise. Abruptly, a vehicle changed lanes in front of them. Barry immediately became immersed in driving more carefully. He ignored the voices from the radio, concentrating on the road. Minutes passed.

"Barry!" Amy blurted.

"What?" He looked around, expecting to see an accident or a dangerous driver.

"Listen to the radio," she ordered.

"...about to wrap up this edition of the Reiter Report. Mr. Lomax, we appreciate your patience with our questions. Audience, I apologize for running out of time. I would have preferred to put each of you on the air with Mr. Lomax." Barry shrugged.

"Keep listening," Amy demanded, turning up the volume.

"Later today, we hope to be able to report further findings in the tragic accidental death of Dr. Karakashian who had agreed to take part in today's broadcast. Also, one of our investigators will report the details about B.J. Nottingham's death. Yesterday, we accused Mr. Lomax of hiring Mr. Nottingham. It now appears that one of Mr. Lomax's associates did contact the young man, but he never appeared for the audition. As we said, his wrecked rental car and another vehicle were recently found on the side of the road in the hills near Nashville. His body and that of the other driver have been identified by the drivers' licenses found in their clothing."

"We've got to go find this Lomax person," Amy stated with finality.

"Why?"

"He hired Beej," she whispered.

"B.J. is dead Amy," Barry reminded her. She remained silent; the radio show continued.

"...today for the Elvis Concert. Thanks to Mr. Lomax, we have press passes. We will report our experiences tomorrow, live from the L.A. Memorial Coliseum. The tempo in Los Angeles has already picked up a notch with caravans arriving from all over the western United States. It might be a relief to have the concert over, given the press coverage of revivals, meetings, establishment of churches dedicated to Elvis, and all the other strange and weird occurrences reported during the last week. Network coverage will start shortly, with the flight of Hound Dog 2 from Memphis."

Barry switched off the radio, fearing the announcer would mention B.J. again. "Please, Barry, please," Vanderbilt pleaded. "Lomax will know if Beej is dead."

"Okay," Lockwood snapped. "We'll try to see this Lomax guy in L.A., but he's going to be busy. Tonight, we are going to be on a plane to Memphis, understood?" Vanderbilt nodded, dabbing at the tears with a shredded tissue.

FORTY-FOUR

Elvis jockeyed the thirty-six-foot long motorhome through the Coliseum parking lot. Only 8:10 a.m. and still a full eight hours before the concert hit the airways, the lot filled rapidly. Jack recognized some of the vehicles ahead of them as they pulled into Exposition Park surrounding the Los Angeles Memorial Coliseum from Figueroa Street.

Excitement disguising their exhaustion from the rapid cross-country trip, people in dusty cars, pickups, vans, and campers sporting license plates from Arkansas and Tennessee waved at the Colonel and Elvis. Elvis smiled and returned the greetings. Shafer sat, fatigue gnawing at every joint; pain a constant companion. In addition to the vehicles from their own caravan, Shafer saw convoys of vehicles with license plates from Wyoming, Idaho, Washington, Colorado, almost every state west of the Mississippi River. Gaunt, subdued, he sat in the passenger seat and stared at his surroundings.

The RV rolled smoothly over the speed bumps and the small hills in the contoured lot, weaving in and around the stampeding automobiles. Elvis handled the wheel expertly, apparently knowing exactly where they were destined, "You know where you're going?" Shafer asked, bewildered by the number of turns, which left the caravan far behind them in the main parking lot.

"We've got a reserved spot, in the back," Elvis replied. "Colonel, there's a folded, blue document in the glove compartment. Could you hand it to me, please?"

Shafer leaned forward and pulled open the walnut-grained panel in front of him. A folded sheet of blue paper fell into his hands. He placed it in Elvis's outstretched right hand. Presley's left hand spun the wheel of the bus to the left; he braked to a stop in front of two uniformed guards. With a flick of his left index finger, Elvis pressed a button and dropped the electric window. "Morning, gentlemen," he said pleasantly, while leaning far out the window and presenting the blue piece of paper to the guard who reached for it.

"Colonel Jack Shafer," the man in the gray uniform called to the second guard who held a clipboard and lounged, sitting on the yellow traffic gate which blocked their path. Pushing his cap back, the second security officer scanned the list in his hand. Wordlessly, he nodded and then lifted the gate with his other hand. Pivoting on a squeaky hinge, the long yellow pole moved. The slender end rose into the air in front of the RV; the short, squat, heavy end rotated downward. Once the gate attained a vertical position, the watchman kept it in place by jamming his boot next to the counter weight where it nearly touched the ground.

The first sentry spoke to Elvis, "Hope you enjoy the show, Colonel."

Elvis, still leaning out the window, looked over his left elbow, which jutted from the motorhome above the guard, "That's the Colonel," he jabbed his right thumb at Shafer, "I'm his chauffeur." With that he saluted the guard and gunned the engine.

The man stepped away from the vehicle with a grin on his face, thinking he had been told a secret, "Have a good day." His words were never heard over the roar of the 230 horsepower Cummings diesel. The motorhome accelerated into the celebrity parking lot and a reserved space at the far end. The second man stepped away from the counterweight; the yellow pole dropped slowly into its original horizontal position. The men returned to their bored stances, arms crossed and leaning against the guard rail.

Elvis parked the motorhome within a long line of RVs and other large vehicles. They sat, parallel to one another, in a single row, arranged so that they could pull forward to leave the lot, without needing to back up. Shafer had difficulty ignoring the other buses and large motorhomes. Many exhibited wild paint jobs and fancy decorations.

Presley tapped Shafer on the shoulder, diverting his attention from the scene painted on the flank of the converted bus parked next to them. Jack forced himself to tear his eyes from the realistic painting of a pack of timber wolves prowling in a forest. "It's beautiful, isn't it?" Presley said.

"Damnedest thing I ever saw," Shafer replied. "Reminds me of the nose art on World War II aircraft."

Presley laughed. "That bus is as big as a bomber."

Shafer calculated, then replied. "Not really, but it's darned close in size to my helicopter." He turned to face Presley, a scowl on his face. "How long are we going to be here? You promised me we'd get to San Diego quickly."

"Colonel, I guarantee we'll be in San Diego tomorrow." Elvis hemmed and hawed, holding onto the back of Jack's seat and rocking it slightly. "I have to run some errands, sir. Can I show you a couple of things before I go?"

"Like what?" Jack asked.

"I have to talk with some people, make some arrangements...."

"Not that;" Shafer snapped, "what do you want to show me?"

Content not to explain his absence, Presley instructed Shafer in the use of the generator, the television, and the remote satellite dish which sat on the roof. He pointed out that he had stocked the refrigerator to overflowing during their last stop at a campground in Nevada.

Shafer had been versed in most mechanical and electronic contraptions invented over the previous thirty years. Comprehending technical knowledge was a survival skill necessary among helicopter pilots. Their aircraft frequently resembled camels: mechanical flying beasts designed by committees. Shafer paid Presley a modicum of attention; he managed to absorb the important details. The balance of Shafer's attention remained focused on the pain, which increased geometrically as the blood levels of his medication began to drop. "You done?" he asked, impatiently.

"Almost," Presley answered. "I refilled your prescriptions for you, also. Wasn't easy with the original doctor being in Tennessee." Shafer nodded in silent thanks. "If you feel better, later, you can walk around the campus of the University of Southern California. It's nearby. The guards have orders to coddle you, sir."

Racked by waves of pain, Shafer managed to smile, "Just like at Graceland, huh? How did you manage that, anyway?" Another thought flashed through his mind. "How is it you can get all these people to go along with your delusions?"

"I have friends in high places." Elvis grinned. He reached forward and grabbed Jack by the arm, pulling him from the seat. Left arm around Shafer's back, hand clamped tightly to the colonel's left side, Presley assisted Jack to the rear of the motorhome. He lowered the old man to the edge of the double bed. Shafer moaned as electrical jolts shot up his back, reverberating up and down his spinal cord.

He grimaced. "Jesus," he winced, holding his ribs with folded arms, squinching his eyes closed, and tucking his chin to his chest in an attempt to keep from moving. When he opened his eyes, Elvis stood in front of him, holding out the pain medication and a glass of water. Shafer washed the pills down his throat with the water. He handed the glass to Presley. "Thanks, son," he said.

"No problem, Colonel." Elvis placed his right hand on Shafer's head. A warm sensation radiated from his hand, like ripples in a pond. Shafer felt the heat echo inside his skull and warm his brain. The warmth spread down his spinal cord, beating back the icicles of pain radiating from his lower back and hips. The pain disappeared. Shafer fell asleep, slumping forward into Presley's waiting arms.

Gently, Elvis lifted Shafer, cradling the thin, wasted body as a parent would a child. He laid the Colonel's head softly on the pillow and covered his body with the down comforter from the foot of the bed. "Sweet dreams," he whispered.

FORTY-FIVE

Attorney Jeff Nordstrom predicted a crowd for the event. He underestimated the mob's size by a factor of ten. Local television commentators suggested a hundred thousand people were on hand for the departure of Hound Dog 2. The airport authority used the opportunity to raise some much needed cash. Privileged observers crammed the airport viewing deck on the second level of the Memphis International Airport Terminal. Nordstrom among them, they were spectators willing to part with a thousand dollars and spend a cool evening in a sleeping bag, with no guarantee of seeing Elvis Presley.

From his vantage point, Jeff could see thousands, maybe tens of thousands, of onlookers crushed against the chain link fence that surrounded the field. What seemed to be a battalion of the Tennessee Army National Guardsmen formed a human chain inside the metallic one. Nordstrom doubted the Guardsmen would have been capable of controlling the mob, if the chain link fence had given way under the surge of loyal Elvis fans and converts to Presleyism.

In one hand, Nordstrom clasped a portable color television. Its flat three-inch screen depicted the scene as recorded by the myriad of cameras installed by the networks. Occasionally, Nordstrom saw the back of his own head on the tiny screen as he flipped through the local channels. He attempted to find updated relevant information about the departure of Hound Dog 2, Elvis's executive jet. The plane had been renovated and made flight-worthy by Turner-Disney. Rumor had it that a million dollars gave the old aircraft wings and a current flight certificate. Total cost included the airlift by the big Air National Guard helicopter, which some observers estimated at twenty thousand dollars.

With his other hand, Jeff pressed the single earphone more tightly into his ear. The din, caused by the babbling crowd surrounding the terminal, made it almost impossible for him to hear. He increased the volume on the tiny television until the vibrations hurt his ear drum. Still, he had difficulty understanding the announcer.

A hundred yards in front of him sat the refurbished aircraft. It squatted on the cement apron, wearing a new coat of white paint with blue and red trim. Her call letters, N 777 EP, sparkled brightly in the brilliant sunshine reflected from the white concrete.

An honor guard surrounded the plane. In chrome helmets and tan uniforms, they stood at attention awaiting the arrival of Elvis's motorcade. The flight crew, in dark blue uniforms, stood next to the fuselage of the aircraft. Nordstrom assumed they sweated mightily. Cotton ball cumulus clouds in a clear blue sky completed the picture postcard setting. Only the humidity and heat of a typical Memphis summer day spoiled an otherwise perfect scene.

The jabber that made it so difficult for Nordstrom to hear changed in character. He began to detect low rumblings of oohs and aahs from along the perimeter fence. Both the volume and the intensity of the background noise diminished rapidly, until it ceased. The television blared in his ear. Nordstrom quickly lowered the volume. On doing so, he heard an announcer explain the reason for the silence.

A caravan of white limousines approached Exit 23, from the west on Interstate 55. The Elvis Procession arrived. The network borrowed its camera from NASA. Nordstrom's television displayed the scene, still miles away. The camera, which routinely tracked the space shuttle into orbit, followed every turn of the ten-car cortege.

In front of the terminal, nine of the cars stopped. The tenth automobile continued moving until it reached a gate manned by the guardsmen. Swinging inward, the gate opened and admitted the vehicle onto the flightline. Nordstrom watched, alternatively, on the television and directly in front of him. The white stretched limousine parked parallel to the Jetstar II, near the port wing tip.

A four-wheeled cart rolled into a position parallel to the car, pulled by a tractor normally used to haul luggage to and from larger aircraft. The driver parked the tractor between the limousine and the four-engined jet. Sitting on the cart was a folded tent.

The honor guard unfolded and erected the elongated canopy between the automobile and the side door to the aircraft. Hidden from view by the tent, several men exited the limousine. They went directly under the white canvas, which engulfed the side of the car closest to the aircraft. Except for their legs, from the knees down, the persons embarking on the aircraft were invisible to the crowd. The canopy hid them from the throng's view as they walked the ten yards to the plane and boarded it. Most of the legs were clothed in black. The lead pair wore white trousers and white shoes.

"Elvis. Elvis. Elvis," the multitude chanted, intent upon seeing Presley, if he indeed entered the jet. Fanatics, six people deep at the fence, surged forward straining the fence to its limits. Stretching, the metallic net bulged inward. Cameras caught images of guardsmen reaching for their rifles. Fortunately, the wire held.

By then, the flight crew boarded the airplane and started the Jetstar II's engines. The sound level rapidly approached a hundred decibels on the deck where Nordstrom stood. He imagined the people closer to the flightline would soon be deaf.

Guardsmen removed the chocks from under the main landing gear. A man, wearing large red ear protectors and holding two flashlight wands, stood twenty yards in front of the little jet. He wig-wammed with his wands to direct it to the active runway. Slowly, the wheels on the landing gear began to turn. The plane rolled away from the terminal and the crowd, toward Los Angeles. The multitude began to realize that they had been denied visual access to Elvis. Their chant became a plea; its volume rattled the concrete structure of the terminal and the deck on which Nordstrom stood. "Elvis! Elvis! Elvis!"

Hound Dog 2 trundled along the taxiways to the runway. For a brief moment, it squatted on the end of the runway. Then, the aircraft rolled onto the runway and tested its engines at full throttle. Releasing the brakes, the pilot allowed the plane to accelerate forward. The jet raced down the concrete strip and leaped into the sky from the middle of the airport, chased into the air by the chant of, "Elvis. Elvis." No one in the crowd departed until the jet could no longer be seen by the naked eye. Nordstrom watched the television screen until the NASA camera lost sight of the plane, one hundred-fifty miles west of Memphis.

Before Jeff returned the pocket television to its case, the scene on the screen shifted to Texas. A similar crowd awaited Elvis at another airport. The crew of Hound Dog 2 planned to refuel in Amarillo on their way to Los Angeles.

FORTY-SIX

Bustling with emotion and excitement, Lomax paced back and forth between Austin and the large window. Hands in his pockets, he strode to and fro, a big grin on his face. He clutched an unlit cigar between his teeth and alternately made the far end dance up and down by rocking his teeth. During the sixty minutes since the Reiter broadcast ended, he paced the room at least forty times.

Austin watched his boss, mesmerized by the boundless energy at his disposal, but smart enough to realize Lomax's mood would eventually change. The flights of fancy usually crashed, accompanied by, or as the result of, bad news. Never having seen Lomax with a more lofty disposition, Austin hoped he would not be present for the next unscheduled landing of Air Lomax. The higher Lomax flew, the deeper the resultant crater.

"Have you figured it out, yet, George?" Lomax asked as he snatched the Havana from his own mouth. He stopped directly in front of the window and spun to face Austin. With his right hand he pointed the cigar at Austin, a game show host seeking the winning answer.

Austin did not know the question, much less the answer, but he always played along in hopes of tranquilizing Lomax. "No, sir. You are going to tell me, aren't you?"

"It's all in the reports you procured from the Tennessee State Police." Lomax pointed to a rolled-up pile of fax papers on his desk. He recited the sequence of events. "In a driving rainstorm, our B.J. Nottingham had a head-on collision with a laundry truck based in Nashville. The truck recently had been at Graceland, during which time the mansion found itself on the receiving end of a well-aimed lightning bolt. Take a bow, my boy. Nice shot."

Lomax put the large Cuban cigar back into his mouth and rubbed his hands with glee. "I couldn't have planned this; it had to have been fate." He continued his soliloquy, "The lighting bolt ignited an underground LPG tank. The subsequent explosion blew the corpse out of its grave and onto the top of the truck. Unaware of the new passenger, the driver of the laundry truck drove toward Nashville."

"Where he collided with Nottingham, killing B.J. and himself." Austin finished the story. "The state troopers found Nottingham's body and that of the driver. Both bodies had been partially devoured by wild animals and scattered around the countryside, but their identifications were found intact. What happened to Elvis's body?"

Lomax yanked the cigar from his mouth and stared at Austin in disbelief. "Who did you see in the video from Las Vegas, George?" he asked. Confused, Austin shrugged. Lomax answered for him, "That, my boy, is the finest Elvis impersonator on the planet, B.J. Nottingham. And he is working for me, for us, for Turner-Disney."

"How could that be?" Austin asked before the light finally lit inside his head. "They found Presley's body! After a week in the elements, they couldn't identify much. Since they found B.J.'s clothing, they assumed the corpse belonged to Nottingham!" The phone on Lomax's desk rang.

Laughing and nodding his head, Lomax answered, "Lomax." He pointed his cigar at Austin to calm his jubilation so he could hear the individual on the phone. Lomax's smile quickly disappeared, replaced by a scowl. "Have them wait there; I'll send someone for them." He slammed the receiver onto the base, bouncing the phone into the air. It settled onto the desk with a clatter. Austin waited. He knew he watched an ego stalling in high flight.

Biting off the end of the cigar, Lomax spit it deftly into the trash can six feet away. He lit the cigar slowly, deliberately, spinning it with one hand while the flame licked the opposite end. Tilting his head back, he blew a cloud of smoke toward the ceiling. "Where are Jaworski and Gutierrez, George?"

"Downstairs in the employee cafeteria. They were going to check with me before driving to the Coliseum to search for Nottingham." Austin stood, placing himself at parade rest, staring straight ahead, maintaining his military bearing. He waited for the remainder of the bad news.

Lomax sat on the edge of his desk and spoke in measured tones. Carefully, he instructed Austin, making certain his lieutenant understood the importance of his mission. "Find 'Ski and Goody. Take them with you to the front lobby. There, you will find Ms. Vanderbilt and her private detective. Do not, repeat, do not let them leave this building, George." Lomax puffed on the cigar, and then removed it from his mouth. Launching himself from his desk, he strode several steps and stood directly in front of Austin. He pointed the glowing end of the burning roll of tobacco in George's face, an inch from the tip of Austin's nose. Austin stared through the smoldering cigar, to a point on the brown hills visible through the window. "Over the phone, just then, their message to me was this: 'We know B.J. isn't dead.'"

Lomax crushed the cigar in his hand. The burning embers fell to the floor, where he stomped them into the carpet. "I want them in my office, George. With Vanderbilt in our grasp, we can corral Nottingham. We can make sure he plays our game, with our rules. Don't let them get away. Got it?"

"Got it," Austin spat between his gritted teeth, the way Lomax loved to hear a response.

"Move, man!" Lomax commanded; Austin spun and walked briskly out the door.

FORTY-SEVEN

Lockwood returned to the hardwood bench. He sat next to Vanderbilt on the uncomfortable seat. Exhaustion hung like a heavy weight from each limb. Even with the extra sleep gained by staying in the hotel longer than they planned, depression sapped his strength. His inner drive seemed stalled with no incentive to search for Nottingham.

Vanderbilt stared at the vast openness of the lobby, decorated in excessive Californian opulence. She spoke to Lockwood without looking at him, her despair evident from her tone of voice. "Well?" she asked.

He pointed at the elderly security guard. The man occupied the centrally-located, elevated, circular mahogany desk, in the middle of the terrazzo floor. Lockwood spoke quietly. "It took ten minutes to get a message past Lomax's secretary. I had to bait him some to get a response."

"Bait?" Vanderbilt looked surprised. "How do you bait Turner-Disney?"

"Not Turner-Disney, Lomax," Lockwood corrected her. "I suggested that we knew B.J. wasn't dead."

She sniffled, catching some tears as they ran down her nose. "I wish it were true, Barry. I don't think I can live if Beej is dead."

One of the six doors in the bank of elevators across the room slid to the side. Catching sight of a familiar face when the door opened, Lockwood sprang to his feet. "Let's go!" Barry urged in hushed tones. He grabbed Vanderbilt by the arm. Pulling her to her feet, he started for the exit, dragging her behind him. He glanced repeatedly from the main entrance to the elevator, head swivelling rapidly.

"Barry!" Vanderbilt exclaimed. "You're hurting me. Where are we going?"

"No place." A stranger's voice spoke from a position directly behind Lockwood. Barry felt the unmistakable thrust of the cold steel muzzle jammed into his back. He tried to turn his head to see his assailant. "Look straight ahead. Walk to the middle elevator," the voice said. "I think you've met our elevator operator."

Another man clamped a tight grip onto Vanderbilt's other arm. Barry felt her skin turn cold with fear as the four of them walked awkwardly toward the lift. The two men bunched themselves closely behind Lockwood and Vanderbilt concealing their weapons from others in the lobby. "Good morning, Mr. Austin," the guard at the central desk said, as they passed within speaking distance.

"Morning, Arthur," the man behind Barry replied. "Mr. Lomax will see his guests upstairs. Let me know if anyone else comes in. All right?"

"I'll do that, sir," the white-haired and mustached old man in the tan watchman's outfit answered. He returned his gaze to the television monitors stacked in front of him.

The elevator doors slid silently and swiftly closed with a solid thump. As the insides of the mirrored doors presented their reflective surfaces to the five occupants, Amy gasped. She recognized two of the men as having been in the car behind them in the desert. The man operating the elevator sported a shaved bald spot of the back of his head. A row of fine sutures held together the three-inch laceration. Vanderbilt could not take her eyes off the wound, knowing what caused it.

"Hey, 'Ski,'" the man holding her arm said to the operator, "she's admiring her handiwork."

A burly man with almost no neck and close-cropped jet black hair frowned at Amy's reflection. "Wait until she gets to admire my handiwork," Jaworski sneered. His coal black eyes bored into Vanderbilt until she looked away from the mirror.

"You'd better not harm a hair on her head...." Lockwood started

to defend Vanderbilt. Simultaneously, he received a punishing elbow to the ribs from the man in front of him and a punch in the
kidneys from the man behind him. Reacting to the blows, he curled
up and bent over, for protection. Uncoiling he lashed out, hitting
the man behind him with an elbow to the solar plexus.

Austin gasped for breath and dropped his gun. Before Barry
could retrieve it, the man holding Vanderbilt yelled, "Hold it. If
you touch that gun, I'll shoot her."

Barry hesitated, then stood upright. He raised his hands in
surrender. "Don't touch her, you...." With nauseating suddenness,
the elevator stopped unexpectedly.

"Wrong floor, you idiot," Austin growled at Jaworski. "Don't
let the door open." Austin retrieved his weapon from the floor.
Slipping the pistol into his coat pocket, he kept it trained on
Lockwood. The other two men struggled to conceal their weapons
in case the door opened.

"There's something wrong with the elevator," Jaworski responded. The door to the elevator opened. A single gentleman
stood in the doorway. He wore a white suit, white shirt, white tie,
and white shoes.

"This elevator going up?" Elvis asked.

The five people on the elevator each took one step backward,
in unison. "Beej!" Vanderbilt squealed. Breaking free from her captor,
she wrapped her arms around his neck. "We thought you were
dead." Realizing their predicament, she attempted to push him
from the elevator, "Run. They've got guns."

Presley stared calmly at the four other men and entered the
elevator. The door slid silently closed behind him. He extracted
himself from Vanderbilt's grasp. Gently, he pulled her hands from
around his neck and placed them by her side. One by one, he
stared at the three thugs with piercing eyes. Then he saw the pain
in Lockwood's expression. "It's okay, momma, we're all going to
the same office. You men can lay off the heavy-handed stuff, now.
Lomax will be upset if someone gets hurt unnecessarily."

In silence, the group rode the elevator the remaining short

distance to Lomax's floor. Elvis stood to one side and invited the thugs out first, "After you, gentlemen. Lead the way." Reluctantly, they exited first. When Amy and Barry reached the door, he motioned for the two of them to follow the three men. Vanderbilt glared at Elvis. Presley seemed not to notice. Taking Lockwood's arm, Vanderbilt trudged up the corridor, past the secretaries, and into Lomax's office.

At first, seeing the three subordinates return without their quarry, Lomax rose to his feet. Face beet red, he prepared to explode at Austin. When Vanderbilt and Lockwood let themselves into the room, his anger turned to confusion. As Presley closed the door behind them, Lomax's face beamed with delight. "Well!" he nearly shouted, ebulliently. "The rumors of your death are exaggerated."

"You might say that, Mr. Lomax." Lomax put his hand out to Elvis; Presley ignored it. "I haven't much time, sir. Since we are among friends here, I thought we could conclude our business." Elvis waved at the motley crew assembled next to Lomax, and to Barry and Amy.

Ever the business man, Lomax walked swiftly to a position behind his desk and pulled out his chair. Seating himself, he looked upward, at Elvis, "And what do you propose?"

Presley pointed to the rose-colored arm chairs and indicated to Vanderbilt that she should sit. Lockwood took the other chair, warily checking the armed men in front of him. The men had not had the inclination or taken the time to disarm him. He squeezed his left upper arm close to his chest and felt the reassuring bulge of his shoulder holster and weapon. Then he leaned forward, hands on knees, feet on toes, ready to spring into action, when necessary.

"Relax, Mr. Lockwood," Elvis entreated the detective. He placed a hand on Barry's right shoulder. Casually, he pushed Lockwood backward, off his toes, and deeply into the chair. He turned his attention to Lomax. "For starters, I think you owe me some money for services rendered to this point."

"Absolutely," Lomax agreed. "Five hundred thousand dollars.

You didn't follow the script exactly, but I understand you had an accident on the way to Memphis."

"Minor problem," Elvis continued. "I would also like to be paid in advance for the performance today. I don't want to come back here afterward. You probably understand my reluctance to return. It's unlikely you'd want to be seen with me, either."

Lomax leaned back in the chair and swung his feet onto the desk. He placed his hands behind his head. A skilled poker player, he was still unable to keep from smiling. "Well, B.J. I can call you B.J., can't I?" Elvis stared at Lomax without responding. "I think you would have to agree that I have you over a barrel here. Let me propose something to you. Instead of paying you the million dollars after the performance, I'll let you return here and pick up your fiancee. Then, if the performance is good and if it goes without incident, I'll let the two of you live. Does that sound fair?"

Vanderbilt yelled, "Beej, don't be a fool! They'll kill us all!" Elvis put a finger to his lips, silencing her without a word. He strolled to the large picture window and stood near the huskier of the two thugs. From his vantage point, he looked out the window at the surrounding buildings and Beverly Hills, as if contemplating the offer.

Deliberately, he reached into his coat pocket. He ignored the sound of pistols being cocked behind him as Austin and his henchmen pulled out their weapons. Elvis removed a palm-sized tape recorder from his pocket and showed it to Lomax. With his thumb, he pressed a button; up flipped a tiny cassette tape. "Your offer, and your complicity, have been duly recorded."

Elvis removed the micro-cassette and flipped it to Barry, who caught it and pushed it into a pocket. Austin went for the tape; Lomax waved him off. Then, Presley tossed the tape recorder through the air toward Lomax. All eyes in the room followed the flight of the machine as it arced toward the expensive, polished wood desk.

Before Lomax could drop his feet from the desk and deflect the machine, Amy and Barry heard a loud crack. Elvis's fist landed against the side of Jaworski's jaw. The man crumpled to the floor, unconscious. A high kick landed on Gutierrez's left temple. He followed 'Ski onto the floor. "He who hesitates, meditates horizontally," Elvis intoned.

Austin spun to point his pistol at Elvis, but found himself staring down the barrel of Lockwood's automatic. Austin released his grasp on his weapon; it dropped to the floor with a thud.

Elvis walked behind Lomax's desk. Trembling, Lomax scooted the chair backward, out of Presley's way. Reaching under the desk, Elvis pulled a black valise from the kneehole and set it on top of the desk. Splitting open the top, he surveyed the money stacked inside. "Looks about right," he estimated.

"You'll never get away with this, Nottingham," Lomax said, cowering in the corner.

"The name is Presley," Elvis growled between clenched teeth. "In case you don't know it, yet, the FBI is recording our conversation. They'll play it for you at your trial." Presley picked up the phone and smashed the plastic handset on the desk. A red electronic bug dangled at the end of three green wires. "Not your typical phone company accessory," Elvis said.

Austin panicked at the sight of the eavesdropping device. He turned to run from the office. Lockwood caught him by the arm and spun him toward the desk. Presley stepped from behind the desk. George took one wild swing at Elvis; it missed badly. After bringing a knee up, into Austin's crotch, Presley dispatched the agonizing thug with a karate blow to the jaw. Austin fell over the unconscious body of Gutierrez.

Leaving Lomax to cringe in the corner, Elvis strode to the office door, opened it, and held it for Lockwood and Vanderbilt. "We need to leave. The FBI and the police will be here, shortly. I can't be delayed; there's a concert I have to attend."

In shock, Vanderbilt placed her hand gently on Presley's muscular arm, an arm stronger, more wiry, than B.J.'s. "Beej doesn't know karate. You're not Beej, are you?"

"Sorry, little momma." Elvis bowed his head in apology.

"Is...is he really dead?" she asked, afraid to hear the answer.

Elvis tilted his head as if listening to distant voices. His eyes stared blankly at the wall behind her. After a moment, he righted his head and focused his eyes on Vanderbilt. "Not that I know of," Elvis replied. "Take these. He might be at the concert tonight." Presley shoved two concert tickets into her hands. "Now get on out of here." Ignoring the staring secretaries, Lockwood and Vanderbilt ran to the bank of elevators. Before entering one, they turned to ask Elvis which floor he wanted. He had vanished. The stairway door closed silently behind his departing shadow.

FORTY-EIGHT

Having lived in Southern California in years past, Jack had grown used to mild tremors and loud noises. Nothing could have prepared him for the continuous, raucous sound that assaulted the motorhome. A constant foot-pounding rhythm shook the RV at each point where the eight tires met the asphalt. The vibrations reverberated through the chassis, air shocks, and electromagnetic springs to the polished aluminum of the body. Every glass and dish, every free-standing object inside the motorhome, rattled. Pandemonium filled the stadium next to him. It invaded and irritated every nerve fiber in his body. He sat in the passenger side captain's chair and watched the fireworks and laser beams dance across the darkening late-evening sky.

The visual onslaught added to Jack's sensory overload. Distraught, he called to Elvis, "Why can't we park somewhere quiet tonight? This will drive me nuts."

Presley stood in the corridor, dressed in black leather from head to toe. He wore black wrist bands and a black headband. His coal black hair complemented the outfit. His eyes twinkled and his dimples deepened as he smiled. "I promise you, Colonel, it will be much quieter in about two hours." He pointed to the ten inch color television perched between the two captain's chairs, mounted in the dash.

On the screen a man sang with a voice which sounded similar to Elvis's voice. Dressed in a white jump suit, he looked very much like Elvis. Camera shots of the audience revealed screaming teenagers, grandmothers, and people of every age between the two. Shafer heard them well enough, singer and screamers both, even with his poor hearing and with the television volume turned off.

The public address system in the Coliseum had been tuned to address all of Los Angeles, the entire country, the whole world. Or, so it seemed.

"It's on every channel," Jack said disgustedly. He stabbed at a button on the monitor. The screen went blank, turning a smooth gray. Above his head, Elvis heard the whir of machinery as the satellite tracking system repositioned itself, aligning with another satellite. Momentarily, the same scene flashed onto the television. "See? It's been going on for five hours."

"Well, it's time for the finale," Elvis replied, looking into the mirror which covered the bathroom door. He positioned the collar of his shirt. From his breast pocket, he pulled a pair of dark sunglasses. "Wish me luck," he said as he pushed his way out of the RV, into the well-lit parking lot.

Jack almost missed his exit, incensed and exasperated by the noise trespassing his personal space. He waved weakly at the disappearing form of Elvis. Too tired to move, sedated from the narcotics, he lay in the stuffed chair merely aware of his surroundings and the damned noise. If he had watched the monitor, he would have seen what 115,000 spectators saw in person. Millions more people, throughout the world, viewed the celebration electronically.

High above the crowd in the press box, Turner-Disney employees took orders from the director of the show. The initial film footage, short clips from Elvis's movies, played on the end zone screens while enthusiastic fans filed into their seats. Following the film clips, many of the excellent Elvis impersonators performed his better known songs. Frequently, the crowd had been moved to tears and cheers. The laser show and fireworks were meant to be a grand finale.

A video tape, recorded earlier in the afternoon at Los Angeles International airport, played across the monstrous flat screens high above both goal posts during the fireworks. All the fans, those on the turf facing the in-the-round-stage constructed at the center of the field and those crammed into standing-room-only space in the concrete tiers and sky boxes, craned their necks to see the video.

On screen, the camera recorded the arrival of Hound Dog 2, its taxi to the flight line at LAX, and the opening of its door on the ramp. Several men in dark business suits and the flight crew exited the plane. Elvis did not disembark. The director meant for the video to be symbolic of the fact that Elvis would not be in the Coliseum in person, that he would be there in spirit. The next order of business was to stop the video, turn on all the stadium lights, and announce the show was over.

Running his hand across his throat, the director pointed at the young man who labored over the electronic control panel. He then raised his palms like an orchestra leader asking for more volume, meaning for the stage manager to raise the lights. The young man pushed the slide bar forward; the stadium remained dark, except for two spotlights.

Crossing, the spotlights met in the middle of the stadium seats, about halfway to the top on the side opposite the press box. Within the lights was framed an entrance to the stadium. The aisle from that entrance led to the fifty-yard line of the football field. A man stood where the two light beams crossed.

"What's this?" the director asked and shot a glance at Lomax, who stood quietly in the background. Lomax remained unusually inactive all evening. The director suspected sabotage of some sort. Alone, without his usual bodyguard for support, Lomax looked at the director and shrugged, as if to say, "Not ordered by me."

"Try the lights, again," the director ordered. Nothing happened. "Put a telephoto on him, let me see a monitor." A crew member spun a monitor to face the director. "Switch the telephoto camera to this monitor." Hands flew; the monitor filled with the dark crowd and the crossed light beams. The picture looked like a dark Jolly Roger flag flying within the confines of the stadium. Gradually, the image enlarged and the focus improved."

"Holy shit," four or five technicians said at the same time, "Elvis." A beaming face radiated at them.

"Nottingham," Lomax whispered disbelievingly, staring at the picture, "you son-of-a-bitch." Lomax screamed, "Put the cameras on him! Broadcast this! That's as close to Elvis as you're ever going to get!" Lomax lunged at the director, in case the man missed his directive. Needing no encouragement, the director and producer began barking orders. Lomax caught himself and held back, not wishing to interfere.

Seeing the image of Elvis displayed on the end zone screens, the crowd began to chant, "Elvis. Elvis." Within seconds, most of the crowd deciphered Presley's precise location in the stands. Presley began to walk down the aisle, arms spread wide, reveling in the adulation. The spot lights remained on him, tight as cross hairs on a hunting rifle. Chairs opened wide when he reached the grass field. Elvis sauntered to the stage and climbed the short stairway.

Once at center stage, he waved both arms overhead, then held both hands palms down to silence the crowd. For ten minutes, the chant continued, finally ending as almost every patron became hoarse or choked with tears. Presley clamped a wireless microphone onto his black shirt. "I missed my flight," Elvis apologized. The crowd erupted again; the chant returned; he waved them silent.

"I have a message for you from a higher being," Elvis said in a rock steady voice. "Miracles do happen. The vector for the miracle of my presence is a being I call Mega. Each and every one of you, each and every living creature on this planet, from the smallest virus to the largest whale in the ocean is a part of Mega. Mega is not your God. God created the entire Universe. Mega occupies a small, infinitesimal corner of that Universe.

"Mega has no proof that God exists, and no proof that He, or She, does not exist. But, Mega is on the threshold of being able to explore the Universe and, perhaps, to meet with other intelligent beings or, at least, to communicate with them. We can expand into the solar system, or we can stay home, pollute our planet, and drown in our own waste.

"If that happens, Mega will probably not die. Man will. Another intelligent species may arise and take on the challenge to explore the Universe. However, it is possible for us to squander our planet's resources to the extent that Mega will be permanently trapped on Earth, sentenced to wither away and die. If it does die, so will the collective memory of millions of beings: your ancestors, your relatives, and you. Mega asks you — the people of the world — for a thousand years of peace in order to explore the solar system and the Universe, to seek other Megas, to search for God. Have no loyalties except to your planet's lifeform — *Mega*. Not to family, clan, nation, religion, nor even species.

"Earl Brown wrote a song I like very much. No one has sung it yet, tonight; I would like to do so now." He turned to the orchestra, "*If I Can Dream*," he said and gave a count of four.

Too soon, the song ended. "I wish I could stay longer," Elvis said, obviously emotional. "I would like to have all my brothers on stage with me for one minute, so I can thank them." Most of the entertainers already fought their way to the edge of the stage and surrounded the platform. With the invitation extended, they swarmed onto center stage, a full regiment of Elvises in elaborate costumes, colors, and capes.

In the front row nearest the stage, standing in front of bench seats planted on the natural grass, Vanderbilt stood on tip toes. She studied the scene, squeezing Lockwood's hand, "He's got to be here, Barry. He's got to be here. Where's Beej?"

On the big screen, seventy yards away, the camera showed Elvis shaking hands with each impersonator, "Thank you, brother," he said, or, "Bless you for traveling so far." Several men looked enough like Presley to be his brother. With one individual, Elvis threw his arm around the young man's shoulder. On the big screen, the two images could have been clones. The crowd murmured in wonderment, "Be healed, cousin," Elvis blessed the man.

"It's him. It's Beej," Amy squealed and broke free from Lockwood's grasp. She managed to run about twenty feet before herd instinct ignited the crowd. As one single organism, it rose to its feet and surged toward the stage. The Elvises disappeared within the sea of humanity. Vanderbilt never found B.J.

Lomax knew he succeeded. If only briefly, he placed Elvis among the living again. The success would be countered by an even larger failure, if his newest gambit backfired. In silence, he handed a slip of paper to the technician typing at a keyboard in the press box. The words he typed appeared on the screen, both in the stadium and on television screens throughout the world. "Type this," Lomax ordered.

Without questioning his boss the man entered the message. His fingers flew across the keyboard. Until he transmitted the message to the screen, he never interpreted what he typed. As he watched the words roll onto the screen, the typist read his message. The full weight of the bulletin became apparent as it slowly slid to the top of the screen to make way for the sign-off and credits.

"Turner-Disney Broadcasting Corporation, Incorporated, has decided to donate the property known as Graceland to a nonprofit foundation whose name will be determined later. It is the wish of the Board of Directors of Turner-Disney that any profits from the operation of Graceland go into an escrow fund. This money will be disbursed according to the wishes of Elvis Presley's dearest friends, his fans."

Lomax thought his gift would eventually become the Vatican of the Preslian Church. He calculated that no one would believe Turner-Disney staged the ruse to make a profit, if future profits never came to T-D. What's more, the value of T-D's stock would remain high, linked to its integrity rating with the American people, and to the tax write-off available to the company after such a donation. Initially, the board was certain to disagree with his actions. However, with the public having read the proclamation, they would have a hell of a time rescinding the offer. Few board members would complain loudly. The Graceland debt had been paid off. The board members' wealth, on paper at least, increased several-fold.

FBI agent, Jon Sorensen stood in the stands near the press box, waiting for Lomax to emerge. As he read the words moving across the end zone screen, he reached into his pocket. He pulled from his suit coat several folded sheets of paper. Deliberately, he tore the search warrants and arrest papers into tiny pieces and threw them into the air. There, they joined with thousands of other pieces of confetti that swirled through the air, in the Coliseum and throughout the world. Joyful celebration became the order of the day. "God is Infinite. Mega is Great. Elvis is their Prophet," he said to himself.

FORTY-NINE

The white clouds hung low in sky. The morning scud provided more protection from the sun than Shafer wanted. He felt chilled, occasionally catching the spray from the bow of the boat as it crashed through the small swells several miles west of Mission Bay, San Diego. Elvis piloted the small outboard powered craft. Jack wore a life preserver over a sweat suit. Presley wore the white suit and blue shirt he wore in the rain storm when he first met Shafer. Jack clasped a warm mug of coffee and shivered. On the deck, between his legs, he cradled the canister that contained the worldly remains of his wife.

The smell of the salt spray reminded him of sailing with his wife, of the laughter and pain that was Annie. Mired between tears and joy, he sat on a stack of flotation seat cushions, back against the forward bulkhead. He stared over Presley at the shore-line, which rapidly became invisible within the mist. Eschewing his usual morning dose of narcotic to be fully alert while performing this last ceremony for his wife, Jack felt the numbing pain spreading from his lower back to the rest of his body. Within the hour his knew the discomfort would be incapacitating.

Abruptly, the small boat entered a fog bank. Isolated from the shore, Shafer could see only fifty feet from the boat in any direction. Elvis cut the throttle and set the motor at idle. "How's this, Colonel?" he asked. "No one else around. You and Annie are back in the Pacific."

Shafer elevated himself to his knees, careful not to lose control of the cylinder. He looked around. The sea was glassy smooth; the boat rocked gently. It was private enough; they could return quickly to shore and to his medication. "Looks good to me," he answered. "Are you sure we are far enough out?"

"I would guess ten to twelve miles, sir." Elvis stood. Balancing himself gingerly, he walked slowly toward the bow of the boat and Shafer. "Do you need a hand with that?"

Shafer sat again, hard. He tugged at the cap on the cylinder, unable to remove it. "It's pretty tight. Would you mind?"

Kneeling, the younger man grasped the end of the canister with one hand and gave it a twist. The lid sailed off and ricocheted around the boat. "No problem." After a moment, of silence, Elvis said, "Colonel, before we scatter your wife's ashes, I have a confession to make."

"Sure, son. What is it?" Shafer sat cross-legged on the deck, arms and legs folded around the cylinder to keep it from toppling over and spilling within the boat.

"I'm not really Elvis Aaron Presley," Presley said. He looked at Shafer, a mournful expression on his face.

"Well, according to the news on the television and radio this morning, you surely fooled a lot of people if you aren't. Don't worry, son; we can fix that. We can find you a good psychiatrist."

Elvis pulled the metal tube from Shafer's hands, interrupting him. "You still don't understand, Colonel. I wonder if anyone does, even after all the publicity. I am not *the* Elvis Presley, I *am* the collective memory of Elvis. I am Mega's memory: the memory derived from all the human beings, living and dead who ever knew Elvis. Like this is the collective memory of your wife." With a heave, Presley launched the canister into the air. As it rose high into the sky away from the boat, it tumbled end over end spewing ashes in every direction. With a splash, it landed in the water and sank immediately. The ashes floated downward from the sky to the surface of the ocean. They disappeared also, swallowed by the Pacific.

Shafer watched in dismay as the cylinder vanished along with the ashes. "I wanted to recite her favorite prayer, son."

A large splash along the side of the boat distracted Shafer. He turned his head expecting to see the spreading circles of waves made by a fish breaking the surface. Instead, he looked into the eyes of a beautiful young woman. She clung tightly to the gunwale of the boat. Adorned in a pink chiffon dress, rivulets of water running down her face from her wet head, she smiled at Shafer. "You mean the Lord's Prayer?" she asked.

"Oh, Jesus Christ, I'm hallucinating. It's Annie!" Shafer shrieked. He reached for her with his trembling fingers and touched her wet head, felt the braided ropes of hair, the smooth skin, and her smile. He wailed, "Annie, Annie. I love you."

She grabbed his hand and squeezed tightly, "And I love you, you rascal, John Henderson Shafer."

"I'm going to be joining you soon," Jack whispered. "Death stalks me, too." His wife, smiling with the full lips and perfect teeth from thirty years before, pulled his hand to her lips and kissed it gently.

"Colonel," Elvis interrupted, "I've got to be going."

"What?" Shafer turned his head to see Elvis peeling off his clothing. Presley folded the white suit neatly in the bottom of the boat. Wearing only his zebra striped boxer shorts, he stood in the stern of the boat. With a wave, he stepped off the edge of the vessel and onto the smooth water, where he stood without sinking. Reaching a hand down to Annie, he pulled her to the surface of the ocean. She giggled like a school girl and twirled under his arm like a ballet dancer. The wet dress threw water at Shafer, who stared with his mouth open. "Where are you going, son?"

"With Annie. Back to Mega." The two stood side by side in front of Shafer, gently rising and falling as the swells rolled under their feet.

The old man shook his head in disbelief, "How will I get back to San Diego?" he asked.

"You are drifting into shore with the tide," Elvis answered. "Do nothing and you'll be back in two hours. To get there quicker, crank up the engine and aim for the inlet when you can see the shoreline. It's easy, kind of like navigating a helicopter." Presley laughed. "Oh, by the way, I deposited your money into a Swiss bank account: The International Bank of Bern. The account number is your social security number backward."

"I don't have any money. Besides, dead men don't need any," Shafer countered.

"You are not going to die for a long while, Colonel. You may have some prison time coming, however. In the penitentiary, you'll find freedom from your disease. Use the money and your peaceful time to spread Mega's message. Keep the motorhome, too. Later, it'll come in handy." Elvis Presley and Annie Shafer, still holding hands and smiling at one another, walked away from the boat. As they disappeared into the mist, they sank slowly into the sea. Neither answered Shafer's calls. Too weak to move, he sat in the boat as it drifted toward shore. After the fog lifted, he throttled up the motor and piloted to shore.

Two men in suits waited for him as he struggled to tie the boat to the pier, on his way to return the boat key to the rental station at the hotel. One man reached into the boat with a muscular arm and hoisted Shafer onto the wharf. "Are you Colonel Shafer?" the man asked, flashing a police detective's badge.

"Yes," Shafer answered weakly.

"Where's your accomplice?" the second man asked.

"Who?" Shafer looked at the man. He did not recognize him.

"Elvis," the first detective elaborated.

"I wish I knew," Shafer sighed.

"Are those his clothes?" Shafer nodded, staring at the white suit and blue shirt. "I think you should come downtown with us, sir. I'll have a man get your things from the motorhome for you." Shafer nodded glumly.

FIFTY

"Mr. P., telephone." The army sergeant passed the portable phone to the white-haired man sitting at the poker table.

Only slightly annoyed, the older gentleman stacked his cards and laid them face down on the table, "I was gonna fold, anyway," he drawled. He took the phone from the sergeant, "Thanks, man."

Wandering away from the group of young men in crew cuts and ill-fitting civilian clothing, the older man spoke quietly into the cordless phone. "Hello? Oh, hi, baby-girl. How are you? Yeah, took us by surprise, too. Your step-mom and I were in Switzerland when it happened. Don't have a clue, sweetums. Look, we'll be in Palm Springs next week. Your momma is going to be there at least one day. You wanna bring the kids down. Okay, it's a date. Kiss my grandbabies for me. Love you, too. Bye." He put the phone down in its charger.

"Hey, Elvis," a young man bellowed from the table, "you want in on this hand?"

The white haired man smiled, dimples still visible in the weathered, wrinkled, mildly overweight face. "Lieutenant," he replied, "that's Mr. Elvis to you, and no thanks." Elvis laughed and walked away from the table leaving the room.

Another voice asked quietly after he left, "Do you think he believes in Mega?"

****

Unsteady on his feet, his clothes fitting more loosely than ever, an emaciated Jack Shafer stood quietly next to his court appointed lawyer behind the wooden table. A single prosecutor stood to his left behind a similar table. The jury box remained empty of jurors, occupied only by a single remotely controlled television camera. Shafer's involuntary muscle tremor forced him to clasp his hands behind his back to keep them from shaking visibly.

In front of them, the judge entered the small courtroom from behind the bench and settled his great weight carefully onto his chair. Donning his reading glasses, the judge peered momentarily at several type written pages clasped in his chubby fingers. He then asked Shafer if he had anything to say before he pronounced judgement upon him. Shafer and the lawyer stood. Jack shook his head, no. The lawyer told the judge there would be no statement by the defendant.

"Colonel Shafer," the portly judge began, "I have read your plea bargain agreement with the prosecuting attorney. In it, you have admitted your guilt to the possession of several stolen items, to wit: two firearms and clothing, the property of Graceland Mansion, the Estate of Elvis Presley, and/or Turner-Disney Productions. I have also listened to your court appointed attorney's pleas for leniency, in that any sentence longer than six months would be essentially a life sentence. Having seen the x-rays and other medical evidence, and having heard testimony from physicians about your terminal prostate cancer, I have to agree with that prognosis.

"Unfortunately, however, I also have to weigh judgement upon you and your actions. Your refusal to cooperate with investigators in the matter of the desecration of the grave of Elvis Presley weighs heavily in that judgement, as does the fact that his body has never been recovered. Your inability to name your accomplice, or to explain how the clothing in which Mr. Presley had been interred was found in your possession on a small boat in San Diego, California confounds me, and the prosecutor.

"In light of all these facts, I am afraid that I am forced to make an example of you. Although I cannot sentence you for crimes that the State of Tennessee refuses to prosecute, I can dispense the full measure of the law allowed for those crimes for which you pleaded guilty. I have taken into account your previous record, your exemplary service to your country, and the possibility that your disease process may have interfered with good judgement.

"You are hereby ordered to serve two years in confinement. Henceforth, you will be imprisoned in the state penitentiary until the completion of your sentence. There will be no chance for parole. You are dismissed. In one hour, you are to surrender yourself into the custody of the bailiff." The judge grasped the gavel with his meaty hand and raised it into air.

"Your honor, I protest!" the defense attorney bellowed.

With a glare, the judge stared at the attorney and slammed the gavel down with a loud crack, "Case dismissed, counselor."

Outside the courthouse, reporters mobbed Shafer and the defense attorney, shoving microphones, cameras, and tape recorders in their faces, "Comments?" they all asked.

"I have only one thing to say," Jack began. "For the first time in two years, I don't feel any pain." He smiled broadly at the reporters. Suddenly very lively, he bounded down the steps ahead of his attorney.

Confused look on his face, the attorney murmured, "No comment." He hurried down the steps to catch his client.

****

Lomax talked quietly with the FBI agent. They sat in the sunlight on the patio of the outdoor cafe. The plastic furniture under them wobbled. In a third chair, a man sat between the agent and Lomax. Face and hands covered by bandages, his identity remained impossible to guess by passers-by. Curious, some stared briefly in his direction, then looked away repulsed by thoughts of what horror might exist under the gauze.

"The agency does not want to destroy an icon of the entertainment industry. The American people might think McCarthyism has returned," Sorensen said. "My supervisors are capable, however, of prosecuting this case. It will require forcing Dr. Karakashian to testify against his will," he nodded toward the bandaged man at the table. The psychiatrist's eyes gleamed. "You might understand our difficulty in doing that. Your movie company is in the process of lionizing him. It's a great story. He saved the lives of his office personnel and the driver of the tank truck, only to need rescuing himself. By the way, we know the driver was a Hollywood stunt man, also employed by T-D."

"So, what are you saying?" Lomax asked in a quiet voice.

"The federal government has decided on a second course of action. If, as the new CEO of Turner-Disney, you divest the corporation of certain properties which give you an unfair advantage over some of your rivals, then we will not prosecute you for the Presley fraud, or the attempted murder of Dr. Karakashian."

"Which properties?" Lomax asked. Sorensen pulled a folded list from inside his coat pocket. He handed it, still folded, to Lomax. Lomax opened the piece of paper slowly and read the FTC's list deliberately, concentrating on each entity. "I'll think about it," he said, politely.

****

A bearded young man stood next to the red Mustang convertible that the best man parked illegally. It sat, two wheels on the sidewalk, in front of the Catholic Church. Dressed similarly to a medieval monk wearing a hooded cloth robe and leather sandals, the man clutched a wooden pole. Attached to the pole, a large sign declared, *Believe in Mega*, on one side, *Mega's Millennium*, on the other.

Watched in fascination by several nuns as they stood on the cathedral steps waiting for the new bride and groom to emerge from the chapel, B.J. Nottingham knelt, as if in prayer, at the left rear of the car. From somewhere within the robe, B.J. removed a bumper sticker. He rubbed the chrome with the sleeve of his habit, carefully polishing the bumper in preparation. After removing the wax paper backing to the sticker, he pressed it firmly onto the bumper. *ELVIS SAVES*, it read in big bold gold letters on a blue background. A lightning bolt with black letters TCB adorned one corner of the sticker.

Wistfully, the monk stood and patted the rear fender of the Mustang, also decorated with placards, shaving cream, and long strands of tin cans. The crowd, which gathered around the car, cheered as Amy and Barry appeared at the top of the church steps. Jeff Nordstrom, the best man, used a blast from an air horn as a starting signal. The wedding party pelted the bride and groom and each other with rice.

Leaving his bride in Nordstrom's care, Lockwood ran to the far side of the car and climbed into the driver's seat. Jeff opened the door for Amy. Before she could slip into the car a voice behind her asked, "May I kiss the bride?"

Amy Vanderbilt-Lockwood spun, recognizing the voice. She threw her arms around B.J. Tears flowed from her eyes. The two kissed tenderly, briefly. Holding her gently by the shoulders, B.J. pushed her carefully backward into the passenger seat. Conscientiously picking up her train, he handed it to her. Lovingly, he patted her hands. He looked into her eyes, then he looked at Barry and back to Amy. "Take care of my Mustang," he ordered. He closed the door solidly. Barry gunned the engine and peeled into the street, followed by numerous well-wishers, and the nuns' waving hands.

****

"Folks, we have an exciting interview scheduled for today. This is Gale Reiter, from the Preslian Radio Network. Later this week, Jack Shafer — Father Jack, to many of us — is scheduled to be released after serving two years in prison. We have an exclusive interview with Colonel Shafer. He just published a book, *Letters Written From Prison*. That conversation coming up, after these messages...."

The beginning...